NO ESCAPE

Lexy surveyed the destruction. The bed's paneled headboard and tester were still standing, but the posts rivaled the leaning tower of Pisa. The reason was plain. One of the side rails had come loose from the baseboard, and the mattress, box springs, pillows, and linens had fallen through the high frame to the floor below. Quite a plunge. These inn guests had to be very fit. She moved toward the bed. A smell of coconuts rose from the tangled sheets. They were fit and inclined to use scented lubricants. Nothing so unusual in that.

She began to pull the covers away from the mattress and froze when she saw the corner of a shiny red paperback book peeking from under the quilt. Her empty stomach clenched. There it was: *Workout Sex*, the book that had taken over her life, made her the target of sex-seeking scum of the male gender and made her buy an inn in Drake's Point. Somehow it had followed her.

SEXY LE XY

Kate Moore

LOVE SPELL      NEW YORK CITY

For the true believers—
Loren, Allison, and Kevin, and Pamela Ahearn.
And the great Brain Trust—
Barbara Freethy, Carol Culver, Diana Dempsey, Lynn Hanna,
Candice Hern, and Barbara McMahon.

LOVE SPELL®

April 2005

Published by

Dorchester Publishing Co., Inc.
200 Madison Avenue
New York, NY 10016

ISBN 0-505-52623-9

The name "Love Spell" and its logo are trademarks of Dorchester Publishing Co., Inc.

Printed in the United States of America.

Visit us on the web at www.dorchesterpub.com.

ACKNOWLEDGMENTS

Drake's Point is a fictional northern California town, but many people helped answer questions along the way to give the setting its authenticity. The mistakes are mine, but thanks go to Kay Golden for her memories of growing up by the Tyne, and British food favorites; Jeff Symonds of Rich Price and the Foundation for his knowledge of pop music history; Linda Armao for a timely Italian phrase or two; and Estes Park Wellesley Seminar Group for locating a CD of elk mating calls.

Prologue

I think I can. I think I can. Lexy Clark shifted in the grip of a skinny redheaded techie in black. He had one hand firmly clamped on her upper arm and one hand on the door in front of them, listening intently to his headset and mouthing a countdown. *Ten, nine, eight . . .*

At one he was going to open the door and shove Lexy out onto the set of *The Stanley Skoff Show,* the show that claimed to test-drive everything the American consumer bought, from salad dressings to phonics programs.

I think I can. I think I can. She could hear the audience laughing at the warm-up patter, an audience that included her family and closest friends. Her agent Tess Gibson had put the show in the tour schedule at the last minute when Skoff, a self-proclaimed consumer watchdog, issued her one of his challenges. Tess had been excited about it. *Are you kidding? Air*

1

time in the L.A. market while we're negotiating the video deal?

Lexy told herself it was just one more appearance as a "sexpert." She wore her signature workout clothes—black Lycra below-the-knee shorts and cropped red tank top, her currently blonde hair in a neat ponytail. She could always demonstrate some basic stretches. People tended to underestimate the value of stretching in their workouts. She knew the drill—suggestive questions from the host, flirty answers from her. That was the first lesson of her public life: No host wanted serious fitness information from "Sexy Lexy."

The sound box fixed to her Spandex waistband wobbled, and she reached back to secure it. Did the show have a wheel or a dial or a meter? Morning shows rarely had wheels, but afternoon shows often did. Even *The Ellen Show* had a wheel. In Lexy's experience anything that spun, flashed, or rang posed a serious threat to a guest's dignity, but she hadn't checked out Skoff's show. She had been too busy breaking up with Colin.

Surely, Tess would have mentioned a wheel when she insisted that Lexy do the spot. *If Stan Skoff has issued a challenge, you've got to do it. He reads the names of people too chicken to show. You don't want that. Not when your book is doing so well.* Lexy had agreed she didn't want to harm book sales. She hadn't dreamed that writing a book would change her life so much.

Her palms were sweating. The air-conditioning had clearly failed. The water in her water bra was superheated by now. Escaping steam would not be good for her image. She wondered if the redheaded techie would notice if she wiped her hands on his black T-shirt.

I think I can. I think I can. Lexy squared her shoulders. Her friends, Erin and Kelly, and thousands of women like them, balanced dozens of responsibilities daily with no time to work out. Lexy had written her book for them, and readers had thanked her at book signings everywhere. Stanley Skoff might try to make a joke out of her, but her work was good.

. . . three, two, one. The redheaded techie jerked one arm back, the other forward, propelling Lexy through the open door onto a wide square stage with a functional, office-space look—black leather desk chairs for host and guest, soft gray cubicle walls on casters.

Lexy blinked in the glare of the klieg lights and fixed her best smile in place. Two banks of seats rose to the front, and the audience seemed to be all men. She couldn't spot her family anywhere in that sea of male faces. The crowd clapped and whistled, and started to chant.

"Sex-y, Lex-y. Sex-y, Lex-y. Sex-y, Lex-y."

Lexy froze. Apparently, Stanley Skoff had invited all the hecklers from her book tour, all the men who had suggested positions or missing chapters, who had offered to help her write them. Or maybe he'd gone back into her past and invited everyone she had known in junior high. She managed another step forward.

Stanley Skoff came toward her, mike in hand, and the chant subsided. He had a thin, youthful face with short spiky brown hair, big blue eyes, wire-rimmed

Kate Moore

glasses, and obviously no sweat glands. With his gray suit, white shirt, and red bow tie, he looked like the all-American nerd on his way to a debate tournament or science fair.

"Ladies and gentlemen, let's welcome our first guest today, the guru of getting it on, Lexy Clark, author of *Workout Sex, A Girl's Guide to Home Fitness.*" He held out the red paperback edition of Lexy's book for a camera close-up, and gestured for Lexy to take one of the chairs.

"Now, Lexy, we always begin our show with a few questions. Tell us—what inspired you to write this book?"

Lexy settled into her chair. She had handled that question dozens of times. "I've always been interested in fitness, and when my married friends complained that they had no time to stay in shape, I had to help. One of them said that she only got her heart rate up when the baby climbed on the kitchen counter or when her husband made love to her. And that got me thinking about the perfect workout for couples."

The audience clapped enthusiastically, and Lexy let her shoulders relax. She knew her lines well.

"You wrote the book for people with partners, isn't that right?"

"Yes, studies show that married women with both careers and children tend to exercise less frequently than they should."

Stan picked up the little red book. "And according to your book, the program works best if partners are in a committed relationship?"

4

Lexy nodded. The heat of the lights was more intense than she remembered from other shows.

"You aren't married yourself. Did you have to do extensive research for this book?"

Lexy knew what he meant. He was trying to coax some over-sharing out of her, but she wasn't going there. "Stan, I bet you don't know what zinc can do for you."

He laughed, but she caught the sly gleam in his eyes. He was setting her up. "So how has the book affected your relationships with men?"

Her smile tightened. *You don't really want me to answer that one, Stan.* The book had cost her a boyfriend, and taught her just how single-minded men could be. As the author of *Workout Sex* she had tripped over the men lined up at her door like she was the latest thrill ride at Disneyland. "Stan, let's just say that men like fit women."

His eyebrows rose above the round rims of his glasses, and he leaned toward the audience. "Must be how she got the name Sex-y Lex-y.

"Lexy has quite a fan base. Many of our studio guests today have tried her workout routine, and some are interested in trying out for a part in the upcoming *Workout Sex* video."

The audience chanted on cue. "Sex-y, Lex-y. Sex-y, Lex-y. Sex-y, Lex-y."

Lexy glanced at her watch. The interview segment couldn't last much longer. She should have asked the techie how she would exit.

"Now it's time for the test phase of our show. Lexy, let me remind you how the show works. Behind you is the Skept-o-Meter." Two gray panels on tracks rolled apart to reveal a wall dominated by a huge painted half-circle divided into pie wedges of colors from red to green. A black needle quivered in the red zone labeled, YOU MAKE ME SKOFF.

Lexy scanned the audience. Her no-good, lying agent was out there somewhere, and Lexy had a few words for her.

"Only the response of our studio audience can move the needle on our Skept-o-Meter. Are you ready to prove your claim?" His voice rose to a shout over the Sexy Lexy chant and the catcalls.

"Give it to me, Lexy."

"You're so sex-y."

"I'm ready to show everyone some great stretches—"

"On national television we can only ask Lexy to do a modified version of her workout, but we've put together a few things to help her keep it real." He pulled a black silk pajama top from under his chair and held it up for the audience to see. They roared their approval.

Lexy's mouth felt dry as a stale rice cake.

Stanley Skoff held up her book again. "Here's our challenge: ladies and gentlemen, according to Lexy's book you can throw out the weights and the stairmaster because the only piece of fitness equipment you'll ever need again is"—a drum roll started and a spotlight pointed to another section of panels—"a mattress!"

As the panels parted, a California King bed rolled into view. Reclining on red satin sheets, propped on one elbow with *Workout Sex* in hand, was a grinning shirtless hunk in black silk pajama bottoms. He winked at Lexy.

"Here we have Chip, an experienced personal trainer from Santa Monica. Chip has read your book, Lexy. Can you give him a workout with just this mattress?"

Lexy looked at Chip and heard Colin, her ex. *Lexy, face it, you're the lite beer of sex. Less filling.*

"Now, we never take chances with the safety of our guests, so . . ."

Another drum roll. Two bare-chested Chippendales wannabes in yellow overalls, red suspenders, and fire hats strode out onto the stage armed with fire extinguishers and took a stance on either side of the bed. Skoff grinned at Lexy and turned to the audience.

"Audience, don't go away. We'll be right back to see if Sex-y Lex-y can deliver a real workout."

Lexy forgot book sales, forgot video deals, forgot her agent. She wanted to rip the needle off the Skept-o-Meter and stab Stanley Skoff through his smug heart, but she knew Miss Manners would not approve. Beyond the red sheets, the red fire extinguishers, and the red of Stanley Skoff's tie, in the dark vastness of the studio, off to one side of the bank of audience seats, a small sign glowed red—EXIT. In one word, it was a whole plan. Beyond the sign her driver would be waiting.

She unclipped the mike from her collar, and yanked the sound box from the back of her leggings. The hunk on the bed arranged himself for the cameramen, and the two fake firefighters studied their own biceps. Lexy struggled briefly to pull the wire out of her cropped top and turned to Skoff, who was having his makeup freshened by a technician. "Thanks for having me as a guest, Stan. Sorry I can't stay longer. Bye."

Skoff's mouth opened. "Hey, you can't just walk off my show."

"Stop me."

The hunk on the bed rolled to his feet and blocked her path. "Hey, babe, chill. Let's work out." His massive pecs gleamed.

"No thanks, Skip."

"Chip."

"Whatever." She shoved her sound box and mike at his oily chest, and he stepped backwards, landing with a heavy plop on the bed. Lexy grabbed an extinguisher from the nearest fire guy, pulled the pin, and leapt down the stage steps. She aimed the extinguisher at two audience members who came after her, dodged a cameraman, and dashed into the darkness beyond the lighted set, her eyes fixed on that EXIT.

A sign on the door read, DOOR ALARM WILL SOUND. Lexy hesitated a nano-second and tossed aside her extinguisher. As she pushed the bar on the door, she heard Stan Skoff say, "Guess Sex-y Lex-y is not so sexy after all. Our next . . ." Then the ringing of the alarm took over.

In the hall a uniformed security guard hurried toward her. "Hey, miss, where do you think you're going?"

"As far away from here as I can get."

Chapter 1
A Firm Foundation

"The strong, vigorous movements involved in aerobic sex must be continuously supported with an appropriate frame. A lumpy, sagging mattress, inadequate cross slats, or weakened joints can limit the range and intensity of the workout."

—*Workout Sex*, Lexy Clark

For the first five miles of narrow curving highway Lexy really enjoyed the fog. She felt invisible for a change, and that made leaving L.A. seem like her best idea ever. Her last good idea hadn't turned out exactly as she'd expected. *Workout Sex* had made her financially independent, but sadly, it had also made her a national joke.

The road narrowed to one lane. Dark twisted shapes appeared along the side and faded before Lexy could identify them. She wasn't wearing her contacts, and her prescription dark glasses added to the gloom. Her headlights were as penetrating as a pair of birthday candles, and she downshifted to first gear. Other than navigating her own twenty-foot driveway in Manhattan Beach, Lexy had no experience with first gear. A glance at the dashboard told her she was zipping along at fifteen miles per hour, and she wondered if she might actually damage the engine. Her destination, the tiny town of Drake's Point on the coast north of San Francisco, had to be close, but she hadn't seen a road sign or another car since she'd entered the fog.

The fog turned to drizzle on her windshield, and she flipped on her wipers. As she reached for the defrost switch, a large beast materialized out of the mist. It was Rudolf on steroids, with a sizeable rack of pointy antlers, a scruffy mane of black neck hair, and a wide, brown body. He stepped into the road, and Lexy hit the brakes. The car slid to a stop on the slick asphalt as Rudolf dipped his head and began to graze in the grass on the shoulder. The little spurt of adrenaline subsided as she waited for him to move, admiring the slow careful way he ate. It would be rude to honk. Good digestion was nothing to sneer at.

By the time she was counting her wipers' steady sweep across the windshield, she realized they had gridlock and Rudolf wasn't waiting for any green light. She peered into the fog but couldn't see a way around him. She had come a long way up one of the coast mountains past steep drop-offs. It didn't seem smart to try to pass Rudolf on the shoulder. She inched her car forward to within six feet of him and put on the flashers. A hint that he was holding people up was fair. She would encourage him to glide back

10

into the mist. He lifted his head briefly, peered past her, then dipped again to his snack.

Now he was the rude one. He was just lucky she wasn't the road-rage sort of driver. She glanced at her watch. She had things to do, miles to go, and she had planned to be at the inn by now. She unfastened her seat belt, slipped out of the car, and paused to take stock of her surroundings. The cool, misty air smelled like ocean and dried grass with an unmistakable hint of farm animals. A faint rustling sounded to her right, and she wondered what she couldn't see in the fog. Rudolf looked taller than he had first appeared, but she told herself to be assertive. After all, he was just Bambi's big brother. Taking a deep breath, she squared her shoulders.

"Okay, Rudolf," she said. "You've had your share of that grass, so it's time to move on down the buffet line." She advanced toward him, cautiously. She'd just wave her arms and yell "shoo" or something.

"Don't move." A voice came out of the fog, deep and authoritative. It wasn't God or Obi Wan Kenobi, but Lexy stopped anyway.

Rudolf's head came up and swung around. The black eyes fixed on her. He snorted and his hooves scraped the pavement. Now that she had his attention, Lexy waved her arms at him.

The next instant a large male body flattened her against the side of her car. Her head hit metal, and her breath came out in a pale huff.

"Not from around here, are you?"

"Excuse me, who are you?" The stranger definitely was not God, but she couldn't see who he was because Rudolf was coming their way. The ends of his antlers looked sharp as Freddy Kruger's nails.

"Don't move."

She wasn't moving. She was trapped. Her cheek was pressed against a broad, solid chest. Over the bulge of one flannel-clad biceps, she could see the beast approaching, heading straight for them. Lexy held her breath.

"What do you know about male sexuality?" The voice was deep, and she felt the vibration of it in the pit of her stomach.

"I beg your pardon?"

"It's rutting season." The low voice and the warm breath against her temple sent a pleasant little shiver through her. "If that fellow smells female, he's going to investigate thoroughly."

Rudolf seemed to glide toward them in slow motion, his antlers stirring the fog. Lexy tried not to think about foreplay with antlers. When the stranger pressed harder against her, she didn't complain. Rudolf didn't veer.

"He's coming right at us."

"I've got you covered."

Lexy held her breath and curled her toes. A few hundred pounds of beast flesh just missed her pedicure. Rudolf's flanks rubbed against the back of the stranger, but he didn't budge. His thighs held Lexy's clamped in place, warm strong thighs in worn jeans against Lexy's mostly bare, khaki-shorts-clad legs. The only sounds were Lexy's heart thumping and Rudolf's hooves scraping the pavement.

A moment passed, long enough to raise Lexy's

temperature a degree or two. When the sound of hooves broke off, Lexy stirred. "Excuse me, Rudolf's gone." Time to say thank-you and get on her way.

"Rudolf?" The stranger didn't move. "Hang on. If that fellow's not the monogamous type, his harem will follow."

Lexy swallowed a protest as dozens of shadowy shapes emerged from the fog and flowed around the car, setting it rocking on its tires and knocking Lexy against the stranger. He only curled his big body more tightly around her.

The clop of hooves on the asphalt continued. Rudolf clearly had more than his share of female companions, and Lexy had time to think about the male body pressed against hers. It was definitely big, over six feet judging from where her ear met the man's chest. Lexy was five-seven and rarely felt small except around her older brothers. The man's shirt smelled of sawdust, warm sun on pine trees, and wet grass. And with her nose practically in his armpit, he smelled male, too.

She could hear the steady beat of his heart, and instinctively she counted, estimating his resting heart rate. *Very fit.* She realized that she was clinging with both hands to the loose folds of his shirt above his belt. Though she wasn't touching him directly, her clinging had pulled the fabric of his shirt taut across his belly. She could make an educated guess as to his body fat ratio. His abs were solid but not cut like those of the model they'd used on the cover of her book. She loosened her grasp on his shirt and considered flattening her hands against his sides, just to see

13

how accurate her assessment was. That was when she realized that the stranger was checking her out, too.

The subtle pressure of his body against hers was as intimate as Lycra. Her cropped T-shirt, which had been perfectly appropriate for the late September heat of the valley as she came up I-5, now seemed skimpy. She shivered. A large stranger who frequented remote hilltops in the fog had figured out her cup size.

And he knew she was checking him out. She had a feeling he could hear her thinking.

Okay, she could pretty much tell he wasn't armed. She wasn't in L.A., so he probably wasn't a stalker or a serial killer, and the Unabomber was in jail.

"Lost?"

"Not at all." She'd followed her Mapquest directions perfectly. "I'm headed for Drake's Point."

"Tourist?"

"Hardly."

"Running away, then." He said it with complete certainty.

"Excuse me?" Lexy tried to see whether there were more beasts moving toward them in the fog. Her dark glasses were now covered with beads of moisture.

"Drake's Point's a regular Brigadoon. People think they can pass through the fog and leave the world behind."

Great, the first person she'd met was onto her. "Do we have to continue in this position?"

Lexy felt the laugh shake him before she heard it. He had a nice laugh, warm and easy. "Any position you'd like is okay with me."

He had to say it. He had to be a man. He just couldn't resist the innuendo! She had heard about as many suggestive comments about positions as there were. On Leno, on Letterman, on Oprah, for heaven's sake. She wasn't taking it anymore. Lexy pushed against him. He waited just long enough to let her know she couldn't budge him, then he stepped back.

Cold air washed over her, puckering her nipples and raising gooseflesh on her arms. She yanked open her car door and slipped back into the warm interior.

He knocked on her window. "Hey, in Drake's Point we say 'please' and 'thank you.'"

She cracked her window. He was accusing her of rudeness. "Excuse me?"

"Lady, that was a thousand-pound bull tule elk, and you weren't eager for him to take an interest in you."

"Better a big elk than a big ego any day." She fastened her seat belt and shifted into gear. She lurched forward a few feet, and braked.

The road ahead was as obscure as ever, but clear of beasts. For that she did owe the stranger thanks. To be fair, and Lexy always tried to be fair, he had known what to do in the face of Rudolf, and he had done it. Competence was good. And he hadn't actually done any groping. And he hadn't pointed out her own assessment of his body, which he could have.

She wiped the moisture off her dark glasses and rolled down her window. Taunting males were no threat to her. Sexy Lexy had disappeared. She was Alexandra Clark now, gracious, dignified, and anonymous. Looking back into the fog, she couldn't really see his face, just the dark shadowy shape of him. "Thanks for your help. I'm Alexandra Clark, the new owner of the Tooth and Nail."

She thought he said something, but she stepped on the gas and the rumble of her engine muffled his words.

There, no one in Drake's Point would ever call her Sexy Lexy.

A mile later Lexy rounded a curve and the road dropped down out of the fog. A perfect half-moon of a cove sparkled in golden shafts of light from the distant horizon. A long sloping ridge of the coast range curled around the northern end of the cove, and nestled in its shadow was her inn. Its white walls, dark timbers, and slate roof looked just as they had on the Internet listing. She glanced back at the fog. The rest of California had disappeared. The stranger was right. Drake's Point was Brigadoon.

There was no sign at the fork in the road at the bottom of the hill, but there was a small gas station. Lexy checked her map and turned left, winding west along a blue creek and over a narrow stone bridge until she reached the inn. Lazy smoke curled up from two chimneys, and an old inn sign swung from a pole, with a pair of arm wrestlers grinning at each other, teeth bared, over the words TOOTH AND NAIL. Lexy smiled. Her inn, a genuine English inn transported from Dorset, beam by beam, slate tile by slate tile, was the best thing that had come out of her book.

She paused to admire it. It looked old and comfortable and established, as if it belonged in this particular spot. It was tangible proof of her book's success, of all those sales. Stanley Skoff might joke, but readers proved Lexy had something of value to say. And now she had something of her own, something lovely and welcoming. She had found the inn on an Internet real estate listing that described it as a "relaxing, rejuvenating escape." Separated from the nearest city by a three-thousand-foot coast mountain, it was definitely an escape. With hiking trail access, a lonely beach, and a geothermal spring that fed a series of rock pools, it was bound to be relaxing and rejuvenating. Lexy was sold.

She gathered her financial wizard brothers to ask for their help arranging the deal, and the three of them had regarded her as deranged.

Matt suggested, "Stay at the inn; don't buy it."

Mark was simply puzzled. "Why escape now, Lexy? You're hot. You've never been hot. So scorch a few mattresses and move on."

Only Bob was willing to help. "Sure. We can help you make the deal, but remember, small hotels have a narrow margin. Keep those rooms filled. And don't expect us to bail you out."

What had she expected from the guys, who, when she was seven, had dressed her as Yoda to accompany their Jedi Knights on Halloween and coached her to say—"Try not. Do. Or do not. There is no try."

Lexy sized up the cars in the parking lot. They suggested affluence but not pretension. She pulled in between a tan Suburban with the inn's logo on the side and a dark green Range Rover with a serious bike rack on the back.

17

Florence Locke, her manager, met Lexy in the small but charming lobby. A pair of flowered chintz armchairs flanked a round table draped in a moss green cloth. A high-backed antique wood bench held a stack of inn flyers. Florence was on the Cher side of fifty and just as remarkable. She had deep red hennaed hair to below-shoulder length, a perfect manicure, and a magnificent bosom hinted at by the plunging V neckline of a chocolate brown silk jacket worn over jeans. Lexy immediately liked the twinkle in her manager's blue eyes and the hint of England in her fluty voice.

"I'll have Francisco get your things. Do you want a tour, or would you like to go direct to your room?"

"The tour, definitely."

Florence beamed approval and led the way from the lobby, explaining how the old Tooth and Nail had been brought from England and modernized over the years. The dining room with its ancient slate floors, trestle tables, half-timbered walls, and huge basalt fireplace had once been the meeting place of a group of nineteenth-century horse rescuers. A bright fire warmed the patrons sitting over tea in the quiet room. Outside, the creek curved around a brick patio furnished with intricate white wrought-iron chairs and tables from the old inn's turn-of-the-century days. Clay pots spilled bright orange marigolds and blue lobelia onto each table. Boston ivy covered the west wall, and above the door a late-blooming red rose climbed a trellis. Lexy smiled. Her new life was going to be filled with flowers.

They made a pass through the busy kitchens. A half a dozen people nodded, and Florence promised to introduce Lexy in the morning. Back through the dining room they went into what had been the old taproom with its marble bar and row of tall tap handles.

Florence exchanged a glance with the bartender, who nodded but didn't speak. His long ponytail and full moustache had gone gray to match his flinty Clint Eastwood eyes. His collarless white shirt and plaid wool vest could have come from any century, and Lexy wondered briefly whether he had been part of the original furnishings.

"You mustn't mind Nigel," Florence whispered. With a wink, she added, "He's a bit of a flirt."

Lexy caught the irony. If Nigel had flirted, it was in a past life. Lexy thought he might be effective as Dr. Frankenstein's servant keeping villagers away from the castle door, but apparently the inn drew enough customers to give the dartboard in the corner a well-used look. By the door was a glass case with a replica of a sword that had been used at Waterloo by Captain Harry Clare, later Lord Mountjoy.

"The Mountjoy family in England has the original."

"I love it. This is so not L.A." The place breathed history. Lexy was ready to put on the long flowered skirts and high-collared blouses of her favorite English designer and disappear into her very own Brigadoon.

Florence had become Flo by the time they reached the cozy blue and white parlor where morning coffee was served. She started to explain the arrangement of guest rooms as they returned to the lobby. "Upstairs we have your suite, and our ten guest rooms. All full this weekend."

19

Lexy liked the sound of that. Her inn was thriving, and she would prove her brothers wrong. She had put herself through an online course in hotel management that stressed guest room satisfaction as the key to keeping up profitable occupancy rates. Lexy was eager to see those rooms.

"There you are." A cutting male voice came from the stair landing above them. A man and a woman in black spandex cycling shorts and close-fitting red and yellow jerseys came down the stairs, arms wrapped around each other.

"What are you going to do about our bed?" The cyclists stopped a few steps above Lexy and Flo.

"Mr. Ramsdorf, sorry. We appreciate your patience." Flo glanced at Lexy.

"Flo, honey, we had this conversation an hour ago." Ramsdorf's thin, sharp voice was grating.

Flo tried again. "Can we put you in another room if the Sackville bed can't be repaired today?"

Ramsdorf removed his hand from his partner's bottom long enough to adjust the chin strap of his helmet, a vented black road helmet that tapered to a sharp point at the back. "Let me spell it out for you, Flo. We're going for a ride, and we want our bed restored to full functionality by the time we return." His companion giggled.

"Of course. We'll get to work on it straight away." Flo's courteous smile never wavered.

"I should hope so. We're paying how much a night?" He snapped his fingers.

"Two hundred dollars." The female cyclist had a squeaky, sucking-on-helium voice.

Lexy glanced at Flo and stepped forward. She knew how to deal with people like Ramsdorf. She had met dozens of big donors at Pacifica College where her mother taught classics and her father coached basketball. She had watched the college president deal smoothly with people who talked too much about the tuition they paid or the money they gave.

"Excuse me. I'm Alexandra Clark, the new owner here. What seems to be the problem?"

Ramsdorf's gaze swung from Flo's cleavage to Lexy's shorts and cropped top. "The problem is our bed broke this morning, and you people can't manage to fix it."

"The bed is broken?" Lexy had slept in dozens of hotel beds. Hotel beds didn't break.

The woman bobbed her helmeted head. "The mattress plunged right to the floor. We coulda been killed."

Lexy offered them her most gracious smile. This was *her* inn now. She didn't know its former policies, but she had to act. It was guestroom satisfaction or vacancies. "How stressful for you. We'll do everything in our power to get you back into bed, and if for any reason we can't, your stay will be on us. Absolutely no charge."

At the mention of no charge, Ramsdorf's annoyance evaporated. His expression turned smug. He and his partner descended the remaining steps. "We'll be back."

Lexy fixed her smile in place and stepped aside to let her first guests pass. They waddled to the door, the plastic cleats of their cycling shoes clicking on the slate tiles.

When the inn door closed behind them, Lexy turned to Flo. "I hope I didn't overstep."

Flo shook her head. "Not at all."

"Does the inn have a policy?"

"We've never had quite this problem."

In the same instant their glances met in perfect understanding, and they let their tight smiles collapse.

Flo passed their common judgment. "Those helmets are a major fashion crime."

Lexy nodded. "Insect-head is not a look just anyone can wear."

"Oh dear, Alexandra. We rarely get that sort. Most of our guests are very lovely people."

"How did they break the bed?"

Flo rolled her eyes. "We gave them an antique English four-poster with an excellent mattress, high-thread-count Egyptian cotton sheets, and a lovely comforter, and they treated it like the ring of a World Federation Wrestling match."

"Can you show me the damage?"

"There's no rush. We're waiting for Sam."

"Sam?"

"Sam Worth. Usually we have to wait a day or more for someone to come over the mountain or down the coast. But with Sam back in town, there's no delay. Sam can fix anything."

"You've called him already?" Lexy was definitely beginning to appreciate Flo.

Flo nodded. "I left a message. He's up on the mountain today. We'll catch him when he comes down. Do let's have a look at your room and have some tea first."

Up on the mountain. Lexy had a sinking feeling. She had met a man up on the mountain with that capable, fix-it kind of competence, and sawdust on his person. "I'd like to see what needs to be done first." She followed Flo up the oak-paneled stairs, down a hall, and into a quaint room with high sloping ceilings and mullioned windows thrown open to the sea.

Against the inner wall was a tall mahogany bed with a rose tapestry comforter and hangings. Lexy surveyed the destruction. The paneled headboard and tester were still standing, but the posts rivaled the leaning tower of Pisa. The reason was plain. One of the side rails had come loose from the baseboard, and the mattress, box springs, pillows, and linens had fallen through the high frame to the floor below. Quite a plunge. The two cyclists had to be very fit. She moved toward the bed. A smell of coconuts rose from the tangled sheets. They were fit and inclined to use scented lubricants. Nothing so unusual in that.

She began to pull the covers away from the mattress and froze when she saw the corner of a shiny red paperback book peeking from under the quilt. Her empty stomach clenched. There it was: *Workout Sex*, the book that had taken over her life, driven away her boyfriend, and made her the target of sex-seeking scum of the male gender. Inside the back cover was a photo of Sexy Lexy as a blonde in black spandex and red cropped top. She'd done everything she could think of to cover that blonde woman's tracks. Coming to Drake's Point was the last step of her plan, and somehow the book had followed her.

Flo came up beside her. "Each of our beds comes from England. We name them." She sighed. "Imagine that pair of sticks generating enough heat and excitement to bring down the Sackville bed and the cheek to want another go at it."

"They did seem to be an athletic pair." Lexy nudged the little red book with her toe, pushing it deep under the bed.

Chapter 2
Food, Drink, and Sexual Fitness: No Aphrodisiacs Needed

"Good nutrition is essential to good sex. Feeding the libido as well as the body means getting enough vitamin B, magnesium, ginseng, and zinc to boost the adrenal glands' production of testosterone, the hormone of desire."
—*Workout Sex*, Lexy Clark

The second time Sam Worth met the new owner of the Tooth and Nail, she was on her hands and knees reaching under the collapsed mattress of the four-poster bed in room 7 of her inn, her bottom in the air. She had changed from the shorts and T-shirt he'd seen on the road. He stood in the doorway, allowing himself time to consider the view. A long, cream-and-blue flowered skirt fell softly across the sweet curve of her backside. He wondered what had sent her looking under the bed.

She started to pull back from the depths of the collapsed bed, so he gave a warning knock on the door jamb. Her head snapped back so fast she conked it on the frame. Something red disappeared under her bulky Irish fisherman's sweater, and she crossed her arms over her ribs, hiding the thing. Her startled gaze dropped from his face to his shirt. There was no doubt she recognized it. Her deep brown eyes expressed open hostility. She was clearly a woman who should not play poker or go into undercover work.

"I see you made it safely down the mountain, Alexandra Clark."

"You." He'd had friendlier greetings from the highway patrol.

"Sam Worth." He didn't offer his hand. She was clutching the thing under her sweater as if her life depended on it.

Her dark hair was pulled up in a ponytail, with loose bits curling around her face from the fog and from sticking her head under beds. It was the kind of hair with deep red highlights to it. He already knew how soft that hair was, and he had an accurate memory of the slim shape now hidden by the bulky sweater.

"Looks like you could use some help . . ." he said. ". . . Again," he added, just to rile her.

"I'm not sure I needed help up on the mountain, but thank you."

"Maybe I was saving the elk." He crossed to stand beside her. She smelled good, like spicy flowers. "Did you attack the bed, too?"

Her chin came up, and the ponytail bounced. Whatever else she was hiding, it wasn't her feelings.

"A pair of guests brought down the bed." She cast a rueful glance at it.

"I'm impressed," he said. She shot him a glare. "Do you want it fixed?"

"Yes." Her sense of humor was as undeveloped as her chest. She had plenty of frankness though. She was checking him out again, just as she had up on the ridge. It wasn't the city singles-bar status check. He knew women who could get a man's profession and after-tax net worth in a single glance. Alexandra Clark's look was thorough, scientific and sexy—way beyond the thirty-second biological mate test. He checked her out right back. When he had first seen her in the headlights of her car, he'd had the impression of a sweet bottom and long, curvy legs. Now he added great bones, a determined chin, and serious need of a wonderbra; a dangerous combination as far as he was concerned. Her mouth with its full lower lip was like a signing bonus.

She swallowed, and he resisted the impulse to grin. That little swallow was her body's *yes*, one thing they could agree on, and it adjusted his thermostat up a few degrees. So much for thinking that a woman's personality could make a Worth man immune to her. So much for thinking he was through with women. He turned to get his toolbox.

"Wait. What are your rates? Do you have references?"

That stopped him. She thought he was the local handyman. He grinned at her over his shoulder. "No one around here charges less, and everyone in town will vouch for my work."

* * *

With Sam Worth out of the room, Lexy paused to recover a bit of her normal brain function. Her book said that fitness was sexy, and he was proof. She had been unable to resist checking him out. His hair was the golden brown of the late summer hills. There was a teasing intelligence in his blue eyes, a sexy promise in his smile, and a hint of vulnerability in his crooked nose. And she had been sucked into that golden boy ease of his when her whole plan was in danger. She needed to think.

The corners of the book under her sweater poked her breasts. She wanted to march downstairs and toss it in the big fireplace. She wanted to watch the pages brown and curl and turn to ashes. This was her new start. She was not going to let *Workout Sex* follow her here. She was taking her name back from the reporters and the TV hosts who had made a joke of it.

But the insect-heads in black Lycra would be back, and they wanted the "full functionality" of their bed. If the book went missing, they would probably insist on a strip-search of the inn to find it. *We've been robbed*, they would say. *Someone's taken our copy of* Workout Sex *by Lexy Clark*. They would be loud, rude, and insistent, and everyone would hear about their loss. *Oh, that book*, her staff would say, and someone would remember seeing Sexy Lexy on Oprah or Leno or even Stanley Skoff.

Lexy opened the armoire and slipped the book into the outer pocket of a suitcase on the floor. It was funny, really. Publishing her book had brought her full circle, back to the nickname of her junior high years when she had first understood the meaning of "irony." She still remembered Mr. Fisher's definition—*the use of words to signify the opposite of what they usually express; ridicule disguised as praise.*

Her older brothers understood irony. Lexy's writing a book about sex was, as her brother Matt put it, *hi-LAR-ious! Lexy's having sex? Since when?* Her friends couldn't believe it either. How had Lexy dared to give them advice about sex?

She hadn't meant to. She had intended to write a fitness book about a normal activity in which married people engaged. Her friends had certainly hinted often enough that sex was one of the good things about marriage. And all her friends were married, with careers and babies. She and her friends still talked since they'd married, but the conversations had gone from over-sharing of intimate sexual detail to complaining about overwork, stress, and burnout. Lexy had listened for months to laments about no exercise, no sleep, and weight gain. Kelly and Erin despaired that they had gone straight from camisoles and low-rise slacks to denim skirts with elastic waists. Lexy had seen the perfect solution, a way to fit regular exercise into those busy schedules.

Somehow in the editorial process her book had become *Workout Sex*, she had lost the girlish "ie" in her name and become "Sexy Lexy," with all that label implied about sexual readiness and prowess. *Bring on the fire extinguishers.* Being Lexy meant being "on" all the time. It meant thrusting her enhanced chest for-

29

ward and smiling until her cheeks hurt. It meant turning up the volume on her normal personality until she didn't quite recognize herself. It meant being suckered every time someone called her name and she turned expecting a familiar face. Those moments were some of the hardest, keeping a smile in place when a stranger stared back at her.

Of course, her public life wasn't all bad. Many, many women thanked her for writing the book. They told her how they had given up on exercise and how the book gave them the courage or the encouragement to try the workout—and how their husbands suddenly turned very supportive. Those women had given Lexy the courage to go to the next book signing or talk show.

In spite of the hype, or maybe because of it, she hadn't had sex in the nine months since her book came out. The whole "Lexy" image portrayed her as a sexually confident woman, a woman who could take on any man in a sexual encounter, bring him to a cardiac-arresting climax, and be ready to do it all again five minutes later. Even if she had met a man who was genuinely interested in her, Lexy could not have become involved with him because she could not live up to her own hype.

So, she had touted the benefits of regular, vigorous sex with a regular partner, answered questions about it, and lain on the floor of TV studios while hunks did push-ups over her Spandex-clad body. Meanwhile, she had turned away offers from men who thought she was the Energizer Bunny of sex until she had just lost interest in the subject. And that was fine, because sex didn't seem exciting anymore. She didn't miss it. It was about as exciting as flossing before bed. She didn't always floss, either.

Sam Worth came back with his tools as Lexy closed the armoire doors. He cast her a curious glance, stripped off his flannel, and lifted the mattress out of the frame as if it weighed nothing, his lovely muscles outlined by a faded gray T-shirt.

Lexy quelled the unexpected flutter in her stomach, but her throat went dry. She had a thing about arms. She was pretty sure there was no biological basis for the feeling. It was learned behavior all the way. Impressionable girls were exposed to T-shirt–clad male bodies repeatedly in high school, and arm lust inevitably developed. It was like collateral damage that went with the diploma. She should write a book about it, except she wasn't going to write any more books.

Sam Worth leaned the mattress against the wall and reached for the box springs. Lexy stood stupidly, watching his back, wondering what was happening to her. His T-shirt stretched over cute deltoids, nice trapeziuses, and beautiful lats.

"They broke some slats. I'll cut some new ones and reattach the side rail."

"Will that make the bed strong enough?"

"What are you afraid of?" He looked back at her over his shoulder. "Another night of head-banging, mosh-pit sex?" Lexy swallowed. For a moment Sam Worth's gaze seemed to get stuck on her throat. Then he cleared his own. "Yeah, that could break the bed."

31

Not what she wanted. "So, can you make it really strong so it won't give way again?"

He looked from the bed to her, one eyebrow cocked. "Am I missing something here? A new inn policy—rent by the hour and change the sheets frequently?"

"Of course not." She caught his grin, annoyed that he could get to her.

It wasn't her fault that the cyclists had broken the bed. She and Colin had tried all the moves in her book while they were still together, and they'd never so much as popped a mattress coil. The book specifically warned readers to begin with a firm mattress. It was true that a late-night comedy show skit involving her book and a well-known politician had ended with a collapsed bed, but that was comedic license.

Sam Worth turned from her to the bed. "I think I can work something out." He shrugged those broad shoulders. "If they break it again, I'll be back. No extra charge."

"Fine." Like that was a good idea—having him come back to move his lovely muscles for her.

Sam signaled Nigel at the bar to pull him another brew. The taciturn Englishman nodded.

The bed busters and the inn's other guests had cleared out, leaving the centuries-old taproom to the regulars, and they were mostly all there. Maybe it was the inn's age that made their own history seem so long, even though it had been no more than fifteen years since most of them had left high school. Sam had been one of the few to leave Drake's Point and stay away for any amount of time. Walt Vernon had left, but he'd come right back. Charlie Beaton's one foray into the outside world had ended badly. Meg Sullivan had never left.

At least Meg wasn't in the pub tonight, so there wouldn't be the usual brawl with Charlie over Meg's affections. Tonight Charlie could focus on his consumption of ale and on losing at darts to the guys from the fire station.

Sam wound his way around the small dark tables to the bar, passing close enough to Flo Locke to smell her perfume and look down the front of her silk jacket. He had been looking down Flo Locke's V-necks ever since he'd returned to Drake's Point. He mostly did it to annoy Nigel. Nigel Hammond had to be fifty. He was a newcomer to the scene who had drifted in from somewhere wearing the look of a man who had done a lot of hard living. He could tend bar, quell disputes, and speak Spanish—perfect qualifications for the job of bartender at the Tooth and Nail. Sam had a theory about just where Nigel might have acquired those skills. Eventually the guy would have to figure out how he felt about Flo.

Sam took his drink back to his favorite corner and settled in to wait. He had a bone to pick with Walter Vernon, Jr., Drake's Point's egotistical excuse for a mayor. Vernon had found yet another way to slow progress on the new library: blackmail. That was Vernon for you—anything for Drake's Point. Sam had been knocking down the obstacles Vernon put in his path since May, and in spite of Vernon, the new library was nearly done. With any luck it would open before the old use permit expired. That was the challenge—to beat the deadline. If he got the place open, he believed the Drake's Point town council would issue a new permit in spite of Vernon.

Permits, inspections, correction notices—they were part of building, but no one insisted on more paperwork than Vernon. For every board-foot of Forest Stewardship Council lumber in the new library, Vernon had managed to generate a foot of paperwork for Sam to deal with.

If Sam's company had been building the library, he would have had assistants dealing with the barrage of paper, but if he put the company name on the project, he would have to deal with the press. His green building work inevitably drew press attention, and as a rule, that was good. He wanted to spread the word about the merits of the work. It was just that once the media arrived, they tended to focus on his life and not his work. He needed to keep the library out of the press as long as he could. He didn't want any reporters digging into any local history. So he was on his own, and the piles of paper kept growing on the big table in the old dining room at Worth House.

He hadn't wanted to come back to Drake's Point, but he had been unable to deny the Ladies Book Club. They had been his mother's closest friends, and if they hadn't given up on her dream of having the library built, how could he? They had hounded him in their ladylike way, and when his engagement dissolved, he had caved. He had been at loose ends, having planned some time away from his business for an extended honeymoon. Instead, he had come back to Drake's Point.

Big mistake. Nothing like going home to remind you that you can't go home again.

He filled his palm with roasted pumpkin seeds from the little cup on the table. There weren't many working farms left in Drake's Point since Vernon had become mayor. Even Meg Sullivan's father, who still grew pumpkins, mostly left them in the fields for tourists to pick later in the fall. It was Meg who turned the seeds into Drake's Point's favorite snack, roasting them to buttery, salty crispness.

All in all it was a pretty tame evening for Drake's Point. The dart game was still friendly, Flo was catching glances from Nigel, and Vernon had yet to show up. Then the glasses started rattling in their rack above the bar.

"Someone's having a good time." One of the boys from the fire station drew a laugh from the darts players. The glasses rattled some more, and everyone was looking up when a heavy thump made the ceiling shudder. "Now, that's what I call getting laid."

"Oh, rubbish. They're done it again." Flo was up and out of her seat, heading for the guest rooms.

Damn! Sam thought he'd fixed that bed. Then he had to smile. The new innkeeper would be needing his services again. He heard the angry bluster of her disgruntled patron at the top of the inn stairs, and smiled. And she'd claimed *Sam* had a big ego! It sounded as if she was dealing with a guy who'd had his super-sized.

Sam's amusement was just fading when Vernon

walked in. He was an obvious sort of guy; nothing was understated about Vernon, from his tasseled loafers to his silk sports coat, Italian tie, and gold watch. He greeted the regulars, ordered a CC Manhattan from Nigel, and leaned back against the bar, waiting for everyone to suck up to him.

Sam didn't move. "Vernon, back off Amadeo."

Vernon picked up his drink and strolled over. "What do you mean?"

"You're ruining him because he agreed to do some cabinets for the library. That's low even for you."

"Farming is tough business. Not everyone's cut out to make a go of it." Vernon slid into the chair opposite Sam's and arranged the cocktail napkin under his drink.

"Amadeo's been farming his place for fifty years."

Vernon sipped his drink. "It's not my fault he uses too much well water. You're the green builder. You know we've got to be environmentally conscious this near the coast."

"You used city funds for a study to say the salmon were endangered by his water use."

"Just doing my duty."

"Just keeping everyone in Drake's Point under your thumb."

Vernon sipped his drink. "Worth, you can't come back here after fifteen years and tell everyone what to do."

"Maybe I should get a silk suit first."

"You left. I stayed. I've kept this place going." Vernon drew himself up into his champion-of-the-people pose.

Sam had to laugh. "You mean you've kept everybody else down. Even you can't be so deluded about your character. You're a greedy, self-important bastard, like my father, only not as charming."

Vernon clinked his glass down hard. "Listen, Worth, you want some sound advice? You can't rewrite history. Your mother was a stripper who spread her—"

Sam snagged Vernon's tie and yanked. The mayor came up out of his chair like a big salmon and landed gasping on the table. Pumpkin seeds and bourbon went flying. Sam gave Vernon's tie another savage tug.

"My mother was the president of the Ladies Book Club. She raised the money and oversaw the design for a town library."

"There's not going to be a library with your mother's name on it in m . . . this town." Vernon spoke through gritted teeth.

"Vernon, let's get one thing perfectly clear. You are not making a profit out of anything I build." Sam released him. Vernon slid back into his chair, brushing pumpkin seeds off his jacket and straightening his tie.

Bourbon dripped on the floor.

"I should charge you with assault."

"Do it. I'm sure Chief Brock would be happy to oblige."

Charlie Beaton ambled over from the darts game and stood next to Sam. Apparently it was his night to be on Sam's side. "Vernon, try not to be such a worm."

Not possible, Sam thought. Malice twisted Vernon's face as the mayor weighed his options. They were locked in a battle that had started years ago, only this *time*, Sam meant to win. He waited for Vernon to back down. There would be nothing so clean as a direct fight with Vernon.

Chapter 3
Some Muscles to Tone

"Taking a few minutes each day to condition stomach, hip, and thigh muscles increases sexual fitness."

—*Workout Sex*, Lexy Clark

Worth House was the biggest house on the highest hill in Drake's Point. Sam took his morning coffee out onto the old porch, where he could see over the tangle of his mother's neglected garden, down the hill, across the town, and far out to sea. There was no fog this morning.

He hung his big double sleeping bag over the porch rail to air and stretched out the stiffness in his back. For weeks he had been sleeping in the library at night. Better to wake up with a stiff back than to give Vernon a chance to damage the place.

The click of dog nails on the boards of the porch made him turn. "Missed you yesterday," he said. Winston, his big golden retriever, stopped a few feet away and looked Sam over. Winston might give the impression that he was easy-going, but he didn't miss much. "Your breakfast's ready."

Winston ignored the offer and shifted downwind of Sam. Winston never did anything so obvious as sniff. He just shrewdly put himself in a position to assess Sam's adventures, moving in, slowly processing each thread of scent on Sam's person.

"You missed a chance to go up on the mountain yesterday. Amadeo didn't show up for work, so I went to check on him. I assume you had other things planned." When they'd first returned to Drake's Point, Winston had checked out all the bitches in town and settled on one pale blonde lab, Vernon's dog. Sam thought her a rather flighty character, but Winston was courting her steadily, waiting for her season, letting her and all her other admirers know she was his intended. The whole process required frequent absences from home.

Now Winston stopped, his concentration total. Sam was wearing yesterday's flannel shirt, and he had a pretty good idea which scent was going through that canine brain. "Yes, I met a woman. Nothing to get your neck hairs up about. Go have your food, and I'll tell you about her."

Winston waited just long enough to make it a matter of his choice rather than Sam's command and trotted off to the kitchen. Sam could understand Winston's wariness. The dog's experiences with women hadn't been pretty.

The previous March, Julia Flood Stoddard, a fourth-generation San Francisco deb, had brought Winston home to the house she and Sam were sharing in Pacific Heights, complaining that the dog had been foisted upon her. She had been playing charitable lady when a vicious television person had trapped her into taking the dog on camera in front of God-knew-how-many people. She'd had no choice, but what was she going to do with a stray? Sam had discovered Winston locked in a broom closet off the garage. And maybe because Sam hadn't tried to keep him, Winston had stayed.

And Winston's staying had been the beginning of the end for Sam and Julia. Sam had been sorting through the wreckage for clues ever since. She had been the perfect choice for him. More important than safe sex was safe love, and Sam practiced the latter. He liked women who weren't affected by his looks: snotty, cool, independent women, the kind who didn't get hurt when the inevitable breakup came. *Not women with vulnerable brown eyes.*

Julia had been as thin and refined as anyone outside the British royal family could be. Nothing jiggled, swayed, or bounced when she walked. She didn't scream, moan, or sweat when she made love. She was an unmusical girl, none of the usual passages of air through the pipes of the human body escaped her. She had a sneeze as soft as a whisper, and she was incapable of a snort, burp, or fart.

She had surprised Sam by being interested in marriage. He hadn't thought of himself as a good candidate, but he had believed they might last a few years—as long as most marriages did anyway. They were like parallel lines that could go on forever without meeting. She was smart and ladylike, with an easy knowledge of all the details of her world, and she liked educating Sam. In her company he got quite good at spotting an inferior gown or a knock-off handbag.

But Julia and Sam had faded as Winston and Sam hit it off. Man and dog liked sleeping with the window open at night, getting wet and sandy at the beach, and taking long walks in the fog. Then the announcement of Sam and Julia's engagement had sent an interested society columnist digging into Sam's past. He didn't know which Julia had objected to more—his father, Ajax Worth, or his mother, Cherry Popp.

Ajax Worth had been big and brash, as unrefined as the Oklahoma crude oil he'd once brought out of the ground, and as shrewd and calculating as the racetrack totalizer he had invented. Racetracks used computers now, but Ajax Worth had made millions on a device that displayed the changing odds and results to the betting public. He had been rich enough to buy anything he wanted when he met Cherry Popp.

Cherry had been a star on the stages of San Francisco's raunchiest O'Farrell Street theaters. There she had done things with an ice cream cart and a cherry popsicle that had raised the admiration of hundreds of men. Thirty-five years later, reporters loved the story of the son of Ajax Worth and Cherry Popp aspiring to the inner circle of San Francisco's oldest families. Julia had not been pleased. She had given Sam his ring back.

By that time, Sam had figured out Winston's history. The dog had been on his own for some time. He hadn't meant to get captured, caged, and exposed to public pity as a wretched specimen of neglect or abuse. So when Sam left the city, he offered Winston a place in the back of his truck. Winston had bounded up without hesitation, and they'd headed for Drake's Point. Their two-male household suited them both. And sometime in the months since his return to Drake's Point, he'd started talking to the dog, really talking, in complete sentences, whole paragraphs. That was probably a sign he should not ignore, an early warning that he could go seriously crazy if he stayed in Drake's Point too long.

He should finish the library and head straight for the city. At Worth Construction headquarters he would have dozens of people to talk to.

And he should start dating again. The thought depressed him more than talking to the dog.

Winston wandered back out from the kitchen, did a bit of minor grooming, allowed his head and ears to be stroked briefly, and settled down on the porch facing Sam, his big lion-like head on his front paws.

"You want to hear about her?"

Winston gave him a steady gaze, not impatient, but not relenting either.

"She's not from around here—L.A. dealer frames around her license plates." Alexandra Clark had that caffeinated L.A. edge to her. The whole flowered-skirt, cardigan-sweater thing didn't fool him. She moved too quickly, took things on too directly. And that was the good news. She'd never stay in Drake's Point. He'd give her a month, six weeks max, to become thoroughly frustrated with the pace of life here. She wouldn't get the place. Most outsiders didn't. They started looking for the movie theater, the drug store, the mall. They wanted cable with a hundred stations, and good radio reception. They wanted working cell phones, fast Internet access, convenience stores and espresso machines. And they hated the power outages and mudslides of winter. Meanwhile, he had a month to get her out of the church-lady skirts and into one of her inn's beds. He smiled at the possibilities.

The birds started up, and Winston shook himself, reminding Sam to keep the story going.

"You're wondering how the elk got mixed up in it? She was having a conversation with him, trying to encourage him to graze elsewhere. We can't give her any points for common sense, but we've got to give her big points for directness and guts." He did admire the way she took the world head-on.

Winston sat up.

Sam tossed the last of his coffee over the porch rail. "Relax. I'm not planning to buy another ring anytime soon. There's work to do." Still, things were looking up. There was a new single woman in Drake's Point, and she didn't know his history. October was off to a good start.

Violeta Montoro stared at the broken bed in room 7 and knew what was wrong with her marriage. The bed smelled like promises, like the piña coladas she and Emiliano had drunk those first days in San Francisco in a hotel overlooking the bay. At eighteen she had married Emiliano Montoro, the smartest, finest boy in San Lazaro. Emiliano promised they would leave the village and the fish nets and find a better life. Violeta pulled at the sheets, refusing to remember that time.

Now they were living in another small village, and she was cleaning hotel rooms, not staying in them. Now the lousy guests were breaking the beds and leaving no tip, and how was she going to fill her savings jar with enough money to make a better life? Now Emiliano was studying all the time, learning English, and she was still struggling to understand the manager's orders. Now she was wondering every day—what if he found his new life and didn't want her anymore? Even now it was hard to tell whether Emiliano wanted her, with all the studying and the tiredness. Now she and Emiliano were falling into an exhausted sleep without so much as making their bed bounce now and then.

She gathered the coconut-smelling sheets into a big ball, and something fell out, landing on her foot. Violeta reached down and scooped up a red paperback book. On the cover the torsos of a man and a woman met, his arm around her for modesty so that the breast did not show. Violeta knew one word of the title: *"Sex."* She flipped the book open. The couples in the illustrations danced in the sheets.

Violeta looked from the book to the bed. So this was why the gringos broke the bed. They left no tip, but they left their book. She would take it home, and if Emiliano wanted her to read English, he could teach her to read this book. And they would make their bed bounce again.

* * *

From somewhere below came the smell of butter and sugar meeting in a heated encounter. Lexy fell back on her floor mat and abandoned her abdominals. Core work and breathing, those were the foundation of her program. But this morning her workout wasn't going well. Horizontal positions felt sexy instead of disciplined, and push-ups reminded her of Sam Worth's arms. Pelvic thrusts were out of the question. Even her long, lean thighs routine made her think completely irrelevant thoughts about Sam Worth.

The warm, sweet smell grew stronger.

Someone was baking. Lexy remembered baking. She didn't do it herself, but random baking and shopping were her mother's main maternal impulses. Whenever her professor mother finished a scholarly article, Lexy and her brothers would be treated to cylindrical loaves of heavy, brown, seed-studded bread. Worse, whenever her mother finished a semester, she seemed to remember that Lexy was a girl, and insist that they go shopping. Her mother's fashion sense was as trendy as her coffee-can bread. Lexy had been scarred for her entire secondary school social life by the black and white polka-dot jumpsuit with stirrups that she had worn to her first middle school dance. Even in the eighties that jumpsuit had been a fashion crime. The label "Sexy Lexy" had been sarcastic, and it had been superglued to Lexy through high school. She'd been voted least likely to ever make the *Sports Illustrated* swimsuit issue.

She thought she'd escaped the old label, working at

Pacifica. In the academic world people cared about different labels, and no one read *Sports Illustrated*. She had worn fitness gear and dated Colin. The Sexy Lexy label had disappeared until she wrote the book. She'd probably been a little silly yesterday to be so uneasy about its showing up in Drake's Point. After all, innkeeping and promoting fitness were such entirely different fields, that even with the similarity of names, no one in Drake's Point would connect her with *that* Lexy Clark. Still, she was glad that her editor and agent had insisted on that blonde hair for her publicity photo on the inside back cover. At the time it had seemed a blatant falsehood, but now it allowed her to distance herself from the Lexy Clark who had written "that book."

Lexy lay back on the floor to admire her lovely room. More chintz, lots of pink flowers, a soft moss green carpet. The book and the cyclists were gone, and her new life could truly begin. She jumped up and pulled back the curtains from the mullioned windows and pushed them wide open. No fog, just a fresh, ocean-scented breeze.

Her first task was to get the bed in number 7 repaired again. She needed that room available. The question was whether to call Sam Worth or not. She pondered it as she showered and dressed.

She followed the good baking smells to the large sunny room off the kitchen where she found ten handsome people in tan Tooth and Nail T-shirts gathered around a long pine table. Plain in all their faces were the unmistakable features of their Aztec ancestors. In front of them was spread a very English breakfast—bacon, eggs, tomatoes, toast, scones, blue and white pots of cream and marmalade. Steam rose from the spouts of two white teapots.

Calculating the caloric content of the meal would involve higher math than Lexy remembered.

Flo greeted her. "Welcome to morning coffee, a tradition for the staff here."

Lexy smiled and tried not to breathe the fat-laden vapor. "Good morning." All the heads nodded.

"They don't speak much English," Flo confided.

Lexy tried not to look dismayed. She had looked forward to working closely with her staff. Her tourist Spanish would get her a beer or a bathroom, but she didn't know how to direct a whole staff without being able to speak to them. "Who translates?"

"Nigel, the bartender. And Violeta's husband—when he's here—is completely bilingual."

At a few words from the man at the head of the table, each employee produced a green card.

"How do they know what to do?"

"Oh, they all came together, except for Violeta." Flo indicated one unsmiling girl. Violeta had smoldering dark eyes and a sullen beauty. She had already returned her card to her jeans pocket. Flo went on. "They worked for an Englishman who had a large house in Cuernavaca. They produce a proper tea, and they run the inn like a house party on a lord's country estate."

Okay, Lexy had to learn to run an inn and speak Spanish. But on the plus side, if her staff didn't speak

English, if they didn't watch television or read books in English, they had never heard of *Workout Sex* or its author. That was another sign that she had come to the right place. She gave them all her warmest smile. "I'm Alexandra Clark."

Everyone smiled back, except Violeta. Flo moved around the table naming people—the chef, his assistant, two waitresses, the bus boys, the upstairs and downstairs maids, and a pair of groundsmen.

Ernesto, her chef, pulled out a chair for her. Everyone began passing food her way. She thought the first words she needed to learn in Spanish might be *fat-free*.

At noon a pair of potential guests stood in the vestibule ringing the bell, and Flo was missing. Guests had come and gone. Rooms were cleaned and readied for their next occupants. The patio was blown clear of leaves, the tables in the dining room set with fresh flowers. Lexy had mastered opening the inn's reservations system, but she had not accomplished the one task she had set herself: fixing the bed.

There was one Yellow Pages for Drake's Point, and it did not list any carpenters. The nearest one in the inn Rolodex was several miles up the coast and didn't answer his phone. So the bed in number 7 still wasn't fixed. Lexy did not want to lose the unexpected guests. They were a sweet couple in their seventies in tweeds and sensible shoes with binoculars around their necks. She was sure they would never break a bed. Putting them in room 7 would make up a little for the two days of revenue lost when the cyclists left.

Sam Worth appeared to be the solution to the problem. He apparently did lots of work in town, and he had promised not to charge more for a second visit. She could hire him quite legitimately, as a business woman needing a carpenter. Still, he might gloat, and she had a feeling that she might be calling him just to watch those arm muscles work. Maybe the fog or the encounter with the elk had short-circuited her brain. She had not devoted so much mental energy to a man in months.

First she had to find him.

Asking the sullen Violeta about Flo produced a series of incomprehensible hand gestures that left Lexy perplexed and Violeta looking even more cross than she had at breakfast. Without Flo, Lexy had no idea how to find Sam Worth. Without Spanish she had no idea how to find Flo. She finally tried Francisco, the bus boy, who handed her a note.

Dear Alexandra,
    Gone to town for the post,

                                          Florence Locke

Lexy settled her tweedy guests in the dining room, explaining her temporary short-handedness, and headed for town. She needed Flo, Sam Worth, and a Spanish dictionary.

A block west of the inn, the road split into two branches. Beach Street curved south around the cove, and Ocean Avenue wound west toward the end of the point. The fog of the day before had disappeared, and the Pacific sparkled in the sun. Odors of green growing things mixed with the salty tang of the sea in the cool air. On each side of the cove a handful of narrow streets fanned up the hill from the main road. Faded Victorian cottages with listing white-columned porches poked up through dark pines and cypress trees. Redwoods grew in dense groves in the folds of the mountain slope. Lexy headed left along Beach Street.

She liked the lazy, weekend feel of the place. Dogs looked up from porches as she passed. Cars passed with surfboards piled on top. A motorcyclist in black leather rumbled by on a big bike. A spiky-haired teenager wove around her on a skateboard, defying the perils of the cracked sidewalk. Old cars listed right and left along the curving street.

Flowers obviously loved the place and were allowed to run wild in the gardens. Frothy white heads of Queen Anne's Lace and golden wild fennel swayed in the breeze. Pink roses wound themselves around fences and chimneys, and clover and poppies sprouted in the cracks of the ancient sidewalks. Shameless pink Naked Ladies on their slender brown stalks made their late summer appearance in bare stretches of brown dirt. Patches of blackberries overran every vacant space. At the top of the hill a graceful old mansion with extensive ruined gardens overlooked the town. Lexy took the flowers as another sign that she had come to the right place. Her new innkeeper wardrobe was all about flowers, from her flowered high-cut briefs to her crocheted collars. No more black Spandex for Alexandra Clark.

She stopped in front of one pale yellow house to

admire its colorful terraced garden. Rims of white porcelain pots overflowed with floppy nasturtiums and balls of orange and yellow lantana. Purple cosmos, spiky lavender, and fingers of cat mint grew around the base of each pot. Pumpkin vines laden with ripening orange globes curled along the spaces between the rows of pots.

Nasturtiums reminded her of ideas springing up. She hadn't had any good ideas on her book tour, but she would in Drake's Point, she felt sure. Not that she was planning to write another book, but she stooped and gathered a handful of pale, green nasturtium seeds for her pocket.

Maybe she would write a short guide to Drake's Point for inn visitors. The lovely garden with the white pots would be the first stop on a self-guided tour. A guitar chord sounded from inside the house, and Lexy lifted her gaze from the garden. A collection of strange white guitars hung in the windows of the glassed-in porch. The hidden guitarist began to pick out a tune, and recognition hit her. The instruments were toilet seats. She looked back at the flower pots—toilet bowls, all of them.

She felt a little silly to have missed the obvious and vowed to be more skeptical. Drake's Point wasn't exactly Brigadoon after all.

About halfway down the block, the flag fluttered over the roof of a low, gray-shingled building where a group of women gathered on the porch. As Lexy headed their way, she spotted Flo among them, her gaze on a building under construction across the street. A single hammer pounded rhythmically. The women on the porch kept their eyes on the building while they spread dishes on a long table covered with a blue-checkered cloth.

Three identical blonde teenagers with bare midriffs, cropped black pants, and besotted looks on their sun-pinkened faces never turned from the building across the street as they passed a plastic snack bag back and forth.

When Lexy reached the porch, she saw an abundant lunch spread on the blue-checked cloth. There were plates of thick sandwiches on wheat bread, bowls of green salad with bright cherry tomatoes, cakes, and brownies.

Flo, who had been so attentive and helpful an hour earlier, barely spared Lexy a quick glance. "Oh Alexandra, you must have got my note. I've got the post. There's a big envelope for you from Star Media."

"Thanks. Actually, I'm looking for Sam Worth."

A small round woman with short white hair in a bob smiled at Lexy. "You've come to the right place then, dear." She pulled the plastic wrap off a large bowl of salad. "I'm Dawn Russell, the mayor's assistant. You must be the new innkeeper."

Lexy shook the offered hand.

"We're the Ladies Book Club of Drake's Point. Everyone, meet our new innkeeper."

For a few minutes Lexy shook hands and tried to connect names and faces. Most of the ladies of the book club were contemporaries of her mother, but they didn't look anything like her mother's academic friends. Their sun-browned faces were full of character and earthiness; their figures were lush. They wore their gray hair long, and dressed in faded jeans and work shirts with big bands of silver and turquoise and wide woven leather belts, and they didn't fit in any of Lexy's usual categories for women. She saw no signs of lurking mini-vans and no hidden designer bags.

She wasn't sure anyone actually noticed her. They all kept looking across the street. The blonde clones continued to pass their snack bag back and forth. It was full of pumpkin seeds—a great source of zinc.

Dawn caught her glance. "Forest, Leaf, and Meadow are our newest members. They've just joined, but they're so determined to help."

Lexy tried to imagine how the three zinc-consuming zombies might help a book club. It was a stretch.

Only Dawn seemed able to tear her gaze away from the building project. "The mayor would like to welcome you to Drake's Point today, Ms. Clark. May he drop by the inn this afternoon?"

Lexy issued an invitation for tea. She supposed she would join the Drake's Point Chamber of Commerce.

The hammering stopped. Every pair of female eyes shifted to a point behind Lexy. The clones exhaled a common sigh and curled their blue-painted toes over the edges of their pink flip flops.

Lexy turned to see what had them gawking. Sam Worth stood on the porch roof of the new building opposite them, below a half-shingled turret. He pulled his white T-shirt over his head, wiped his face with it, and tipped his head back to take a long drink from a plastic bottle. The sun gleamed on his bronzed shoulders and picked out golden highlights in his hair. Beads of bright liquid trickled down his long torso. A leather tool belt rode low around his hips.

Lexy's brain melted in her skull and dribbled out her ears.

"Here." It was Flo's voice. "Eat this. You need to keep your strength up."

Lexy put out her hand to take whatever Flo offered. She put it in her mouth and let her teeth sink into avocado, cheese, bacon, mayonnaise, and soft sweet wheat bread full of seeds. She caught the crumbs with her tongue.

"That's the iced tea I made for him," said a voice behind Lexy.

"It's my turn on Monday," said another.

"We made the brownies," said the teenaged clones together.

The crackle of the plastic bag being passed between the clones snapped Lexy out of her trance. She swallowed and put the sandwich on the porch rail. She had just consumed an unhealthy dose of fat grams because a small-town hunk who knew his power over the local females had removed his shirt. Worse still, she was going to have to ask for help from him. He was obviously used to sucking up female adoration like a power-vac. It was a mortifying blow to her idea of her new self, the poised, assured businesswoman, not to mention that the three clones could be seriously damaged here, exposed to such a man at an impressionable age. Lexy could at least divert their attention from the tool belt.

She stalked down the porch steps, and halted abruptly at the curb to avoid colliding with a woman

cyclist, who swerved around Lexy on a yellow bicycle. The woman was way younger than most of the
book club ladies but equally lush and earthy with
carroty red hair in a long braid down her back. She
was dressed like a cowgirl in a blue western shirt,
jeans, and cowboy boots.

"Hey, Sam Worth," the woman called up to him
without a glance at Lexy.

"Hey, Meg Sullivan," he called down.

They clearly knew each other in a way that made
Lexy feel foolish for even her fleeting thoughts about
Sam Worth. She had obviously misjudged his interest
in her the day before.

"I've got your pumpkin seeds at the store." Meg
waved and then rode off out of view.

Pumpkin seeds! Lexy looked back at the clones with
their bag of seeds. Apparently, everyone in Drake's
Point was getting plenty of zinc, and no one had read
her book. As comforting as the thought was, it meant
that none of them knew the invigorating effect of all
that zinc on the adrenal glands.

She marched across the street. The new building
was a handsome updated version of the Victorians
around her. A wide welcoming porch stretched the
width of the first floor. The upper story had a pair of
round turrets at each end and a row of three gabled
dormers in the middle. Now that she looked more
closely, she could see that the building was unfinished inside. Its wide double front doors were
propped open, and sunlight made bright patches on
the plywood sub-flooring. Insulation lined the still-
exposed framing of a single large room.

Sam Worth was applying shingles to the second story. Shading her eyes with her hand, she tilted her face up to him.

"Mr. Worth, do you have a minute?"

He lowered the water bottle and wiped his mouth with the back of his hand. "Ms. Clark, do you need that bed fixed right away?"

"How did you know it was broken?"

"I was in the pub last night. Everyone in Drake's Point knows your guests had quite a workout."

Lexy's mouth dropped open, and she shut it abruptly. She told herself he didn't know about her book. "Workout" was only a phrase, not an intentional reference. "Apparently you're the only carpenter in town."

"Looked elsewhere, did you?"

"Does your employer mind your entertaining a female audience while you work?"

A puzzled look crossed his face, then he grinned at her, the kind of grin that told her she'd gotten something about the situation wrong. "My *employer* encourages it, insists that I keep them happy."

No wonder he understood the behavior of the bull tule elk. He was one of them. He had his harem grazing nearby, gazing in awe at his . . . antlers. He unhooked the tool belt and slipped it from his hips. There was a collective gasp from across the street. Lexy's stomach did a somersault. He swung down from the roof, landing lightly an arm's length from Lexy.

At close range in warm sunlight a shirtless Sam Worth was good to look at. Lexy's resting heart rate sped up. She had thought herself impervious to shoulders and pecs after her tour. Nicely put together males had come on to her at each stop, offering to help her develop more workout techniques. Sam Worth was something different. He wasn't oiled, shaved, or sculpted, and he did have those arms. He looked—natural.

"Did your bed-breaking guests finally leave?"

"Last night late."

"Relieved, huh? What did you have against them? Did they uncover your dark secret?"

Lexy swallowed. His tone was teasing, but she didn't trust the shrewd look in his eyes. "What makes you think I have anything to hide?"

"In those church-lady outfits of yours? You have everything hidden."

"It's called modesty. You might not be familiar with the concept." Her gaze dropped to his chest.

He laughed and took another swallow of water. "Got you to look."

"It might have been an accident. I had to see why everyone was staring. And these clothes are vintage Laura Ashley."

He was staring, at her lips. "You've got something on your . . ."

Lexy rubbed her lips together.

"Let me." He reached out and touched the corner of her mouth with the tip of his finger; no pressure, just dizzying contact. Her lips tingled, and her nerves sent hot little messages to parts of Lexy that were already paying too much attention to Sam Worth. She took a quick step back from him. He should not be

58

having such an effect on her. Lexy knew the whole physiological progression of sexual attraction—the body check, eye contact, voice exchange, hand contact. It was a perfectly logical sequence, but Sam Worth's casual touch put the process into hyperdrive. She thought about his unregulated consumption of pumpkin seeds.

"The bed." The word came out breathy.

"You know, I thought I fixed that bed so that the 49'ers could scrimmage there."

"Can you fix it again?"

"Today?" He glanced up at the unfinished building.

"This afternoon. A new couple showed up. They don't have a reservation, but they'll stay the night if I can get that bed fixed. It would be great to make up the lost revenue."

"You let that other pair walk!"

"Only fair."

"I was thinking you ought to charge them. They broke the bed twice."

She shrugged. Let him think she was crazy. She wasn't going to explain why she needed to have them gone. He had already made jokes about secrets and workouts. She wasn't going to give him any hints about her past.

"You have an interesting way of doing business, Ms. Clark. I'll come up to the inn after lunch." He headed toward the admiring crowd on the porch. "Are you joining us?"

She shook her head. "You should skip the pumpkin seeds. Trust me, they're overkill."

* * *

Two hours later, Lexy's potential guests were still out bird-watching. Sam Worth hadn't arrived, but Mayor Vernon had. He gave her his card, but insisted right away that Lexy call him Walt. They had a corner of the inn's dining room to themselves.

Walt had a baby face with a square brow, pointed chin, and a head of springy brown curls. He reminded Lexy of someone, but she couldn't think who. He spoke with a slow deliberation that made Lexy want to finish his sentences, and he looked as if not so much as a chromosome of his person was out of place. Not like Sam Worth.

On the whole she decided she had handled her latest encounter with Sam Worth rather well, so she should not be distracted by thoughts of him now. It was just that she expected him to show up any minute to repair the bed.

"Alexandra, thank you for agreeing to meet me and allowing me to be the first to welcome you to the business community here, and to say, I hope we can work together."

Lexy pulled herself back to the present. This was the mayor, and she had a business to run. His formal manner conveyed his sense of her as a fellow businessperson. Here was a man who would invite her to a Chamber of Commerce meeting, not to a workout on a mattress.

"I hope it's not too presumptuous of me to ask you to get involved right away."

She was going to say "not at all" when her chef Ernesto appeared and left them a silver tray full of scones and clotted cream, pieces of dark rich chocolate layer cake, and dainty heart-shaped sandwiches with visible mayonnaise. Under cover of the table she pinched the flesh at her waist with her thumb and forefinger. Not bad. She was still probably under seventeen percent body fat.

"Now that's a tea!" Walt beamed at her. "You could get top dollar for that tea. Imagine the revenue if people came over to the inn after shopping in town or visiting an art showing at the gallery."

"There's an art gallery in town?" Lexy had missed that.

Walt straightened his tie. Silk, Italian. Lexy had the feeling he would know which wine to order with dinner and where one could find the best risotto in Tuscany.

"There could be." Walt gave her another earnest look. "With your help. Drake's Point is on the cusp—I won't say of a boom, but of a revival. The tourist dollar has never been more vital." He loaded a plate with two of the little sandwiches, a scone, and a piece of layer cake.

Lexy's stomach contracted painfully. She hadn't eaten since the bite of sandwich at the noontime Sam Worth viewing. She focused on a small compote dish filled with blueberries and melon.

"What can I do to help?" She might be hungry, but she wasn't going to miss this opportunity to establish her connections to other businesspeople in Drake's Point. She reached for the compote dish, but Walt beat her to it, and she took a cucumber sandwich.

Walt flashed her his high wattage smile again. "I like your attitude, Alexandra. There's a group of local businesspeople who have found a great location for a collection of shops that we think will really boost our local economy. And we wondered if you'd be willing to help us get the project going."

Lexy nodded. "What sort of shops?" Before she purchased the inn, Lexy had made sure that Drake's Point didn't have a bookstore. In fact, she knew it didn't even have a library.

Walt reached for his briefcase and drew out a clipboard. "Well, an art gallery, of course, and a gift shop to sell local crafts, and perhaps a clothing store."

Lexy tried her sandwich. It was delicious. She could picture a quaint shopping area in Drake's Point within walking distance of the inn. Her guests would probably find an art gallery more charming than the toilet bowl garden.

Walt turned the clipboard her way. "What I have here is a citizens petition to convert this prime location to commercial use. Can I get you to sign?"

"Of course." Lexy wiped her fingers, took the clipboard, and started reading the description of the property at 39 Beach Street. There were "whereases" to spare in the legal jargon of the document.

Sam Worth's voice interrupted her reading. "I wouldn't sign until you know old Vernon a bit better."

She looked up, and he was standing there, the complete opposite of the mayor in fashion sensibility. Mayor Vernon was looking like the *Thomas Crowne Affair*, and Sam Worth was looking like *Cool Hand Luke*. If he frowned any harder, the mayor was going to need a botox treatment. "Worth, you're interrupting a private conversation."

"Sounded more like a snow job to me."

Okay. These two men hated each other. Lexy didn't need her B.A. to figure that out. There was clearly some history between them. She tried to ease the tension. "Walt was just filling me in on local business issues."

"Very civic-minded, our mayor. I'll just fix that bed for you, Ms. Clark."

But he didn't move. Then Ernesto emerged from the kitchen with a large ice-filled platter studded with oysters, pink centers surrounded by the ruffled silver edges of their shells. More zinc.

"Hola, Senor Sam." In a stream of Spanish, which apparently Sam Worth understood, Lexy caught the English words "mad rivers." With his gaze on Lexy, Sam Worth took an oyster and swallowed. Lexy watched his throat move, and she thought about all that zinc and what it would do for his already extreme testosterone levels. "I'll be upstairs, Ms. Clark."

Across from her, the mayor cleared his throat. "Now where were we?"

"You were talking about working together to promote the economy of Drake's Point." Lexy was surprised she remembered.

"You know, Alexandra, you do want to be concerned about occupancy. That's what drove the inn's last owners out. The more attractions Drake's Point can offer, the better for the inn. Our citizens initiative is the first step."

Lexy turned to the page where the signatures began. There were four. "How many signatures do you need?"

"We're just getting started. By the end of the month, we'll have hundreds."

"Alexandra?" Flo interrupted, sounding distressed. "The cyclists have called. Apparently they've left some book behind, and they want us to FedEx it to them at their next stop."

"Book?" They'd left *Workout Sex* behind, somewhere in the room where Sam Worth was repairing the bed. Lexy was standing before she knew it. "Mayor Vernon . . ."

"Walt."

"Walt. Do excuse me, please. There's a matter I have to resolve."

"Now? But—"

"Immediately."

"Fine. I won't take a minute more of your time. Just sign, and I'll be on my way."

Lexy scrawled her name and headed for the stairs.

Chapter 4
Stretching

"Habitual tension can lead to stiffness in the hip, back, and pelvic regions. A combination of both static and dynamic stretching before you begin your workout increases the range of motion available and prevents injuries."
— *Workout Sex*, Lexy Clark

Lexy found Sam Worth on his back on the floor, half under the broken bed, his long jeans-clad legs stretched out into the room. Good. She couldn't see his arms. Where was the book? She couldn't crawl under the bed to look. "So, how's it coming?"

"They snapped the screws right off."

"Is that bad?" Lexy peered over the rim of the bed, and scanned the patch of visible floor.

"Once I get the frame secure, I'll put more slats in. It'll be sturdy as a trampoline."

"I don't think that's necessary." She lifted the heavy bed curtains. Nothing.

He slid out from under the bed. "Expecting a tamer

breed of guests today? No one inclined to violent lovemaking?"

"An innkeeper doesn't speculate about her guests' use of the furniture." Lexy glanced at the pile of bedding in the corner. Violeta had stripped the bed. If she had seen the book, most likely she would have tossed it in the trash.

"Looking for something?"

"The last guests left an item behind."

Sam Worth left the room, and Lexy went to the heap of bedding. She shook the sheets, blankets, and spread. Sam came back with a armful of lumber, plugged in an orange extension cord, and stretched out under the bed again.

Lexy focused on her search, ignoring the brief bursts of sound from his drill. She opened the armoire. Nothing. The bathroom was equally bare. She tried the bureau drawers. Empty. She shifted the cushions in the window seat. The book wasn't anywhere. The bed-breaking cyclists must have taken it with them. But Lexy would see that her agent sent them a new copy. Just in case.

She turned at the snap of wood fitting snugly as Sam Worth shoved the new slats into place.

"Done." He slid the box springs over to the bed, tilted it up over the frame, settled it into place. The mattress followed. Then he stood back and looked at her. "I think you should test it."

"Test it?"

"Give it a good bounce, make sure it won't collapse."

"Not necessary." She stepped back.

"Are you sure? You don't want a lawsuit." He closed in on her, edging her up against the bed.

"I've got a good lawyer."

He looked grim. "Never involve a lawyer in anything you can do yourself." He caught her by the waist and swung her up. Her bottom landed on the firm mattress. Looking up at him, she bounced lightly.

"You call that a test?"

She bounced again, harder. The bed barely moved under her. "It's fine."

"Move over. Let's give it a real test."

Lexy scooted over as he climbed up beside her. She felt the bed dip under his weight then return as he stretched out.

"Nice canopy." He crossed his hands behind his head and closed his eyes. His brows and lashes were much darker than his wheaten hair. Involuntarily, her gaze slid down his body. He didn't move. He had the stretching part of Lexy's fitness routine down fine. He lay, utterly relaxed, while Lexy's whole body snapped to attention.

His eyes opened again. "What do you think they were doing when the bed collapsed?"

"I don't want to know." Lexy flopped back, but he had started her thinking, picturing Sam Worth getting fit.

"Have you ever broken a bed?"

"Of course not."

"At least they weren't swinging from the canopy, but you can't rule that out. Maybe you should put up

67

a sign." He stretched out one beautiful arm, pointing. "Right up under the canopy. 'Antique English beds. Suitable for missionary position only.'"

"Not necessary."

"I don't know. You think it can stand a real work-out?" He rolled onto his stomach and did a few rapid push-ups, an effortless flex of those arms. He had smooth firm skin in which the veins made rugged lines. Lexy imagined tracing those lines with her fingertips.

He collapsed beside her again. "Now that's a bed that won't break."

She checked out his fit body again. If there was a person who didn't need her book, it was Sam Worth.

Then a depressing thought occurred to her. Maybe her book had been so successful not because it was helpful to women but because it fit the psychology of men. They saw sex as an athletic endeavor, a work-out. They liked scoring, winning, crossing the goal line. Her brothers certainly did. "How much do I owe you?"

"Nothing. This one's on me." He rolled toward her on his side and his eyes had that knowing look.

"What?"

"Poor Ms. Clark. We met yesterday; we're in bed today. Not a record, but pretty good."

Lexy sat up. "I hate to prick your ego balloon. But we're *on* the bed, not in it."

He laughed and rolled to his feet. The bed felt empty without him.

"If it's ego balloons you want to prick, Walter Vernon's got the biggest one around."

She scooted to the edge of the bed, her skirts hiking up around her thighs. He checked them out with undisguised interest. *He likes my legs*, Lexy thought. She tugged at the offending skirts. He scooped up his flannel shirt and shrugged into it, a movement that emphasized his broad shoulders, and he caught Lexy watching him.

"You know I'm not some female elk that's going to be impressed by the breadth of your antler rack."

He offered her a hand. "You're more impressed by brains than brawn?"

She let him help her off the bed. "And by modesty, humility, and a considerable number of other things."

Sam looked pleased. "That's a cheering thought. Vernon won't stand a chance."

The fog rolled in at five, heavy and low, obscuring the horizon above the cove. Waves broke and crashed somewhere beyond Sam's vision. There was no wind and no hint of a sunset, only a deepening gloom. The cool air was just what he needed after another encounter with Alexandra Clark. He tossed a stick into the shore wash and waited for Winston to decide the game was at an end. They were both wet and sandy.

The dog trotted by Sam with the stick, a sapling really, as thick as a hockey stick and twice as long as Winston himself. He pranced up the beach with it and deposited his prize in a pile of driftwood against the dunes. Game over. Winston returned to Sam, gave himself a good shake and turned toward home.

Sam shook his head. "I'm going for a run. You go

69

ahead." He settled on a big piece of driftwood to pull off his work boots and socks.

Winston planted himself in the sand in front of him.

There was no fooling the dog. Sam hadn't run in weeks. "It's exercise. You've been getting the workout here. Now it's my turn."

Winston shifted downwind of Sam and cocked his head to one side.

"There's nothing to explain. Yes, I saw her, at the inn. Nothing happened. She's skinny and dresses like somebody's grandmother." He was not going to mention to his dog, no matter how intelligent, that he'd had Lexy Clark on that bed. Fully clothed, on top of the covers, though he'd been thinking naked and under.

He did some stretches. Who was he kidding—testing the bed?! She certainly got him heated. But the bed test also had been a moment of clarity. They were *going* to have sex. The question was when. The answer, because he was a gentleman, was when she was ready. Sam didn't think he was vain, just attuned to other people's signals. He had had to rely on nonverbal cues all through school, and not much got by him now. Her awareness of him put all his senses on alert whenever she was around. It seemed fair to encourage her.

Winston didn't budge. Sometimes Sam thought the dog could read his mind.

"It's just a run. I've got some bones for you from the inn."

The big ears came up.

"For a dog, you've got a black, suspicious heart."

Winston shook himself again, spraying sand and water, and trotted off.

On Wednesday morning Flo was rearranging a large slippery stack of old magazines in a corner of the inn's tiny office. She wore another cleavage-enhancing silk jacket, this one a deep green. The office appeared to be organized by a piling rather than a filing system. There were piles across the back of the desk, on top of the actual filing cabinet, and along the floor. It was something Lexy planned to work on. She was an organizer, a fan of the Dewey Decimal System and the Periodic Table. A good filing cabinet was her idea of an indispensable piece of furniture. She could have Sam Worth build some shelves.

The magazine tower threatened to collapse as Flo worked her way down the stack. Lexy put the Star Media manila envelope, with its glossy photos of *Workout Sex* hunk candidates, back in her drawer. She reminded herself to call her agent to send a new copy of the book to the bed-breaking cyclists.

A more immediate problem was getting billing information out of Sam Worth. On Monday he'd come to the inn again, at Flo's suggestion, with a big orange industrial-strength vacuum cleaner to remove the muddy tracks left behind by several bird-watching guests. From the bottom of the stairs she'd had a good view of that strong back and those beautiful arms at work. But he had sucked up the dirt and left with a grin and a cocky assurance that he'd "charge her the usual."

It bothered her. She had the feeling that he knew

something she didn't know; that he was humoring her, letting her think she was in charge. It was like playing games with her older brothers—exciting at first, fun to be included, but humiliating in the end when she lost, as she inevitably did, when they pulled out some rule or skill she hadn't realized the game required.

Eventually she would get the hang of how things worked in Drake's Point, and Sam wouldn't be able to flash that knowing smile at her. Flo was probably her best source of information.

"By the way, did Sam Worth leave a bill with you the other day?"

Flo laughed. She set a big clump of travel magazines on the only clear corner of the desk as she looked through the rest of the pile. "Oh, don't worry about Sam's bill. You can square things with him any time."

"Doesn't he need the income?"

"Sam? No worries there."

"He's from Drake's Point originally, isn't he?"

"His father used to own most of the property in town."

The magazines on the desk slid to the floor, and Lexy made a catch and helped Flo to reorganize. "*Used* to?"

"Sam's parents died when he was seventeen."

"So Sam owns most of Drake's Point?" Maybe that explained the amount of attention he got from local females and his attitude toward billing.

Flo shook her head. "Most of the town belongs to Vernon now, but Sam still has his mother's house.

You've seen it. The big white one at the top of the hill."

"Is that why Vernon and Sam don't like each other?"

"Oh, I don't think Sam bothers about property at all. He doesn't like the way Vernon treats his tenants—very vile—and they have had words over Vernon's attitude toward Cherry, Sam's mother. There's a good bit of history there." Flo took a big pile and dumped it in the corner wastebasket. She had worked her way to the lower end of the floor stack. "I know that article is here somewhere."

"What are you looking for?" Lexy really wanted to ask about Cherry. Cherry did not sound like a mother's name. All the mothers she knew had proper maternal-sounding names like Ruth or Susan or Ann or Helen, not Cherry.

Flo waved a magazine with a spectacular cover photo of the sun setting beyond a rock strewn beach. *"Bay Area Magazine's Guide to Small Hotels.* They're sending a reporter and a photographer for their annual visit this weekend." She handed Lexy the magazine, folded open. "Here's last year's spread."

Lexy scanned the brief blurb next to a small indistinct photograph of the inn and felt her temper stir. "A rustic ten-room inn with modest amenities. Some appeal for the Birkenstock-wearing eco-tourist. Not much to do in funky little Drake's Point except hug redwoods and gawk at endangered birdlife." There was half a silver star next to the review.

"Funky?" They had seen the toilet bowl garden. "Rustic? Who are these people?"

"Jackie Gold and Jayne Silver. Last time, they said the menu was all that's boring in British food."

"Boring?" Ernesto's food, boring? Lexy's temper was hotter than the chef's salsa. "When do they arrive?"

"Saturday. They have an interview with you. Then they check out the menu, the local attractions, any nightlife, and of course the accommodations."

Travel writers. They probably knew nothing about fitness, so they wouldn't know anything about her book, so she didn't have to hide from them. She wanted them to eat those words about the Tooth and Nail.

"We need a battle plan." How could she get two travel snobs from *Bay Area Magazine* to appreciate Drake's Point? Her inn *rustic?! Funky?!* She shook the offending magazine. "Flo, I'm going to read their other reviews, and we're going to put our heads together and come up with a plan to knock their socks off." Her carpenter's bill was the least of her worries. The reputation of her inn was at stake. She would give those reporters guestroom satisfaction!

As Lexy headed for her room with the *Bay Area Magazine* she heard Violeta Montoro singing. The song came and went in snatches as Violeta moved in and out of room 7, newly empty with its bed intact.

Violeta smiled at Lexy, a big, happy, the-world-is-a-wonderful-place smile. "*Hola, Senorita Clark.*"

Lexy stared at the changed girl. Without her frown, she was stunning. Lexy managed a greeting in her tourist Spanish, and reminded herself that she

74

needed to get a Spanish dictionary in a town that had
neither a bookstore nor a library. It was something
else to ask Flo about later.

An hour later, Lexy headed for Drake's Point's only
general store with a plan. She had read the *Bay Area
Magazine* cover to cover several times, and had made
notes on the inns and small hotels that rated a full-
page spread. She had figured out the silver- and gold-
star rating system. At Pacifica, she had listened to
endless travel stories from big donors and traveling
academics who dropped the names of eco-guides to
Belize, Tuscan trattorias, and Greek isles with obscure ruins; but Jackie and Jayne were a different kind
of travel snob. They would be horrified at the thought
of climbing, rafting, or trekking to enlightenment, or
even to a good risotto in obscure corners of the globe.
A kayak would terrify them.

No, they were looking for luxury. Two of their favorite words were "boutique" and "jacuzzi." They
wanted to be pampered, and they wanted to shop.
To please them, the Tooth and Nail needed to offer
some Spend-and-Spa mix of amenities. Lexy
reached this conclusion as she passed the toilet bowl
garden.

That's when the dog started following her. He was
a golden retriever with a big lion-like head. He
stopped when Lexy looked back at him and started
again when she moved on. Lexy did not have the best
experience with dogs. In Manhattan Beach she had
devised a route for her morning run that avoided
large barking dogs likely to erupt from yards and

driveways. She turned to face the beast. He stopped a polite distance behind her.

"Hello, dog. Are you lost?"

He had no tags that she could see.

"Can I help you find your owner?"

The dog shifted his position slightly, sizing her up, but not showing any desire to come closer.

Lexy tried firmness. "It was nice to meet you. I'll be on my way now." She started off again, and still the dog followed. When she looked back over her shoulder at him, he dropped back a little. Lexy really couldn't object to his using the sidewalk, and she was reasonably confident that Drake's Point wasn't the sort of place to enforce a leash law.

She passed the new building. There was no hammering from within and no women lined the opposite porch. It was too bad it wasn't finished and filled with trendy boutiques.

Lexy followed Drake's Point's main street to the end of town. She passed a few commercial establishments, a small café, a bait shop and kayak rental place, and a real estate office. Drake's Point was no Carmel, but it was pretty. She looked out over wetlands where the creek emptied into the cove. On the right a road led to beach parking, on the left was a big old building with red siding. "Sullivan's Feed Store" read a sign above the yellow porch awning. A yellow bicycle leaned against the building. The door opened, and five Asian men with shaved heads and maroon robes emerged. Each man nodded gravely at Lexy as the line passed. Monks, she thought, one more sign that Drake's Point was nothing like L.A.

Inside, the feed store had more to offer than its name suggested. It was a big open space from the old plank floors to the high roofbeams, divided into sections for different kinds of merchandise, the sort of stuff that reminded Lexy of a hardware store, grocery store, and pharmacy combined. There was even a self-service coffee bar with cases of baked goods and a gleaming coffee roasting machine. At the center of the store was a counter island with a couple of cash registers. The carrot-haired cowgirl with the bicycle and the pumpkin seeds was at one of the registers.

Meg Sullivan wasted no time introducing herself. "Welcome to the coast, the land of surfers, artists, and lost souls. Mostly the artists and the surfers go farther north, and we get monks and the lost souls." She gave Lexy a close look.

Lexy looked back. "Not me. I'm a found soul."

"That's good, because Drake's Point is no L.A. Everyone's bound to know your business, your family, your whole life story after a while."

Lexy frowned. Not if she could help it. She checked out the merchandise. The most interesting corner was devoted to used books, old clothes, and slightly dated appliances. On the wall in big letters above a bulletin board crowded with messages a hand-lettered sign read, WE RECYCLE. An old gray metal library shelf was stuffed with books, and a second sign proclaimed, TAKE A BOOK. LEAVE A BOOK.

Meg Sullivan explained, "If there's something you need, you just put a card up on the board, and if it's in Drake's Point, someone will bring it in within a week. Our self-help shelf is really popular."

"A Spanish dictionary?"

"No problema." Meg grinned. She pulled a purple index card from a box on the counter, wrote out Lexy's request, and tacked it to the bulletin board.

"Now, Alexandra, if you really want to get a feel for Drake's Point, you should try some of my pumpkin seeds." She led Lexy to a table covered in flat woven baskets overflowing with plastic bags of roasted seeds labeled cinnamon, garlic, herb, Cajun.

Lexy thought of the clones salivating over Sam Worth. "Did you know that pumpkin seeds are full of zinc? The trace elements are very effective in stimulating smell, taste, and sensitivity to touch."

"Should I put a warning label on them?" Meg laughed, and Lexy laughed, too, but she wondered what Flo could tell her about Meg Sullivan and Sam Worth.

Lexy offered to buy a bag of the cinnamon-flavored seeds just to support local business, not because she had to worry about her zinc levels. As she put her money on the counter, the feed store door banged open, and a man walked in carrying a big burlap sack of coffee beans on one shoulder. He was thirty-something, lean and angry looking with dark eyes, uncombed chin-length brown hair, a day's stubble, and paint-splatter on his T-shirt and jeans—Johnny Depp on a bad day, a really bad day. He and Meg Sullivan exchanged a glance that plainly said they had a history.

Meg attempted an introduction. "Charlie Beaton, Alexandra Clark, our new innkeeper."

Charlie Beaton did not glance at Lexy. So much for Drake's Point friendliness.

Meg tapped her cash register keys, and the drawer popped open. "What are you doing here, Charlie?"

"Your dad ordered me to roast today, so I'm going to roast."

"You can see we have enough beans. You can roast on Friday."

Charlie stopped and leveled that hostile gaze at Meg. "Fine." The sack of coffee beans hit the floor with a thud that raised dust. "Friday."

"Fine." Meg Sullivan turned back to Lexy with some change, which Lexy almost dropped as she caught the look in Charlie Beaton's eyes once Meg wasn't watching—a look of intense longing. Then he stalked out, banging the door.

Meg Sullivan froze mid-transaction, and even Lexy needed several calming moments to recover from that particular glimpse into the human soul. Quietly, Lexy started talking, explaining about the coming visit from Jayne and Jackie, and waiting for some life to return to Meg's face.

"*Bay Area Magazine* is sending its reporters to check out the inn this weekend, and I want us to go gourmet. I want them to think luxury, think spa."

Meg Sullivan returned from wherever she'd momentarily gone. "Drake's Point and spa. The two words don't exactly go together. Drake's Point and organic, Drake's Point and time warp."

Lexy shook her head. "These women want to be pampered, and they want to spend money."

Meg shrugged her shoulders. She opened the lid of a ceramic mason jar, releasing a rich sweet smell. "Try Malagwi. We get it from Coast Cake and Coffee over the mountain."

"Malagwi? That stuff's worth its weight in gold."

Meg smiled. "Want to use it at the inn? I can get you a deal from the roaster."

Lexy inhaled. "Oh my, yes."

"We also have amazing mud from the sulfur baths just north of town." Meg led the way to another section of the store. Next to the shelves of aspirin and cold remedies were fragrant handmade soaps, exotic shampoos, and jars of mud. The mud looked like jellied combat gear in small medicinal-looking jars.

Meg took in Lexy's skeptical expression. "It has a plankton that boosts the skin's renewal processes. Dawn Russell says it's the next best thing to doing a soak in the springs."

The geothermal springs! That explained the lovely skin of the members of the Ladies Book Club. A trip to the sulfur baths would be just the outing for Jayne and Jackie. "Skin-renewing springs? How close are they?"

"Oh, they're just beyond the cove. There's a path through the rocks."

"Can you walk there from the inn?"

"At low tide. It takes fifteen minutes."

Little nasturtiums of thought poked green stems up in Lexy's brain. The spa plan was going to work. "Is there someone in town who could do a couple of massages?"

80

Meg raised both her hands, wiggling her fingers. "Meg Sullivan's magic fingers are available."

Lexy grinned. "Perfect."

In the next few minutes she helped Meg sort through the vintage clothing items to put on display: the jet bead earrings, Paris scarves, and antique beaded satin bags. With a little cellophane, some pale green ribbon and glitter, they worked up new packaging for the plankton-rich mud. Then Lexy gathered the coffee and some soaps, and Meg rang up the sale. Lexy's last question for Meg was about local artists. Wasn't there anyone who painted? Anyone who had some work Lexy could hang in the inn dining room?

Meg looked down, arranging the bills in her hand until all three Georges faced the same direction. She took a deep breath and said, "Charlie Beaton. He paints."

"The coffee roaster paints?"

Meg nodded.

"Intense."

"Yeah." Meg managed both a smile and Lexy's change. "He has a studio in the back of his grandfather's house. You know the yellow house with the toilet seat guitars?"

Lexy did. "What does he paint?"

"Landscapes. They're beautiful. He . . . Alexandra, you can ask him, but he doesn't usually show his work to anyone."

"Why?"

"He had some bad experiences with galleries in

81

the city. That's when he made all the toilet seat guitars. His career was in the toilet."

"Oh, I thought there might be a statement there.
I'm going to try him anyway."

"Good luck."

The golden retriever was waiting for her when she
came out of the store.

"What am I going to do with you, dog?" she
asked him.

He looked unconcerned.

When she unlatched the gate to the garden of the
yellow house, he dashed past, brushing her skirts.
"Hey, dog!" she called.

He bounded up to the steps of the weathered,
glassed-in porch with all those hanging toilet seat instruments and started barking. Lexy tried to quiet
him, but it was no use. Charlie Beaton appeared,
sullen and paint-splattered, with a welding torch in
one hand and headphones draped around his neck.

"What do you want?" He put down the welding
tool and removed his heavy gloves. Lexy was glad she
had the dog.

"I wondered whether you would allow the inn to
display some of your paintings this weekend. You
could price them for sale, or not, as you wished."

"You haven't even seen my paintings."

"I'd like to." The dog came and sat beside Lexy as if
he were the most obedient dog in the world.

Apparently that triggered something in Charlie
Beaton's angry soul. "Sure, why not." He stepped
back, holding open the screen door, and Lexy hurried
up the steps onto the porch. He led her through the

quiet, dark house, and she had only the quickest impression of old chairs and chests and rugs. They emerged into a large, high-ceilinged room with a wall of tall south-facing windows. It smelled of paint and thinner and empty pans left over a flaming gas burner. Unframed canvasses leaned against the walls, and a jumble of tools lay on an old work bench. A welding mask reminded Lexy of Boba Fett's *Star Wars* helmet.

Charlie steered Lexy around a large metal sculpture, a tangle of tubes and wires that looked vaguely female in a Cubist sort of way. He began to pull canvasses out for her to look at, and Lexy forgot the toilet seats and the metal sculpture. She was stunned that the angry man beside her could paint them. Apparently his dark soul craved the light.

One piece was a ribbon of highway bisected by the double yellow line, swooping and dipping across the tops of rounded grassy hills. In another his subject was an old blue fishing boat, listing to one side in a shimmering wetland. You could see the texture and movement of the grasses. A third was a rocky cove with three smooth pools.

She didn't hesitate. "I'd like to hang these in the inn dining room. Right away. You can price them as you like, but I'd go high."

He laughed. Actually it was more of a snort than a laugh. Lexy didn't change her expression, and neither did the dog.

On Saturday morning Lexy found that being right about Jayne and Jackie did not make it any easier to deal with the women. Obviously, neither had ever been fashion-impaired. Jayne was cool, with an Audrey Hepburn sleekness; her short dark hair had a fringe of bang, and she wore a clinging, cleavage-showing ivory sweater over beaded ivory pants and a wide leather belt with a vintage buckle. Jackie was perky with shoulder-length blonde curls, over-sized tortoise-shell dark glasses, red lipstick, and a loud voice.

They looked at Lexy as if her clothes had expired and she were a fugitive from the fashion police. But Lexy loved her flowers, and she was sticking to her disguise.

Still, she felt they all were competing from the moment the women arrived, and the score was woefully lopsided in Jayne and Jackie's favor.

The women dismissed Charlie Beaton as a "local" artist because he didn't have gallery representation. They ignored the gift baskets Lexy and Flo had put in each room. They missed the views of the ocean, navigating Drake's Point sidewalks in pointy-toed high heels, and now they were taking apart the inn wine list. Guestroom satisfaction was not in their vocabulary.

"A couple of the reds aren't *too* bad, do you think, Jayne?"

"But I don't see a really good *Viognier*, do you?"

V-OH-KNEE-A? Lexy wanted to snatch the wine list back. The night before a nice couple had complimented the inn on one of her selections.

Jackie looked at it, frowning. "You're right. It's so

not sexy. The whites are so"—she gave a little shrug—"ordinary."

Both women looked at Lexy as if she were pathetic, and shared a little smile. Lexy cringed. Obviously, it was fun to despise her taste. Her brothers would have high-fived each other over such a triumph. Lexy felt it was time to play the spa card. She mentioned the skin-renewing hot pools, and Jayne and Jackie perked right up.

According to the tide log they had at least two hours to get to the pools, soak, and return. Plenty of time. The clear, hot, early October weather was cooperating. Lexy sent Jayne and Jackie to their rooms to organize themselves for an expedition. She slipped into shorts, a T-shirt and slides, and packed a canvas bag with thick towels and lotions, bottled waters, and some lovely wedges of melon packed in ice. She grabbed a hat.

Jayne and Jackie eventually re-emerged with their own bags of towels and skin preparations, hats, dark glasses, sparkling flip-flops, and beach wraps. There had been considerable delay finding a sunblock with the proper SPF rating. Jackie had contained her hair under a hat.

Lexy drove to the north end of the cove and parked the inn Suburban as close to the beach as she could get. A well-trodden path led them through brush and across the sand to the jumble of rocks that had broken from the cliffs over the eons. The tide was out. The Pacific sparkled. There was a path of firm wet sand between tall dark jagged mounds of rock. At the base of the rocks starfish clung in shades of bright peach, rusty orange, and brick red. Below the tide line, the rock surface was covered with creatures, most of them closed up, waiting for the tide to come in. An occasional cold puff of breeze tugged at Lexy's hat, but the sun was warm on the crumbling yellow cliff above.

When they rounded the point, the cliff dipped above the tide line into a perfect bowl of smooth gray rocks hollowed into still steamy pools. It was utterly private and serene, with nothing between the bathers and the Pacific. Behind them was a wall of lush greenery unlike the usual stunted, wind-browned coastal brush.

Even Jayne and Jackie were silent for a minute. Then Jayne shrugged. "Well, it's not Canyon Ranch."

Jackie dipped her red-coated toes into the nearest pool. "Oooh. Nice." She slipped the wrap off her shoulders and began to lay out her possessions on the rocks.

Jayne shrugged and picked a pool of her own.

Lexy was out of her clothes and into a third pool while her guests were still arranging their toiletries. It was heavenly. She could feel the tension of the day draining as her muscles relaxed. The sulfurous steam made droplets of moisture bead on her face. Best of all, her guests were silent. Lexy let her eyes drift closed, let the gentle movement of the water sway her resting body. An erotic dream took over, and she saw herself rising from the pool in a swirl of hot mist and stepping naked into the arms of Sam Worth.

Instead, a crashing boom of surf brought her back

to alertness. She opened her eyes and blinked. The sun was very low and bright on the horizon. Time to get back. She hoisted herself out of the warm pool and shivered. The air had cooled considerably. She toweled off and slipped back into her shirt, shorts, and slides.

Of course it took Jayne and Jackie awhile to pull themselves from the warm water, collect their gear, and fix their hair and makeup. They spent several minutes looking for Jackie's tortoise-shell glasses, which had slipped into a rock crevice. Then they set off.

The path was gone. Breakers crashed directly below the pools. Angry water swirled, rising and plunging. All the little creatures on the rocks were open, waving happy tentacles at them. Lexy looked at the cliff. It looked about as scalable as the Cliffs of Insanity in *The Princess Bride*; it was just bits of rock and sand pressed together in a vertical stack of crumbling yellow orange layers. They would have to find their way over the rocks.

Lexy led the way. The rocks were slick, and each woman had an awkward bag to carry. They had to go barefoot, and Lexy tried not to think about the squishy and crusty textures under her toes as she picked her way to within sight of the beach. It was farther than she'd expected. The rock route led out to a flat rock quite a distance from the sand. Waves were crashing at the end of the rock, dousing them with cold spray, and the breeze was stiff and chilly. The red glare of the sun setting behind them flashed in a few windows on the hill above Drake's Point. There was no one at their end of the beach. There were a few cars in the distant parking lot at the other end of the cove, but no people.

Jayne dug in her bag for her cell phone, but could get no service. "What do we do?"

"Someone will come get us, right?" They looked at Lexy.

Even Lexy did not suggest swimming. A nasty stretch of churning water lay between them and the shore, and she knew Jayne and Jackie would never abandon their bags of possessions. Flo did know where they'd gone, and they would be missed. So someone would come looking. The question was: when? Before the waves got higher? And what if a rogue wave came and washed them off their perch?

She was having that grim thought when she saw the dog. He came racing down the beach to the water's edge, stopped and barked furiously. Lexy couldn't hear him, but she could tell he was making quite a racket. He raced back and forth several times in the shore wash, then turned and ran away. Lassie he was not.

Chapter 5
Breathing

"Deep rhythmic breathing is fundamental to a successful workout and to the intensity of orgasm. Draw in a breath slowly halfway through climax and release to extend the peak."
—*Workout Sex*, Lexy Clark

Icy water washed around Lexy's ankles, and strands of hair whipped across her face. The sun's red glow was a fading line on the horizon. They had to act now. They could pick their way back to the hot springs to spend the night, or Lexy could swim for shore. Jayne and Jackie objected. Lexy pointed out that people swam the San Francisco Bay in the Escape from Alcatraz Triathlon, and people even swam the English Channel.

"You can't leave us here."

"I'm going to get help."

"We'll sue."

That did it. Lexy shoved her bag at Jayne and started to pick her way to the edge of the rock, but Jackie caught her arm and held her. "Look!"

When Lexy lifted her gaze to the beach, the dog was back at the edge of the surf, barking furiously. Flo was there, and beside her a man was stripping off his clothes. In a minute he was encased in black. A wetsuit, Lexy realized. Three more men appeared on the beach and formed a line from the sand down into the water. The first man charged into the surf, dove under a wave and came up stroking energetically. A bobbing orange float marked his progress toward them.

When he crested one of the nearer swells, Lexy recognized Sam Worth, his golden hair washed back from his tan face by the waves. He was definitely a strong swimmer, and watching his progress, Lexy realized she had misjudged his intensity. He seemed careless, almost lazy with his teasing and his indifference to time. Now she saw that she had been a little wrong about him.

By the time he reached them, the water had numbed Lexy's feet, and there was little light left in the sky. Sam waited for a surge to lift him and sprang up onto their rock. For the first time in their visit to Drake's Point, Jayne and Jackie were impressed. The wetsuit defined Sam Worth's broad shoulders and narrow hips.

"Ms. Clark, need a little help?" He wasn't even breathing hard.

"You."

"Flo called. Said you might be out of your depth."

"She was going to abandon us." Jackie and Jayne dissolved into complaints and grateful blubberings about how frightened they had been and how insensitive Lexy was, while Sam Worth pulled on the line trailing from his float. From the line he unclipped three life vests. He tossed one to Lexy and personally helped Jayne and Jackie into theirs—just your friendly local bull tule elk expanding the herd.

Still, he was nice to them. Lexy had to admire the patience and humor with which he helped her frightened companions into the water. He managed to tie their three bags together with Lexy's towel to make a flotation device. "We'll use this," he told her.

Their swim through the freezing water was mercifully brief. Jayne and Jackie clung to the orange, bullet-shaped float, pulled along by the firemen, and Sam Worth talked to them the whole way, his voice steady, reassuring, and teasing. Lexy hung on to the floating bundle of tote bags. Sam Worth never said a word to her, but he never let go of her arm. In between icy dark swells tall enough to block her vision of the shore, Lexy had to admit that the hand on her arm was nice.

They rode a long swell into shallow water where her numb feet made a jarring impact with the sandy bottom. In front of her, Jayne and Jackie stumbled into the comforting arms of three waiting firemen. Sam Worth released Lexy's arm as soon as she had her feet under her, and she staggered through the shore wash to dry sand. Flo tossed Lexy a towel, and then the dog barked at her. Lexy was sure she got the message. It was dog-speak for, "*You* idiot, *what were you thinking?*"

Sam Worth came up beside her. "I see you've met Winston."

91

"Your dog?" Lexy shuddered from the cold.

He nodded.

Of course it was.

Sam was desperate. It was ten o'clock in the old Tooth and Nail pub, and he had been the man of the hour for the past three hours. Being a hero was overrated. True, people had been buying him drinks, shaking his hand, and elevating the story of the rescue to legendary proportions, but Charlie Beaton looked ready to kill him, Vernon was consoling Alexandra Clark, and the wrong woman was pressing her chest, hip, and thigh against him.

An hour earlier he had given up trying to peel Jayne Silver off his body. The woman had amazing adhesive qualities. With his free hand he tipped back a brew. He had tried to get her talking, but now she wouldn't quit. Usually, Sam found people interesting when they talked about their work, but Jayne's job—professional snob—didn't have much going for it. She had given him a staggeringly boring account of the failings of several famous resorts, and an equally mind-numbing recital of her battles with Jackie over the number of stars each inn deserved.

The good thing about the conversation was that it made him feel better about the break-up with Julia. Jayne was humorless, and he realized now, Julia had been, too. Maybe "J" was a bad letter of the alphabet for him, and he ought to move on to some other letter. Like "A."

He glanced at Alexandra Clark to see whether she noticed Jayne's attachment to his body. For the second time in two weeks he'd had a chance to get close to Alexandra's skimpily-clad body, but in forty-eight degree waters, the parts of him that most wanted to get close had retreated for warmth. What he'd really had in mind was the two of them in one of the hot springs pools. Now Alexandra was back in her innkeeper outfit, a bulky sweater, long skirt, and high-collared shirt.

"What?" He looked down at Jayne. She'd switched topics on him, and he'd missed it.

"I've seen your name in print somewhere. I never forget a name in print."

Sam shook his head and gave his best impression of local boy carpenter, a role he'd been practicing for Alexandra Clark. But Jayne was starting to think, the mental effort plain on her furrowed brow. He knew she hadn't seen the *Fortune* article about green builders—it was not likely that Jayne read *Fortune*. More likely she'd seen the items in the San Francisco paper about his engagement and subsequent lack of engagement. Time for Jayne to have a conversation with someone else.

Lexy was doing her best not to look at Sam Worth, but his height made her aware of the room's low ceilings and she could pick out his easy laugh in the swell of sound. Jayne, in her cleavage-baring sweater, had applied herself to his body like a long Crest Whitening Strip. His grin flashed in his tan face, the expression of a man enjoying himself. Lexy could just imagine Jayne pumping admiration into his inflated ego every time she opened her mouth. And Jayne's first words

93

when they'd returned to the inn were fixed in Lexy's brain. *Did you see that butt?*

She reminded herself that she'd just left the land of big-egoed males with well-formed butts and well-muscled chests. If she had wanted those particular assets in a man, she could have stayed in L.A. She had come to Drake's Point to find her new path in life, not to find a man. Still, she had to give Sam Worth the edge for those arms. Maybe that's why she was having such a strong physical reaction to him.

She took a deep breath and looked around her pub again. There was a lot going on in the crowded room, and Lexy needed to pay enough attention to get a sense of how the regular customers interacted with outsiders. She also needed a fraction of her attention to respond to Walt's expressions of concern for her safety.

It was interesting to see how easily Sam Worth connected to people, compared to Walt's studied way of doing it. She really had to feel a little sorry for the mayor. People were less likely to be interested in a man who succeeded in the Chamber of Commerce than a man who clearly could succeed in the bedchamber. Meanwhile, Charlie Beaton and Meg Sullivan were involved in a strange dance of attraction and resistance, Charlie glaring at anyone who talked to Meg, Meg feigning indifference even as she gauged Charlie's mood. And the inn's scary silent bartender Nigel watched Flo every time she turned away. And then there were Jayne and Jackie, who had apparently forgotten their objections to the inn's entertainment options.

Mike, Pat, and Tim, the firemen who had rescued the women, were earnestly trying to teach Jackie darts. She made pitiful casts, needing continuous assistance that required a great deal of body contact. The guys helped to position her hips, roll up her transparent sleeves, or guide her arm.

Conversation with Walt encouraged Lexy to take up arranging the items on their table. Cocktail napkins, cards from Jayne and Jackie and Walt, bowls of pretzel sticks, drink stirrers, a box of matches. She hoped she had not been too obvious when Walt stood, excusing himself.

"Alexandra, I'm so glad our volunteers were there when you needed them today." He gave her shoulder a little pat. "I took the liberty of checking your next booking. Have a care. It's Grindstone. And don't forget our committee meeting. Tuesdays! We need you on the team."

"I'll be there." *Just don't pat my shoulder.*

"I'm just going to give the boys my thanks before I go."

Lexy watched him saunter across the room and fall into Jackie's chest.

Then it hit her. To Walt she was sexless. Walt saw a businesswoman, not a celebrity. And that was a good thing, wasn't it? It meant Lexy was free to impress people with her brains and her competence. In a way, Jayne and Jackie had been a test. They were outsiders who might have heard of "Sexy Lexy." But if they had, they hadn't made the connection. Most likely Jayne and Jackie would print another one-star blurb on the Tooth and Nail, and Alexandra Clark's name would appear in a line at the bottom next to the phone number. She had truly escaped.

She looked up again, and Sam Worth was steering Jayne to her table. He nodded to Lexy and turned to Flo.

"Flo, Jayne's got a funny idea that she's read about me somewhere. Could you set her straight?" He shrugged. "Be right back."

The words were kidding, but Lexy didn't miss the appeal in his eyes or the quick escape.

Jayne settled in her chair and leaned forward. "I've read about him somewhere, I know it. I never forget a name in print."

"Well, let me see. What can I tell you? He's our local handyman, born and bred right here in Drake's Point," Flo began. She described the floats he'd built for the city's Fourth of July parades and his prowess in county sports championships in high school. She described in detail the doors and windows he'd fixed recently, roofs he'd patched, his work at the inn. Jayne's eyes glazed over, while Lexy wondered what Flo was hiding.

"Over here in Drake's Point, we're a bit out of touch. I can't think what Sam would do to get his name in print," Flo concluded.

Jayne stood up. "When we get back to civilization, I'll do an Internet search." She headed over to the darts game.

Lexy turned to Flo. "What was that all about?" Before the rescue, Lexy hadn't thought Sam Worth would exert himself enough in any way to make the media take note.

Flo made sure Jayne was out of range and leaned close. "When his engagement ended, a lot of ink was devoted to Sam's family. Newspeople always make a bit of a fuss about his background, and Sam hates it. He's a very private person."

Lexy's breath kind of stuck in her throat. He'd been engaged? "His Drake's Point background interests newspeople?"

Flo suddenly looked a little tight-lipped. "His mother's background, really. She was . . . famous before she came here."

"She was a celebrity?"

Flo nodded. She glanced at Nigel, who appeared to be wiping the bar surface with complete attention. "Fame is tricky for a woman. When a woman becomes famous, like Princess Di even, people don't see her anymore." Lexy looked at her hotel manager with new appreciation. "They see the fantasy. And being people's fantasy makes you daft."

Lexy had to agree, and to wonder how Flo came by her knowledge of fame's downside. Being a public person had made Lexy someone else. What had fame done to Flo, or to Sam Worth's mother? "So Cherry came here to escape?"

Flo was silent for a moment. "Cherry was a good friend to many of us. I wouldn't have mentioned her past, except that Sam is trying so hard to keep her name out of the press right now."

"I'm glad you did mention it." She was. What Sam Worth had said about Drake's Point being Brigadoon made sense now. She understood him better. But if the press tended to show up in his life, she would be wise to stay away from him. She wanted to stay anonymous.

Sam's knee brushed hers as he slid into a chair next to her. "You warm now? You got pretty chilled."

"Yes." She was warm as toast, warm as fleece blankets and hot chocolate.

He immediately started to dismantle her careful arrangement of the table's contents. "So, other than the tide coming in and the unexpected involvement of the fire department, how did your spa plan go? Did they like the hot springs?"

She watched his rugged hands turn the thin pretzel sticks into a structure. "They did, and at least they're not likely to sue us—but I shouldn't have tried to make the inn into something it isn't. If they can't appreciate it for what it is, they can't."

"Wise." He gave her an approving glance. He picked up the business cards and worked them into his project. "They seem to be enjoying themselves now." He glanced over at the dart game, and Lexy followed his gaze. Jackie saw them look and drifted to their table.

"Jayne and I really should come back, Alexandra," she said. "To get more of the spa details and a shot of the hot springs." She took a sip of Sam's beer and turned back to the game.

Sam Worth laughed, and Lexy shook her head. For a few minutes he went on folding and arranging the things he had gathered into a delicate structure with careful, precise hand movements. Then he took his hands away from the arrangement he'd been making, and Lexy was amazed. He'd made a replica of the inn with cocktail napkin walls, pretzel stick timbers, and business card chimneys. For the first time since she'd staggered up the beach, she was too warm. She shrugged out of her sweater.

She felt the change in his attention instantly, how it narrowed on her, how the intensity of it cut her off from the rest of the room. There was really no one else there, just them. His heated gaze interfered with her breathing, causing a little catch in the rhythm. He was affected, too.

After a pause he sucked in a long breath, and exhaled raggedly. "You know, I like rescuing you—the danger, the skimpy outfits, the closeness. But maybe we could get together on dry land without elk or ocean waves."

Lexy swallowed. He was all wrong for her. Dangerously attractive, just out of a relationship, and with a past that drew reporters. Sexy Lexy knew just what she had to say to Sam Worth. "Never."

Chapter 6
Moving into the Target Zone

"At the first sign of sweat, partners should move into the second phase of the workout. Continuous rhythmic activity raises the heart rate to 70 percent of the MHR (maximum heart rate), burning fat and building muscle."

—*Workout Sex*, Lexy Clark

Lexy's mid-morning tea made lovely curls of steam in the chill air of the inn's tiny, cluttered office. She smiled at the homey chintz and Flo's piles of paper. From that first shared glance of understanding over the cyclists, she and Flo had been bonding. Together they had vanquished Jayne and Jackie. They were ready to bring on the next guests—cyclists, reporters, messy bird-watchers, whoever! She and Flo could handle them.

She booted up the computer reservations spread. "Who's Grindstone?" She recalled Walter Vernon's warning.

Flo didn't look up from her Monday-morning bill

sorting. "They're a band. Or they used to be until the late eighties. Did you never hear of them?"

Lexy said no, and Flo sighed.

"Right. You're a bit young for that sort of thing, I imagine. Heavy metal. *Mad Revels, Sweet Mayhem, Bed & Bedlam*—those were their big albums." Flo sounded nostalgic.

Lexy glanced back at the computer entry. "They've reserved eight rooms for next weekend."

"They usually come for Solstice," Flo said. She didn't seem unduly alarmed by the prospect, but she had that tight-lipped look she'd had when Lexy had asked her about Sam Worth's mother.

"So they've been here before?"

"Every year." Flo was holding something back.

Lexy felt the closeness of the past few days evaporate. "Walt warned me about them."

"Oh, you mustn't pay him any mind. They never do any real harm." Flo put down the bills and moved to the window, her back to Lexy. "Well, they do make the occasional miscalculation."

"Miscalculation?"

Flo pointed to a grassy spot under a distant stand of trees. "You know, we should have the septic cleaned before they come."

"The septic?" The abrupt shift in topic left Lexy puzzled.

But Flo didn't notice. She launched into an explanation of the inn's dependence on two septic tanks. She seemed more alarmed at the prospect of eight toilets flushing simultaneously than at guests who'd recorded a series of rock lyrics on the theme of anarchy.

"Who do we call?"

"Oh, Sam will take care of it." Flo turned, the fluty lilt back in her voice at the prospect. "I'm off to get the post. Shall I talk to him?"

"No. Thanks." Lexy distinctly remembered the end of her conversation with Sam Worth two nights before. Asking for help was not a good follow up to *Never*.

Flo looked puzzled. "You'll take care of it?"

Lexy nodded.

"Right then, I'm off."

Flo left, and Lexy reached for the slim Drake's Point phone book with its one Yellow Page. It didn't list any plumbers within ten miles. She sipped her cold tea, pondering her options.

Outside the office a rapid, angry exchange in Spanish intruded on her dilemma. She opened the door and found Nigel holding Violeta back from lunging at Paula, the downstairs housekeeper. Violeta squirmed in Nigel's hold, glaring at the older woman, and Lexy realized she had underestimated Nigel's strength. He said something calming in Spanish. At least Lexy thought it was calming, because Violeta stopped fighting his hold and contented herself with a hostile stare at the other woman.

Paula raised her chin, and her next words made Violeta strain against Nigel's grasp and utter a pithy reply. Paula shrugged and walked off, obviously pleased with the distress she had caused. Violeta promptly turned in Nigel's arms and burst into tears. He made an imploring, helpless male face, and Lexy stepped up and took over. She led Violeta to an old armchair in the office, sat her down, and stroked her back as the girl sobbed. She had gone from defiant to despairing.

Lexy turned to Nigel for an interpretation. "What was that about?"

"Paula said *'What kind of ignorant girl needs a book to keep her husband happy?'*" He looked disgusted. "Paula's mean as a hangover."

Lexy's hand paused in its stroking. *What book?*

Violeta, who had been singing yesterday, sobbed freely. Nigel asked a couple more questions. Violeta's answers came on shuddering breaths.

"Apparently her husband Emiliano has been too tired for sex until recently." Nigel looked supremely uncomfortable relaying that revelation. Violeta said something else. "Actually, until Violeta brought the book home."

What book!? If Violeta brought home a book that had revived her husband's sex drive, Lexy had to ask.

"Nigel, would you ask her if she found the book in room 7?"

Nigel translated, and Violeta hung her head. She gave a watery sigh and looked up again, her big dark eyes brimming with tears.

Nigel asked a longer question. "She says the gringos left it behind, and she borrowed it, but when Paula started teasing her, she gave it away."

"To whom?" Lexy held her breath.

Nigel asked. Lexy felt helpless. She was going to have to step up her Spanish studies right away.

"Violeta put it on the book recycle shelf in the feed store."

"Oh." Lexy made herself sit still, calmly comforting Violeta as the girl's sobs subsided. The feed store was open. People were stopping by for coffee and zinc-filled pumpkin seeds and a chat with Meg Sullivan at this very moment, and maybe they were checking out the new books on the recycle shelf. *Workout Sex, A Girl's Guide to Home Fitness,* the slim volume with the shiny red cover, was sure to catch someone's eye. That person would pull the book from the shelf and flip through the pages and maybe pause over one of the illustrations and start to imagine the possibilities. Then, with a friendly word to Meg Sullivan, the mystery person would tuck the book in a pocket or a bag and take it home.

Lexy had to get to the feed store now and grab the book before it fell into the next person's hands! Relying on Nigel to translate, she told Violeta that she did not consider her an ignorant girl for reading a book, but that she expected Violeta and Paula to work together. They would have to have a meeting to reestablish a good working friendship. She got Nigel to ask whether Violeta felt able to go back to work. When Violeta nodded, Lexy offered a smile of encouragement. Then she headed into town.

She had no luck at the feed store. She chatted with Meg, checked out other merchandise, and accepted a grunted greeting from Charlie Beaton, who was tending the gleaming coffee roaster. The rich, sweet-burnt smell of the darkening beans filled the store. Lexy helped herself to coffee in a paper cup and strolled over to the recycle shelf. The only books with red spines were a dog-eared contemporary romance, a guide to bartending, and *The Ten Thousand Most Common Misspelled Words*.

No other customers were in the store. Charlie Beaton watched Meg and his roasting machine with equal severity. Lexy picked out some daffodil bulbs from open boxes in the garden section, and as she paid for them, she asked Meg, "Busy morning?"

Meg looked up from the cash register and laughed. "It was till now. I think everyone in town has been in here this morning."

"Oh. Well, that's good." Lexy thanked Meg.

Great! Workout Sex was somewhere in Drake's Point, and Lexy had no idea where. She headed back to the inn, trying to tell herself that maybe it wouldn't matter who had the book. Maybe whoever had it would keep it forever, end of story. But somehow she didn't think so. The book would go on plaguing her and causing her trouble even here, where no one seemed to know that the outside world existed. It was like an infection, like the *Andromeda Strain*. It would pass from person to person in tiny Drake's Point until everyone had it and someone connected its authorship to her. She should leave now. Return to the inn, pack up her stuff, head farther north. Alaska might do.

Charlie Beaton was not a morning person. Roasting beans for Sullivan's might help his cash flow, but it did nothing for his disposition. Meg was singing country songs and moving about the feed store, restocking shelves and setting out the day's pastries. Nothing seemed to interfere with her cheerfulness. She stopped to smile and talk to everyone who came in, except him.

Everyone was checking the damn book recycle shelf. Charlie had looked it over a couple times himself, but he hadn't found anything beyond the usual yellowing, yawn-inducing stuff about self-realization, body alignment, and Buddhist healing practices that had been circulating in Drake's Point for ten years.

Nothing had changed in Drake's Point until Worth came back.

If Worth was going to make a move with Meg, why didn't he do it? Then, this time, it would finally be decided. Meg would pick Worth or Charlie, and they could all move on.

She had to know Charlie wasn't going to change sides for her. He wasn't going to let his grandfather lose his farm because Worth wanted to rebuild that damn library, and he wasn't going to feel guilty about it. Worth thought he could fight Vernon. Hah! Look what happened to Worth's family. Charlie was smarter than that. He would do whatever dirty work Vernon asked. Amadeo was frigging eighty-five. When his grandfather was gone, Charlie was out of here.

He kept his scratchy eyes fixed on the sacks of coffee beans and the turning roaster. He didn't care who came and went. Okay, maybe he was not a people person. Maybe that was another reason he was never going to have Meg Sullivan.

* * *

A single hammer pounded somewhere inside the new building as Lexy approached. Sam Worth was working alone again. Lexy had yet to see other workers at the building site, and today none of the usual adoring females had gathered across the street. This time she was struck by the way the new building seemed to complete the line of older houses along Beach Street. It had the same Victorian features, neat patterns of shingles and trim, with handsome newel posts at the base of the porch stairs. Once painted it would fit right in with the prevailing architecture of Drake's Point. Her steps slowed. She weighed her pride against her need for a plumber, climbed the porch steps, and passed through the unfinished front doors. The newly installed windows, still bearing the manufacturer's stickers, were open, and the ocean breeze blew coolly through the rooms. Winston met her as soon as she stepped in the door. He was as cocky as his master, but she silently thanked him for sparing her a long night in the cold with Jayne and Jackie. He turned and led the way toward the sound of the hammer.

Sam Worth had his back toward her—his very nice back, long and strong, the shoulders broad with a slight slope, and the narrow hips hugged by the butterscotch leather of his tool belt. Lexy's steps echoed between the hammer blows, and he turned.

"Hi." It was the best she could do for a start.

"Never, huh?"

Never had definitely been an unfortunate, an undiplomatic, choice of words. It was true that she

108

and Sam Worth had no future, absolutely none, and she had expressed her full conviction of their incompatibility in a single word. But at the moment she had been having a particularly strong reaction to the sight of Jayne applied to his body like a French manicure. The necessity of relying on him to keep the inn's plumbing working had not been on her mind at all.

"You and I are just a bad idea." Honesty, she told herself, was always the best policy.

"I thought the whole rescue thing was going well." He slipped his hammer back into a loop on his tool belt and stood there, a golden-brown package of perfectly arranged muscle and bone.

Lexy felt all that effortless sex appeal interfere with her resting heart rate. He had no right to be so good-looking. "In middle school did you ever read *Zero to Hero, Cam Cornell's Guide to Teenage Popularity*?"

"Pardon?" He looked as if she'd asked about ear wax or nose hair.

"There you have it. You didn't, I did. I took notes." The book had been one of those things her mother had purchased for her—so well-intentioned and yet so wrong. Lexy had dutifully read it, and for a while, had been naive enough to apply its principles to her daily interactions with peers. Big mistake.

"You're going to hold my middle school reading habits against me?"

"In middle school you were already the head tule elk with the ever-expanding herd, and I was . . . lost in the bad-hair-wrong-clothes fog." Basically, they came from different planets.

He laughed. "You don't think we've gotten over

middle school in the intervening fifteen plus years?" He unbuckled his tool belt and slipped it off, draping it over a paint-spattered sawhorse.

Lexy shook her head. She hated that he'd done that. The heavy belt had pulled his jeans low, exposing the masculine curve at the top of his pelvis.

He was taking in her whole outfit, from her running shoes to her long cream-colored print skirt, to her pink-collared shirt and brown cardigan with its crocheted wildflowers. She lifted her chin, daring him to make a comment about her outfit, but his eyes kept sending messages that she knew she had to be misreading.

"Stop it."

"Is it just me, or do you have trouble accepting male attention?"

"Men like you—"

"Whoa!" He held up a hand, traffic-cop style. "What do you know about 'men like me?'"

"Men like you"—Lexy took a breath—"who reek of that whole confident, I've-got-what-you-want-baby sexuality, don't go for women in—"

"—vintage Laura Ashley," he finished for her. He gestured at her outfit.

She nodded.

"Had some bad experiences?

I could write a book. "Scarred for life."

"So why did you come here today?"

"On inn business. I don't have a bill from you for the bed repair, or the stairs clean-up, and—"

"Don't worry about it."

110

"No. It's important . . . to keep our relationship on a strictly professional basis."

That knowing smile curved his lips upward. "I won't make the obvious joke."

"You know what I meant. Innkeeper and—"

"I know what you meant." He closed the distance between them, and his nearness interfered with her breathing again. "You don't like the rescues, but you like hiring the help." She hadn't thought of it like that.

"Show me one scar." The hint of roughness in his voice made Lexy's stomach flip.

"Never." The word just slipped out, and Lexy backed away from him. "Flo says you can do a septic tank clean out."

That stopped him. "You are tough on the male ego."

"Your ego is indestructible. Can you do the septic tank?"

His eyes scanned the unfinished room around them.

"I mean in your time off." She kept forgetting that he had this other job.

"I can make time."

"Before Friday, when Grindstone arrives?"

"Grindstone, the metal band?"

Lexy nodded.

"Never a dull moment at the Tooth and Nail for you, innkeeper."

After Alexandra Clark left, Sam tried to recover the easy working rhythm that had kept him going all morning. He had to stay focused on his task if he meant to complete the library before the use permit expired. He wasn't going to let Vernon win this one.

And Vernon was up to his usual tricks. Another cartload of correction notices had arrived yesterday. Just to read through them would take Sam hours. It would take hours more to figure out how to get around them. But he would. When he finished, there would be something in Drake's Point that didn't belong to Vernon.

Winston was watching him closely.

"You think I caved in too easily?"

Winston snorted.

"Just being neighborly. She's still new in town. And she likes flowers." He hadn't expected the flowers. She liked pretty clothes, but they overwhelmed her slim figure. She had more flowers on her than bloomed in his mother's garden.

Winston settled down, not deigning to reply.

"I know you think she's too uptight. It's the cover-up, whatever she's hiding. She's not used to keeping secrets. She only knows how to shoot from the hip, a very straightforward girl."

Sam could swear Winston's doggy brows lifted.

"And I think Flo's been talking." Flo, Meg, Vernon, Charlie—they all knew his history, or a part of it. "That's what the *never* thing is about. The good news is she thinks I'm a carpenter with a history, and she still can't stay away."

Winston was unimpressed.

"She may be hard to get, but you have to admit

she's no Julia. She gets along with all of my favorite people. Even you."

Winston rolled to his feet and headed for the door.

Sam thought of something else. "She's quick, you know. She doesn't miss much."

But Winston was gone.

Mayor Vernon's Committee on the Future of Tourism in Drake's Point met Tuesday evenings in the Sunset Room of the city hall. The Sunset Room reminded Lexy of her middle school cafeteria, with its linoleum floor, metal folding chairs, and small uncurtained stage at one end—except, decorated by the Rod and Gun Club instead of the PTA. The dark paneled walls were hung with black-and-white photos of the early years of Drake's Point. There were scenes of runners finishing the annual Peak Race, the volunteer fire brigade's BBQ, tug-of-wars along the beach, and Beach Street itself when the only buildings were the feed store and a vanished saloon. There were dozens of pictures of men holding dead things—deer, boar, foxes, turkeys, and big fish. And dozens of antler racks were mounted around the top of the paneling: just the place for the living members of the herd to remember the dead ones.

Ten men sat facing Vernon, who was setting up an easel in front of the small stage. The men passed a clipboard around, each one taking a minute to look at the attached papers. They were rugged and grim-faced and didn't look happy to be there. Lexy knew a couple of the men by sight. Vernon was the only one wearing a coat and tie.

113

A slouching man in overalls and a baseball cap passed the clipboard along and broke the silence. "Vernon, you shot that dog yet?"

Vernon mumbled something without turning around.

Chief Brock said, "No one is shooting any dogs in Drake's Point."

The man in the overalls was undeterred. "That sucker's going to get your bitch one day, Vernon."

"Never." Vernon turned toward the baseball-cap guy, and his angry glare caught Lexy instead.

Lexy managed a smile and hello.

"Ms. Clark, welcome. I didn't see you." Vernon's face shifted back to smooth cordiality.

All heads turned her way, and Vernon hastened to make introductions. Lexy met Mike, who rented kayaks and sold live bait; Felix, the golf pro from up the coast; and Noah Green, the guy in the baseball cap, who owned the gas station. She said hello to the people she already knew, like Chief Brock, who ran both the volunteer fire department of Drake's Point and its tiny police force.

When they settled in the folding chairs again, they all looked at the sketch on the easel. Lexy recognized it right away. "That's the building Sam Worth is working on."

Vernon cleared his throat. "It is."

"What a great location." The room was so quiet she could hear the creaking of the metal chairs as the men shifted in them.

Vernon nodded. "It is for the right mix of businesses, and that's what we're trying to decide.

Alexandra, you had some ideas about businesses that would help the inn."

Lexy looked at her companions. Somehow they did not seem like the kind of guys who wanted an art gallery or a boutique in the middle of town. "Everyone else has more experience than I do with Drake's Point tourism. Maybe I ought to just listen tonight."

"Tourism?" Noah in the overalls snorted, caught a glare from Vernon, and straightened up.

"Green, we don't need your input." Vernon faced the crowd, his hand resting on the top of the easel, a gleam from the overhead lights flashing on his gold watchband. "In Drake's Point either you run a profitable business or you have a hobby. Anyone here have a hobby?"

No one spoke up.

"If we want a commercially viable downtown for Drake's Point, we have to get the right businesses into the new building. Now, how is the petition doing?"

"Forty names," said a man behind Lexy.

"I want each one of you to come up with ten more names before we leave tonight."

Lexy saw it was going to be a long meeting.

By Thursday afternoon Violeta and Paula were doing their jobs without any further outbreak of hostilities, and Lexy had posted Spanish phrases around the mirror in her bathroom. She was particularly fond of *la aspidora* for vacuum cleaner and *limpiar* for clean. She and Flo were falling into a comfortable routine of sharing tasks, so maybe she had been wrong about the distance between them.

In between menu-planning for Grindstone's British tastes, Lexy quizzed Flo about the band's history, and discovered that their first big break had been in 1970 at the Isle of Wight Festival, five years before Lexy had been born. Their hits had come in the early and mid-eighties while Lexy was arranging Barbie's pink furnishings. They had disbanded in 1985 after the drug overdose death of Roger Fripp, their lead guitarist, when Lexy gave up Barbie for running. It was all in the past, but Lexy had a feeling Flo wasn't telling everything she knew. She did reveal the less-than-comforting information that all Grindstone's live performances had featured a grindstone, a large double-bladed axe, and fire.

Sam Worth had completed a thorough cleaning of the inn's septic system, and Lexy knew exactly how certain muscles in his back flexed when he bent and straightened. For all the time she had spent studying diagrams of lats, delts, and trapeziuses, she hadn't really understood the beauty of how they worked till now.

Men who did hundreds of reps on machines in gyms didn't get the same results. The jerky movements gave them bulk, not the long, lean strength that Sam Worth had. The model who had posed for Lexy's book cover had explained his own routine in great detail. He had been particularly pleased with the cut look of his six-pack abs and the low body fat ratio he'd achieved. He had not appreciated Lexy's pointing out that getting his ratio so low might also lower his sperm count.

Sam Worth, on the other hand, had natural good

looks that came from the ordinary movements he made with ease and confidence as he worked, and he was in no danger of lowering his sperm count. The blonde teenager clones brought him brownies. Meg Sullivan brought him pumpkin seeds, and Chef Ernesto offered oysters. With the part of her brain that wasn't devoted to his beautiful musculature, Lexy made a careful accounting of all the hours he worked for the inn. Once again he didn't give her a bill.

Lexy found it hard to forget his suggestion that they get together. Maybe he'd just meant that they should get to know one another, but maybe he meant they should have a thing or a fling. Lexy had never done casual sex, so she ought to find it easy to dismiss the idea. She didn't.

Mayor Vernon's regular presence at the inn's afternoon tea didn't help ease Lexy's mind about her anticipated guests. He informed Lexy of the whole previous history of Grindstone's visits to Drake's Point, the theme of which was fire. Most recently they had managed to burn down the public restrooms on the beach. Of course they had paid to have them rebuilt, but Mayor Vernon understandably felt that the town's public buildings were at risk. And he pointed out that October was peak fire season in California.

Thursday night Lexy dreamed of the mountain in flames, and Bambi's mother trapped by falling trees while a great bull tule elk led the inn's guests to safety. Friday morning she had the smoke alarms in every room checked and made arrangements to have someone on duty at night. Lexy wasn't sure what the

117

weekend's other guests would make of the band, but that worry evaporated by three o'clock Friday when two other parties cancelled. It was her third week as an innkeeper, and she had yet to fill her inn. On her desk was a reply to her latest request for Sam Worth's bill. It simply said, "Never."

Lexy felt her patience snap. She would get a bill from him. First she started afternoon tea, greeting and seating guests. Then she headed for Drake's Point.

Sam's golden retriever blocked her path when she reached Charlie Beaton's toilet bowl garden. At least the nihilistic Grindstone might appreciate the town's familiar landmark.

"Hello, Winston. I don't need a rescue today, thanks." She started around him, but he trotted to an opening in the vegetation between two houses, stopped, and barked. Lexy could see a flight of railroad tie steps. "You want to take me to Sam?" she guessed.

The dog seemed pleased with her intelligence. Overgrown with honeysuckle and blackberries, the steps led up the hill from the town. Lexy couldn't resist filling her hands with a few last berries. Above the first row of houses, she and Winston reached a dirt lane and turned south. They came to a weather-beaten white picket gate in a hedge of wind-bent cypress trees. Lexy opened the gate and stepped into a neglected garden. A brick path climbed past old terraces to a grand white Queen Ann Victorian with a large enclosed porch across the south end. Sunlight flashed off the porch windows.

The house was weathered and the garden untended, but it had an air of elegance and pride of place. Lexy found her view of Sam Worth shifting. He had a past that was different from the past she'd imagined for him. To her he had been a small-town handyman with a sexy smile and a way with women. Now she saw that he was part of the history of the town. Flo had said his family once owned most of Drake's Point, and Lexy wondered how he had come down in the world. What was it like to be a carpenter in a town where one's family had been so important?

Maybe it was like being invisible on the campus where your mother was a famous professor and your father was the basketball coach. But Sam Worth was hardly invisible in Drake's Point. Everybody knew him. Lexy supposed that his situation presented its own set of problems. She had always been in the background at Pacifica. Only with the success of her book had she come to feel that people were watching her and expecting things of her. And those things were mostly bad. But perhaps everyone in Drake's Point had been watching Sam and expecting things of him all his life. Lexy had a sudden thought that maybe Sam Worth's easy charm was actually a way of keeping people at a distance, of giving them a pleasing surface to look at so they didn't look deeper.

The final terrace was a wide patch of shaggy, dandelion-infested lawn bordered by a low rock wall. Once it must have been a perfect spot for garden parties overlooking the sea. A screen door opened on the porch, and she looked up at Sam Worth. Did the man ever wear a shirt?

"Ms. Clark, I *never* expected to see you here." He had a beer in one hand.

"Blame your dog." Lexy looked around. The dog, of course, had disappeared. "And I only came because I *never* get a bill from you."

"I'm behind with my paperwork."

"How much paperwork do you have?"

He seemed to consider a moment. "I'll show you."

"Come in, you mean?"

"Never?" He tilted his head to one side, studying her.

Lexy gritted her teeth. He wasn't going to let her forget that. "Show me your excessive paperwork." She marched up the faded, sagging steps of the porch. A dark blue, double sleeping bag hung over the rail. "You know, if you aren't interested in being paid, you could be working on this place."

"Not till the library's finished."

"The library?" That confused her. "The building you're working on is a library?" He didn't answer, just led the way inside, and she followed him through a large elegant room with a coffered ceiling and a tall stone fireplace. It was unfurnished except for excellent Persian rugs.

"I thought the new building was for shops."

"Shops are Vernon's idea."

"I don't understand." But she was beginning to. Recalling what she'd seen of the building's interior, she realized the layout had not been designed for shops.

He opened a pair of double doors into a paneled

dining room from another era, a time of butlers and maids in black uniforms with white aprons and gloves. A walnut dining table for twenty or more stretched down the center of the room, its whole surface covered with piles of paper, each weighed down by a rock or piece of driftwood.

"Oh my." It was a daunting amount of paper, and it could not be invoices, or Sam Worth had not been paid in years. Lexy was trying to figure out how he had acquired so much paper doing odd jobs when she was distracted by the painting on the end wall of the room. Above another fireplace was a nearly life-size portrait of a woman in her forties. Tall and blonde with handsome features and great cheekbones, she smiled with sweet calm happiness. There were big round pearls in her ears and in a band around her slim throat. She wore a sleeveless white top and a narrow, ankle-length peach skirt. A light white shawl was draped around her shoulders, and her sandal-clad feet peeked from under the skirt. She looked sort of the way Princess Diana might have looked had she reached her late forties, but Lexy had no doubt who she was.

"Your mother?" she asked. Sam Worth had inherited her eyes and brows, her cheekbones and coloring, and something of her disposition, too.

"Yes."

She did not look like a Cherry. She looked as refined and blue-blooded as the room itself. And Lexy could not imagine how she might have been famous except for her beauty. "She's lovely."

"Thank you."

121

Silence stretched between them. Of course, he didn't have a bill for her. It was the toilet bowl garden all over again. Sam Worth wasn't who he appeared to be.

"You don't have a bill for me, do you?"

He took a swig of his beer. "Maybe we could form a partnership. You could help me with my paperwork in exchange for my handyman work at the inn." He had a sly look, as if there were a catch somewhere.

Lexy was conscious of his nearness, of the warm scent of him. "A partnership?" A noise like the low rumble of distant thunder distracted her. "It's a lot of paper."

"But only a temporary arrangement. I'll be leaving when I finish the library."

She got the feeling he was posting a warning sign, telling her not to get too close. "Leaving? Don't you live here?"

"I just came home to build the library."

She stepped back away from the pull of his maleness. "There's something you're not telling me."

"That makes us even. You've been hiding things since you got here." The thunder noise rumbled nearer, and Lexy tried to place it.

His gaze caught and held hers. "So, are you in witness protection? Or are you wanted in ten states?"

She couldn't look away. "You know, you aren't exactly a tell-all, up-front kind of guy yourself. Not about your past."

The thunder noise filled the house until the vibration of it reached into the pit of Lexy's stomach. Then it passed by. "What was that?"

"I think your weekend guests have arrived."

"Oh!" Lexy was overcome with worry. "I have to go. I shouldn't leave Flo to handle Grindstone on her own." She stumbled to the porch door.

"Don't worry. Flo can handle Grindstone," Sam assured her. "Have we got a deal?"

Lexy turned back. Sam stood under his mother's portrait, his hair gilded by the late afternoon light. "Why are you always so sure of everything?"

That smile of his curved up the ends of his mouth. "I know the history."

Five huge black motorcycles crouched like menacing dogs outside her inn, their saddle bags studded with metal. *Heavy metal, indeed.* Inside, the cozy inn entryway was littered with backpacks, duffel bags and guitar cases. Everything was black. Lexy picked her way through the scattered items toward the loud welter of voices in the pub.

Eight large people in leather and chains, with bared, tattooed arms, pierced features, and long neon-colored locks filled the room. Lexy wouldn't call them guests, exactly; more like invaders. In their midst her elegant manager, Flo, lay half-sprawled across the leather-sheathed legs of some descendant of Attila the Hun. Flo's jacket was off, her hair was down, and she was wiping away tears of laughter. The beefy man in black, looking very pleased with himself, had one possessive hand on her waist and another on her thigh.

Lexy could not help a quick glance at Nigel. He was murderously silent. When her gaze shifted back to the group, she noticed another silent person in the room. He had the table in the far corner and was ignoring the conversation, devoting himself to lighting matches. He would light one, watch it flare, and drop it into the film of ale at the bottom of his glass. Lexy thought of Bambi's mother caught in the flames.

Attila's descendant looked up. "Well, hello there."

Lexy gave a small wave. "Hello, everyone."

Flo squirmed upright in the man's hold and managed to make floor contact with her feet. "Alexandra, let me introduce Grindstone. Alexandra is the new owner of the Tooth and Nail, everyone."

Hellos followed from the group, except the punk version of the Little Match Boy in the corner. Flo pointed out the vocalist, Ian Nash, a skinny fellow with green hair; the manager, Ginger Mott, a woman who might have been Flo's punk twin; and the keyboardist, Cliff Cook, whose large hands and forearms reminded Lexy of Popeye. Gram Blackmore, the man with his hands on Flo, introduced himself as the bass guitarist. He tilted his head toward the match-lighter. "Mel Winter, our drummer."

Match-lighting Mel stood abruptly, knocking over his table, and pushed his way through the others to get in Nigel's face. "Bugger off, mate. I don't fancy your staring."

Nigel didn't budge an inch. "I don't fancy your breaking the fire code."

Mel snarled, and Gram Blackmore intervened. "Back off, Winter."

"Let's just do the fire and get out of here."

"Fire?" Lexy squawked.

No one answered. Mel and Nigel were locked in a staring contest.

"Tomorrow night as planned, right?" Gram broke the tension. He looked around at the others. "Remember what we came for—our tribute to Roger." Heads nodded.

"A fire?" Lexy asked.

"Tea and scones, anyone?" asked Flo.

Chief Brock looked in later on the gathering at the Tooth and Nail. He exchanged a few words with Gram Blackmore, but ignored Lexy's imploring look. She had called him to ask whether a permit was required for a fire on the beach. Lexy knew when disaster loomed. She couldn't believe the chief couldn't see it, too. She felt warning lights should be flashing and sirens wailing as she considered the situation in the crowded pub.

Flo was at the center of it all, in the midst of an intense game of darts between the band members and the boys from the fire station. It was clear the firemen did not like Flo playing with the band, and equally clear that Grindstone had claimed her. Lexy now knew why. Ginger had filled her in on Flo's past as the girlfriend of the band's late lead guitarist, Roger Fripp. Fripp's death had broken up the band and sent Flo to Drake's Point. Now they had come to take her back for a planned reunion tour.

Lexy divided her attention between a Flo she had never seen before, the drummer Mel with his limitless supply of matches and hostility, and the murderously silent Nigel. She was prepared to throw her body between Mel and Nigel if need be.

The pub's small round tables were stacked high with empty glasses and littered with red and blue McVittie's Hob Nob and digestive biscuit wrappers. The smells of malt vinegar and pickled onions rose from empty plates, and as the band members came and went between turns at the dart board, they brought a whiff of cigarettes with them. They all took turns roaring off through the town on one of the motorcycles, setting off an explosion or two and roaring back minutes later. Lexy hoped Mayor Vernon was in Tuscany.

All the talk was of the reunion tour or the fire tribute they were planning for Fripp. They kept breaking into raucous song, sucking Flo in with them. When one of the interminable darts games ended and new sides were being picked, Drake's Point's firemen complained. "No fair siding with outsiders again, Flo."

Gram enveloped Flo in large hug. "Outsiders? She's our Flo, she is. And when we leave, she's coming with us."

A startled, torn look crossed Flo's face. Lexy felt rather than saw Nigel come out from behind the bar, a man pushed to the limit. She slipped out of her chair.

Nigel, who hardly spoke, and never above a low volume, shouted, "Dream on. Your stinking band is dead. Over. *Finito.* There's no reunion tour."

Mel immediately stopped lighting matches and swung toward him. "Says who? You've been sticking your oar in our business since we got here, bartender. Shove off." He gave Nigel a shove that didn't move him an inch.

Mel swung, but Gram grabbed his fist. "Leave it, Winter."

Mel shook off Gram's hold. "I won't leave it." He jabbed the air with a finger pointing at Nigel. "He's got a fancy for our Flo, that one."

Flo slid a glance at Nigel, as if for confirmation, but he didn't meet her gaze.

Nigel stuck out a stubborn chin. "You can't suck her into your fantasy. She's got a life here. She's not Fripp's Geordie girl anymore. You can't revive your dead band with her."

Gram finally looked angry. "It's here that she's sodding dead. What the sod is there for her here?"

Another explosion shook Drake's Point, and Flo stepped free of Gram's hold. "Thanks, Nigel. It's my life, I'll decide it. Now, gentlemen, I believe I'm on the fire department's team this round."

Lexy wanted to believe that Flo's words meant she was sticking with the Drake's Point crowd, but her accent had become as pronounced as the band's. And somehow that made Lexy feel they were losing her.

Gram shrugged, but Mel glared at Nigel until he stepped back behind the bar. "Let's just do the bloody fire and get *out*." It sounded like *oot*, and it made Lexy realize that Flo's old life had come back to get her, and that old life had a hold on her. So much for female bonding. The Tooth and Nail and Lexy could lose Flo.

Saturday afternoon Lexy found Flo sobbing in the office in black leather pants and a plunging V-necked, lime-green tank top that bared a double-bladed axe tattoo on her left shoulder. A heavy iron Celtic cross dangled in her cleavage.

Lexy quelled her surprise, pulled the desk chair up close, and handed Flo a box of tissues. "Can you tell me what's wrong?"

The woman pulled a half dozen tissues from the box, trying to restore order to her tear-streaked face. "I don't know who I am today."

Lexy knew the feeling. "What are your choices?"

Flo gave a watery laugh. "There's the old outrageous Flo, the 'Wild Child' of the seventies, celebrated girl of Grindstone's early songs." She gestured to her outfit. "And there's Florence Locke, pillar of the Drake's Point Ladies Book Club."

"Tough choice?"

Flo gave a sigh. "The band's invited me to go away with them. I could start over somewhere else."

"But Ni—" Lexy broke off. She had started to say that Nigel was in Drake's Point. She held her breath. She didn't want to think about the possibility of Flo's leaving.

Flo shook her head. "The new Florence isn't getting anywhere with Nigel, so why not go back to the old Flo?"

"Maybe the fault is in Nigel, not in you."

"He doesn't see me, you know. He sees silk jackets and a manicure and thinks. . . . I don't know what he thinks."

Lexy leaned forward. "Flo, I don't want to alarm you, but Nigel watches you all the time."

128

Flo went on, "It's ironic, you know. I wasn't really that person in Roger's songs, either. And I came here to find out who I was. Now I know, but I feel invisible again."

"Oh, I don't think you're invisible. I think Nigel's numb. Numb Nigel. He's frozen."

"You think he needs to be . . . what? Thawed? Shocked?"

"Definitely."

Flo sat up straight, obviously considering the possibilities.

"Go for it," Lexy advised. And she hoped it worked. She did not want to lose Flo.

"Do you think it's possible to meet a man who sees a woman as she really is?"

Lexy shrugged. In her experience? No. But she didn't want to discourage her manager. Nigel might wake up yet.

At midnight Lexy sat hunched against the cold night air in her thickest sweater and a dark plaid wool skirt. So far the band hadn't burned down or blown up anything important.

A huge bonfire rose in the middle of Drake's Point Beach, sending galaxies of red sparks swirling high into the air. Lexy willed them to burn out before they landed on dry grass or rooftops. Intermittent waves of smoke blew her way, making her eyes water and her throat burn. Her ears rang from the day of erratic explosions. She could see the dark figures dancing chaotically around the fire. Flo was out there somewhere, in leather pants, with her hair down, and unexpected tattoos revealed.

Lexy shivered. She was tired. The bonfire had been burning for hours, and the dampness of the air and sand had seeped through her clothes. Real stars, cold and bright, winked high overhead. Her nose and ears hurt. Deep inside she'd turned to ice, and she kept her jaw firmly clenched so her teeth wouldn't chatter. Apparently Grindstone meant to party all night.

And in the morning Flo might leave. Just like that. If Nigel remained in his silent shell. Her old life called, and she'd answered. Flo had made a list for Lexy of her usual duties, recommended some people who could help out until Lexy hired a new manager, and assured Lexy she had a knack for innkeeping. But the prospect of running the inn without Flo seemed daunting and not so much fun.

A light-colored blur passed her, and Lexy recognized Winston. She would have missed him in the dark, except that he nearly trod on her toes. She heard the sand crunch as someone else came toward her.

Sam Worth spoke. "Worried they'll burn something down?" he asked.

"Town." Lexy managed the word without breaking into shivers.

Sam sank down beside her on the sand with a bundle in his lap just as another blast shook Drake's Point.

"What *are* those?" Lexy asked of the explosions.

"M-80s. A half a stick of dynamite, basically. They're like cherry bombs for grown-ups."

"Oh." She dared only the one syllable before she felt her teeth start to click together.

Sam Worth unwrapped his bundle and shook it out, but she couldn't see the contents. "How long do you plan to keep watch?"

"As long as they keep the fire going."

"All night then." He shifted and spread his bundle across the sand. She heard the sound of a zipper, and realized it was the sleeping bag she had seen on his porch rail. Beside her he slid his big body into the bag, rustling the fabric.

Her teeth began to chatter in earnest, and once they started, the rest of her began to shake, a constant quiver in her stomach and deep tremors of her limbs.

"Join me?" Sam asked.

He waited for a reply. Everything about Alexandra Clark's huddled posture got to him. She was obviously cold, but more than that she was withdrawn, daunted. She wasn't striding forward, taking on the next tule elk or obstacle in her way. The resilience that had given bounce to her ponytail and snap to her comebacks was gone. She was staring at the bonfire but not seeing it.

He rolled and slid in his sleeping bag, warming its surfaces with his body, making the synthetic fabric whisper in invitation. Coming to the beach was one more step in caving in to desire. He wanted her, and he was giving up a night's sleep on the off chance he could get close to that soft round backside of hers.

He lay on his back, staring at the stars and waiting for her to crack. He heard her teeth knocking together, the huff of her breath with some exertion, and the rustle of her clothes—then he felt her tug at the sleeping bag. He rolled onto his side facing her and lifted the bag open to ease her entry. She scooted in beside him and lay there, rigid and shaking, her knees drawn up to her chest, her back to him. He reached his right arm around her belly and pulled her against him.

"Stretch out." He pushed her knees down.

"My . . . toes . . . are . . . ice." Her voice through the shivering sounded like it was underwater. The shock of her cold feet against his warm legs made him suck in a breath.

She gave a shaky laugh.

Fire and ice. Her bulky sweater made a lump where it rode up between them, but Sam cocked his hips into that firm round bottom, applying the hottest part of himself to the job of warming her. He had been piling driftwood on this particular blaze for days. He only hoped she wouldn't notice right away.

Then he buried his face in the hair at the nape of her neck. The wind had tangled her hair and trapped the tangy scent of ocean in her curls, but the soft strands at her collar had a sweet citrus scent. The only skin he had access to was at her wrists and neck. He wanted more; he wanted to spread his hot palm across her belly and lower, but he was pretty sure she wasn't going to encourage that move. He covered her icy hands with his and drew circles on the inside of her wrists with his thumbs.

"Flo is leaving," she said.

It took him a minute to decipher the quavering words and the lost tone. "I don't think so."

"She's out there with them. I hardly recognized her when she left the inn tonight."

"Tattoos showing?"

"You knew."

"Fripp wrote a lot of songs about her. She was his Tyne River Girl."

"I know that song. That was her? She was famous?"

"Fame is not all it's cracked up to be. I think she got lost in his image of her. When he died, she came here to find out who she really was." Sam found Alexandra's hands were warmer, not clenched but starting to open. He pushed his thumbs up into her palms, brushing heat across them.

"Do you think Drake's Point is enough, after someone has been famous?"

"Do they miss it, do you mean?"

He felt her head bob in answer. He said, "I don't think Flo does."

"But she might leave!"

"Depends on Nigel."

"I know. Why doesn't he say anything to her?"

She didn't misunderstand him. She had obviously seen what he had. "My best guess? He has something to hide, like everybody else in Drake's Point." He knew she wasn't going to blurt out her own secret, but still Sam waited, letting her think about it. He let go of her palms and rested his hand against her belly, running a finger along the narrow waistband of her skirt. The folds of her shirt, loosened by the wiggling

133

and shivering she had done, left a gap in her clothing. With a shift of his hand he could touch her stomach.

He did.

He felt her body relax into his, a smooth fit, pliant and yielding, melting to his touch. The wind was dying, and he could hear the breakers—not a big surf, but a regular beat—and the drowsy tumble of stones sucked down the shore in the receding waves.

She wiggled against him, and the heat melted whatever thoughts he had and he pressed closer to her. "What are you doing?"

"Trying to stay awake. I promised Vernon I wouldn't let them burn anything down."

"Winston will bark if anything happens."

She settled against him and stilled. He felt the awareness in her. Clearly, she knew the state he was in.

"I should go." She didn't move. "I just came in to get warm."

"You know we've got a strong attraction going here."

She didn't deny it.

"Are we going to do something about it?"

"Like?"

"Like, get to know each other."

"You like sexy women."

"And you're not sexy? Explain it to me. Maybe it will help."

"You like women with significant cleavage."

Wrong. "Well, I *know* women with significant cleavage. But I'm not in a sleeping bag with any of them."

She changed tack. "You don't like women who give orders."

"Order me to get naked."

"No!"

"Distract me." If he could get her thinking, she would stay. He knew it.

It occurred to him that her style was intended as protection from male attention, as camouflage. He wondered why that was, and how he could get her to show him the real woman. She was pretty in a natural way; not glamorous or sultry, but definitely sweet and wild; a flower growing on the mountain, not in a garden bed.

He recognized that she wasn't as ready as he was for things to progress between them, but he was patient. He knew how to work with the grain of the wood, not against it. The trick was to coax her to go in the direction he knew she wanted to go. Right now he wanted to get her to face him. He was enjoying that soft round bottom, but there were other parts he wanted to connect with. That mouth, for one.

Her shivers subsided to a slight tremor.

"How come you have so much paperwork?"

"So you can help me with it. Are you going to?"

"This isn't making any sense." She rolled to face him.

"Makes perfect sense to me." He slid his arms around her waist and drew her close.

"You're coming on to me, and I'm wearing—"

"—a sweater that's two inches thick and scratchier than a welcome mat. If you want help removing it, I'm right here."

"No, thank you." Her breath fluttered against his throat.

"You know I've got access to just a few square inches of skin here."

"You're just going to have to be satisfied with that."

Never, he thought to himself. And set himself to get her to tip her face up to his.

YES! ☐

Sign me up for the **Historical Romance Book Club** and send my THREE FREE BOOKS! If I choose to stay in the club, I will pay only $13.50* each month, a savings of $6.47!

YES! ☐

Sign me up for the **Love Spell Book Club** and send my TWO FREE BOOKS! If I choose to stay in the club, I will pay only $8.50* each month, a savings of $5.48!

NAME: _____

ADDRESS: _____

_____

TELEPHONE: _____

E-MAIL: _____

☐ **I WANT TO PAY BY CREDIT CARD.**

☐ VISA   ☐ MasterCard   ☐ DISCOVER

ACCOUNT #: _____

EXPIRATION DATE: _____

SIGNATURE: _____

Send this card along with $2.00 shipping & handling for each club you wish to join, to:

Romance Book Clubs
20 Academy Street
Norwalk, CT 06850-4032

Or fax (must include credit card information!) to: 610.995.9274. You can also sign up online at www.dorchesterpub.com.

*Plus $2.00 for shipping. Offer open to residents of the U.S. and Canada only. Canadian residents please call 1.800.481.9191 for pricing information.

If under 18, a parent or guardian must sign. Terms, prices and conditions subject to change. Subscription subject to acceptance. Dorchester Publishing reserves the right to reject any order or cancel any subscription.

JOIN NOW!

Chapter 7
Maximum Intensity: Reaching for the Peak

"Varying positions during this phase of the workout ensures that both partners use all of the major muscle groups. In addition, frequent subtle adjustments in movement add intensity."
—*Workout Sex*, Lexy Clark

Lexy did not want to wake up. Cool air moved across her face, but the rest of her was deliciously warm and rooted to her bed, her arms and legs too heavy to move. Pale light penetrated her closed eyelids, but she kept them shut and let herself sink back in the heavy warm feeling, which narrowed into points of contact with Sam Worth's hard male body. Dimly she realized that they were spooned together. His breath came and went in a warm pulse against her shoulder, and one of his arms encircled her ribs. With her breathing, the hair-roughened top of his arm brushed against the smoothness of her stomach.

She was waking up in bed with Sam Worth! Well, in a sleeping bag with him. But they hadn't had sex.

She was still wearing her clothes. Her shirt had come free of her skirt and was bunched up under her breasts, but everything else was in place.

She didn't remember falling asleep, but her waking mind zeroed in on the hot spots where their bodies connected, spots that sent signals zipping along her nerves, waking other parts of her that hadn't stirred for months. She recognized the languid, charged feeling. She felt sexy. Sam Worth's touch made her feel sexy.

She stretched slightly, testing the feeling, and his body shifted to keep the contact. She felt a hot liquid rush of arousal, and a jolt of energy sizzled through her. She held her breath, but he didn't waken.

All the wires of her body started humming as if a current had been switched on. She felt slick and tingly and . . . hot. If she didn't get away from him, she'd set the sleeping bag on fire.

She opened her eyes. A misting fog shrouded the beach in gray. The smell of ash and charred wood wafted up from a blackened circle where the bonfire had been. There was no sign of Grindstone, but Drake's Point was still standing. She lifted Sam's muscled arm from around her middle, and cool air rushed in over the exposed parts of her. She wriggled free of the bag, trying not to wake its other occupant.

Condensation had dampened her socks where she'd taken them off, so she tucked them in her sweater pockets and slid her feet into her cold shoes. Winston watched her from the other side of Sam Worth's sleeping body.

She prayed he wouldn't bark, and waved good-bye.

But Sam's muffled voice came from the sleeping bag as she stood. "Remember. We made a deal."
What deal?

The fog obscured the mountain and silenced the town. Lexy passed along Beach Street without seeing anyone. Drake's Point really was Brigadoon, where strangers could appear and disappear in the mist.

There were no motorcycles outside her inn, and the only sounds were the familiar ones of the building waking up for another day. Lexy stood outside for a few minutes, listening to a vacuum upstairs and water from a hose splashing against the patio and someone whistling. The door opened and a beautiful young man came out; tall, dark-haired, and green-eyed. He started when he saw her. Then his gaze took in her flowered skirt and heavy sweater, and a wide grin brightened his expression.

"You must be Ms. Clark." He came forward and seized her hands in both of his.

Lexy tried not to gape. Sam Worth was good-looking, but this man was unreal.

"I must thank you. I am Emiliano, Violeta's husband. You have made her happy here." He gestured toward the inn. "Things are much better now." He gave Lexy's hands a parting squeeze and strode off into the fog whistling a pure, sweet melody.

Lexy stood for a minute, dazzled and wondering what things were better for Violeta and Emiliano, then she realized—they had been reading her book. They didn't know it was her book, but the two most beautiful people in Drake's Point had been having *Workout Sex*. If Stanley Skoff only knew. Lexy thought she needed to sit down. She pushed open the inn door.

Flo was at the reception desk, looking her usual polished self—no leather pants, no tattoos. She took in Lexy's awestruck state. "I see you met Violeta's Emiliano."

"Oh my." Lexy sank onto the wooden bench in the foyer.

"He has that effect."

She smiled at Flo—at Flo, who was still in Drake's Point, still at the Tooth and Nail. "You didn't leave!"

"No."

"I thought maybe Drake's Point wasn't enough for you."

"Drake's Point is just right, but it did do to remember that other life, to keep the old fires burning." She laughed. "Especially last night."

Lexy looked at Flo's familiar outfit. "I love that jacket."

"Those leather pants were a torture." Flo gave a wicked grin. "I did want to shake Nigel up a bit, though."

"Did it work?"

Flo sighed and shook her head. "But my decision isn't really about Nigel. It's about me. This is my life."

Lexy still wanted to shake Nigel. "Is the band okay with your staying?"

"Oh, yes. They like to visit the past, but they don't really want to go back."

"No reunion tour?" Lexy wanted Flo's certainty.

Flo laughed. "They talk about it every year, but Gram mostly produces CDs now. Ginger and Cliff have a string of Burger Kings, and Mel has a ranch. They like to pretend they're still ragers, but they're not."

"At least they didn't burn the town down." Lexy smiled. Her manager had turned a corner, and her dangerous guests had disappeared back into the fog from whence they'd come. "Who do we have coming next? Bring 'em on."

The fog did not lift that day, the inn was empty of guests, and the usual Sunday lunch crowd was thin. There was absolutely nothing for Lexy to do except remember or try not to remember her unwise night in the sleeping bag with Sam Worth. *What deal?* She was sure she had not agreed to sex. She had not been *that* sleepy. And besides, she wouldn't have sex with him. Lexy didn't do sex without a relationship. One of the cardinal rules of *Workout Sex*, the one every male reader who'd propositioned her had overlooked, was that the partners had to be in a committed relationship to gain the full benefits of the program.

Lexy and Sam Worth were ships passing in the night—a brief collision and then onward. He was going to finish his work in Drake's Point and go back to the city where he had been engaged to someone else. He was the past of Drake's Point, and she hoped to be its future. He was full of confidence, and she was a C-minus student in assertiveness training.

He thinks you're sexy, a voice repeated in her head. Even now, the way you are.

A cold shower seemed like a good idea, but a run in the fog might be better. She needed to release the restless energy building up inside her, and cool mist on her skin would help. At the very least, it would keep her from becoming too heated. She changed into blue running shorts and a white Pacifica T-shirt, and picked a trail that started on the other side of the creek from the inn and led up the ridge toward the mountain away from Drake's Point. The uphill grade and rock-strewn trail called for concentration.

Lexy focused on her breathing and footwork, getting a nice rhythm going. The cool air smelled of bays and redwoods and grasses. Near the top of the ridge, the trail veered south across an open field. Above her the fog clung to dark stands of redwoods with their long drooping branches, and below her the grassy hills sloped down steeply toward Drake's Point and the ocean. She could see just enough of the trail to keep moving forward at a steady pace. But her thoughts fell into a groove as well, a Sam Worth groove. Maybe he was her chance to discover a new side of herself.

She had been in the sixth grade and wearing her first bra, a band of cotton with a cup size designed to hold brussels sprouts, when boys had started calling her Sexy Lexy. She had known even then that it was not because she inspired desire. She had often been the only girl hanging out with her older brothers and their friends, or with the guys on one of her dad's basketball teams, but her sexual presence had never registered. Until she wrote her book, she had never even caused a blip on the male radar screen. Her bar code didn't scan.

Of course, after the book she'd had old boyfriends call to ask if she wanted to work out. As one of them put it, "I've heard of ways to get laid, Lexy, but this beats them all."

Before the book she couldn't remember really turning anyone on, except in a generic way. Not even Colin. Maybe *especially* not Colin. He had been very pointed about that in the end. *Lexy, you're the lite beer of sex.*

Of course, he had been angry when he said that. Considering that he'd had the benefit of all her research for months, his anger seemed particularly unfair to Lexy. When she'd finally understood, she had been glad to break up with him: He wasn't angry that she was a lite beer of sex—he'd enjoyed it when she tried her workout ideas out on him—but about the book deal. Her advance was bigger than his corporate lawyer salary. He'd even threatened to sue her for half the earnings based on his contribution to her research. She'd told him that test subjects didn't get the Nobel, and she'd found a feisty lawyer of her own. One call from Joan Bird had silenced Colin.

Breaking up with him was one more way the book had made her independent. On the book tour she'd had time to realize a lot about their relationship. She had moved in with him mainly to get relief from the surreal L.A. dating scene. It was a scary world with boyfriend-shopping on the Internet, speed dating, and rules like cell-phone-numbers-only, don't-let-him-see-you-leave-the-bar. Getting her coffee one morning, she had overheard the guy in front of her casually describing how he had broken a woman's nose in a bar the night before. He was into sound effects and repeatedly slammed one fist into the other palm, recreating the satisfying crack of the woman's nose breaking. Lexy had moved in with Colin fairly shortly after that.

Colin was plain vanilla—solid blue boxers, white shirts, and gray pin stripes. He didn't take risks or make jokes. Living with him was safe. But they hadn't really seen anything particular to like in each other. Being together had been like buying the generic brand of everything. Sex with Colin had only been decent when she had the book to think about.

But Sam Worth was a different story. And in that sleeping bag he had been turned on—openly, boldly, hotly. And that had stuck Lexy's sexuality switch in the *on* position. The voice in her head caught the rhythm of her stride, insisting that the sleeping bag had only been a taste, there was more to have and she knew where to get it. *Come on down,* the voice said in a car salesman voice, *have we got a deal for you.*

Of course, making love to him would be using Sam Worth, and that would make her like Colin and all the Chips and Skips who had come on to her while she was promoting her book. And she would not do that. She had standards, after all.

She was feeling pretty good about her ethics when a noise came out of the fog that froze her in her tracks. It was like a whale shrieking—high-pitched, with deeper notes underneath and three sharp barks at the end, loud, urgent, and close. Lexy thought Monstro, thought *Jurassic Park*. She couldn't be sure where the sound came from. She couldn't see anything at the edge of the woods; the unfamiliar trail disappeared into the fog in both directions. Should she go forward or back? She strained to hear the noise again over the rasp of her breathing and the pounding of her heart. The bushes at her feet rustled in the wind. A startled bird exploded from the brush a few feet away and fluttered off into the fog. Lexy staggered back and landed on her bottom.

Then Winston bounded out of the fog. He brushed past her legs and turned to confront her, barking wildly. Lexy scrambled to her feet, trying to quiet him, as something large and invisible crashed through the woods just out of sight. She backed down the hillside, urged on by Winston. When she came to a fork in the trail that she hadn't noticed on her way up, he herded her down it. Once she thought she heard the noise again, but she kept on running, downhill, taking whatever turns Winston chose.

Her heart rate didn't slow until she saw the rooftops of Drake's Point. Winston stopped in front of a grand white house with a circular drive and a white-columned portico. A bronze plaque proclaimed, Worth House. It was even more impressive from the front than from the ruined back garden. Lexy thought she might slip by, but Winston did his barking routine again and the door opened.

Sam Worth appeared, coffee mug in hand, wearing a shirt for once but no shoes. Even his bare feet looked sexy.

145

"Hi. Are we starting where we left off last night?"

No. But you want to. Parts of Lexy other than her conscience got excited at the prospect. "Your dog herded me here."

"Good dog, Winston." The retriever trotted over to sit next to him. "Why?"

"There was something in the woods." Lexy kept her distance. She saw that, under lowered lids, he was checking out her running attire.

"Another encounter with the local wildlife?"

"It sounded like an elephant." She didn't want to alarm him by mentioning that he probably had a T-Rex in his neighborhood.

That slow grin of his lifted the corners of Sam's mouth. "Bull tule elk bugling," he explained.

"Naturally."

"Did you want to come in?" he asked.

The part of Lexy's brain that was still working wasn't sure that was a good idea. *What* was *the deal we made?* she wondered. "Could I have some water?"

"Sure."

She followed him into the house. She could swear the dog looked self-satisfied.

"I'm just passing by," she said. But she watched Sam Worth lean into the sink and run water into a glass, and thought about that sleeping bag.

He turned back to her, holding out a glass. "So we've got a deal? You're going to help me with my paperwork?"

Lexy smiled and took the offered glass. She breathed a sigh of relief. "Sure. How about tomorrow afternoon?"

146

* * *

After lunch the next day, Lexy set off to help Sam Worth with the mountain of paper on his dining room table. The fog had burned off in the warmth of the October day, and a white-haired old man in an ancient suit and European-looking hat came out of Charlie Beaton's garden gate, whistling. He stopped when he saw her and tipped his hat. *"Buona sera, Signorina,"* he said, smiling as if he had caused the sun to come out.

Lexy found herself grinning back.

He opened his hands in a wide appreciative gesture that took in her whole self. *"Beato il poeta per cui Lei e la nuova Beatrice!"*

Lexy had no idea what he had said, but the lilting tone was seductive.

Then he coached her to say *"buona sera,"* and she repeated the phrase in his musical lilt all the way to the feed store. She checked the recycle shelf, but there was no sign of her book. Maybe it had disappeared into the mist. She hoped so. She picked up some brown paper shopping bags and some sticky pads, and asked Meg about the charming gentleman as she bought them.

"That's Amadeo, Charlie Beaton's grandfather on his mother's side."

"Oh. He spoke to me in Italian, I think."

"Flirted with you, most likely."

Lexy nodded. It had seemed like flirting. "He said something that sounded lovely."

"He probably said you were the new Beatrice. That's one of his great lines. I don't know what's up with him, but he's got the twinkle back in his eye."

Lexy accepted the change from her purchase. "Maybe it's those pumpkin seeds of yours."

Meg laughed. "Maybe."

On her way home, at the building site, Lexy saw a stranger with an orange hard hat and a clipboard making an inspection of the building; and from the look on Sam Worth's face, it wasn't going well. The stranger's bulging gut opened little diamond-shaped gaps between the two halves of his shirt front.

Lexy caught Sam's glance, and he motioned for her to join them, introducing her as his assistant. Jay Johnson was the county plumbing inspector, a friend of Mayor Vernon's. A bristling wad of keys hung from Johnson's belt and jingled as he walked. Lexy rolled her eyes at Sam, but she was soon caught up in listening to the way he talked about the building, surprised at his knowledge of all its workings. She had not thought that pounding nails and sawing boards would give him such an understanding of architecture.

They went from the men's bathrooms to the women's rooms, examining the fixtures. According to the inspector, the shape of the new dual flush toilets in the women's rooms wasn't to code, and he couldn't quite grasp that the waterless urinals in the men's rooms actually had pipes running to them in case the system needed to be connected. He had no patience for Sam Worth's explanation of how the building's water system actually purified its own water, either. But Lexy found it sort of exciting. She hadn't realized how sophisticated the new building was going to be.

On the way out, Johnson commented on the dry

wall. It wasn't his area, but was it properly attached? he asked. The little screws were supposed to be so many inches apart.

Lexy was no expert, but she looked at the straight perfect seams joining the pieces and Sam's tight expression and wondered what was up. The inspector told Sam to call for a second inspection when he redid the work. He ripped a long form off his clipboard and handed it over.

She and Sam watched Johnson climb into his truck and pull away before Lexy felt it was prudent to speak. "What was that all about?"

"Just Mayor Vernon making it tough to meet my deadline."

His deadline? "What happens if you don't make it?"

His mouth set in a grim line. "The use permit expires, and the town can pick a different use for the building."

"That's what the mayor's petition is all about, and the Tuesday meetings of his committee?"

"Yeah."

"*Oh no.* I signed." Apparently she had chosen sides in a looming battle without realizing it.

"Don't worry. Everyone will. Vernon has a hold on most folks in Drake's Point."

"But if you finish on time?"

"I think the council will renew the use permit in spite of Vernon."

She looked around again. "There's nothing wrong with the plumbing or the drywall here, is there?"

"No. This building is plumb, level, and square, which is not easy on sand dunes." He ran his hand

149

along one of the seams. "Plumb means it's aligned to a true vertical. Level means you've got true horizontal, and square means the pieces fit together in a perfect 90 degree angle." He laid a level on the top of a half wall in the large main room, and the liquid green eye came to rest in the center of its tube.

"You're not just a carpenter or a handyman, are you?"

His gaze met hers and held. "I'm a builder. I have a firm in the city. We take on a lot of community-based projects like libraries and recreation centers, especially if the clients want green buildings."

"And you let me think you were the local Mr. Fix-It?"

"You assumed, and I didn't correct you."

"Why?" Lexy was sure he was still being modest.

His gaze shifted away and then slid back to meet hers. "How many times have you called me, innkeeper?" He was looking at her long lavender flowered skirt, high-collared white shirt with lace and tucks on the bodice, and her lavender cardigan. But she had a feeling he was seeing her without any of it. "Have we still got a deal?"

"Fine. Let's get to it." She showed him her paper bags.

"You plan to chuck the lot?"

She shook her head and laughed. "Trust me. I can organize anything."

He led the way up the honeysuckle path to his parents' house.

"If you have a tight deadline, why are you working alone?"

"Vernon hassles the subcontractors. Does license

checks on them. Issues parking tickets for their trucks. It helps to know the mayor's secretary. Dawn Russell always tells me when Vernon's out of town."

"So, the library isn't a town project?"

"No."

"Who's paying for it?"

"The Ladies Book Club of Drake's Point asked me to come back and build it."

And you couldn't refuse. She was beginning to appreciate his generosity.

The sleeping bag was again hanging over the porch rail in the afternoon sun. Lexy ran her hand over its warm folds as she went by.

Sam's dining room table looked just as cluttered as before, but Lexy refused to be daunted by the stacks of papers. "Okay, what needs to be done?"

Sam ran a hand through his hair and pointed to a pile of small notes. "A builder has to record his work. The mechanics sheets have to match the architectural sheets. Sketches that show the as-builts have to go with original plan sheets. And then there are plans for all the systems—mechanical, electrical, and plumbing. There are RFIs, requests for information, that have to be tracked down. Vernon's inspector has sent correction notices. There are bills, permits, licenses . . ."

Lexy turned to him. His face was tight, and he wasn't meeting her gaze. He obviously found the paperwork a nightmare. "Okay." Lexy found herself wanting to help him.

"You're sure? Do you need anything? Otherwise, I'll be down at the site. I better get working."

"I'll be fine."

* * *

As soon as he left, Lexy began examining the piles. The table looked the way her living room had when she was deep into work on the book, with piles of different drafts and notes and research tomes everywhere. At least each stack of Sam Worth's papers contained items of the same size and color. She turned her paper bags into baskets to hold the different piles and hummed an old *Sesame Street* tune. *Some of these things are just like the others . . .*

His handwriting was regular and masculine, but Sam seemed to have little concept of how to spell. The blueprints Lexy came across were yellow with faded blue lines and many notations. Still, she was surprised to find a page dated 1990. She had been fifteen. Sam would have been seventeen or eighteen. She looked for a newer set of plans, but didn't find any. If he was building from the 1990 plans, no wonder he had made so many modifications.

When she turned to the notes and sketches in the pile he'd called "as-builts," she realized that there were two sets. One was clearly Sam's work with a scrawled set of his initials on each page, but the others were the work of someone else. Those had the 1990 date, as if the library had been built fifteen years earlier.

At least the bills were up-to-date and somewhat ordered. She set aside the unpaid ones and arranged those that had been paid by the account and check numbers on the invoices. Again, there were two sets of bills, both from recent months. The first totaled nearly three hundred thousand dollars, but the others quickly added up to over a million. It was puzzling. The Ladies Book Club had never raised that kind of money, and the mayor didn't want the library, so who did want it enough to spend over a million dollars to have it built? People in Drake's Point passed a few books back and forth through Meg Sullivan's recycle shelf, but Lexy didn't see the place as a literary enclave.

The click of dog feet on the boards of the porch alerted her to Sam's return. Or at least to Winston's. The porch door opened and closed, and she called out a hello. From the dining room windows she could see the fiery autumn sun low in the sky. Sam Worth stopped in the doorway, looking tired and dusty with his sleeping bag draped over one arm. "You cold?"

She was. "I didn't realize it was so late."

"I'm going to light a fire in the living room and take a shower."

A *shower*? Lexy's stomach did a little flip. "Okay." She waved a hand toward the piles on the table. "I'll just finish up here." She heard both dog and man's footsteps go away, then her hands got a little shaky, and the papers in front of her didn't make sense anymore.

She pushed back in her chair and wandered into the living room, where the only signs of Sam were the sleeping bag and the fire, as if he were camping out in this big empty house. He had spread the sleeping bag on the rug in front of the fireplace. Lexy had a feeling he was going to ask her to join him on it. She curled her toes in her running shoes. She had good feelings about that sleeping bag.

But she still had a choice. Just because she had

153

spent the afternoon getting a sense of his generous vision of the library didn't mean she had to stay for sex.

She went over to the big windows and watched the light fade from the sky, doing a little core work—taking deep breaths and releasing them—trying to think through her options.

Sex with Sam Worth in his big double sleeping bag. It was something new. There would be conversation. Partners were supposed to communicate. Her imagination took things a step further. In her book she had advised using clinical terms to name parts and acts, but what if Sam Worth had other words for things? Short, Anglo-Saxon words—pithy, earthy words? She had heard the words, but she hadn't said them much. Would she still feel sexy, turned-on—or would she just feel embarrassed? And what would he ask for? In the sleeping bag they'd had their clothes on, eyes mostly closed. There was no kissing, unless being pressed body to body was considered a form of kissing.

Yes, kissing was a big deal. Lexy had not written much about it in her book. She had sort of assumed it would happen between the stretching and the breathing. She wasn't a kissing expert.

She knew sexy women did things with their tongues that Lexy had never felt like doing. She'd never wanted to explore Colin's tonsils. She couldn't twist a cherry stem into a knot. She couldn't even fold her tongue in half the way thirty percent of the population could. It was a genetically determined trait, she knew. Every year the students in Pacifica's introductory bio class checked the tongue-folding abilities of everyone on campus, and every year Lexy's tongue failed to fold.

What if the man who made every woman in Drake's Point weak-kneed with desire realized she wasn't sexy? She would let the inn crumble into ruins before she would see that happen.

Winston passed her and sat by the porch door, doing some doggy grooming but clearly waiting for her to let him out. She obliged, and he trotted off into the darkness. She realized she was making herself nervous over nothing. She really was very accomplished at sex. She'd planned all the moves in a great workout. She just needed to remember them. She went back to her breathing.

At the sound of footsteps, she turned. The fire in the hearth danced brightly, making popping noises and sending out lots of heat, and Sam Worth was there in a white T-shirt and jeans, barefoot. Little damp spots on his shirt clung to his shoulders and chest.

Lexy watched him cross the room—easy, unhurried. "Do you want to see what I did with the papers?" she asked.

He shook his head. His look said he had a very different agenda. "Are you ready to give in to the inevitable?"

"Oh, inevitable, is it?" Lexy stiffened her spine and raised her chin. He had some nerve.

He just grinned at her. "Yep. As inevitable as Adam and Eve falling, two people stuck in a small garden with a hot attraction going. There was no way they

155

were going to walk past that apple every day forever."

"Maybe they couldn't, but surely we can for a few more weeks."

He shook his head. "I don't know. Once the attraction takes hold, it's hard to shake."

She had to agree with him that there was a strong pull between them. She was standing in his big empty living room because she couldn't stay away. And she didn't want to admit how often he'd popped up in her dreams and fantasies.

He turned to the fire, taking up the poker. "When you're ready, I'm ready," he said quietly, with his back to her.

Lexy watched the fire's glow outline his rugged build. He prodded the logs, sending a shower of sparks up the flue, all his movements easy and unhurried, as if time might stop for them. He was something new in her experience, a sexy man who invited her participation. Something tight released in her, and she made her dry throat work.

"I'm ready."

He turned back, taking her hand and pulling her with him to the edge of the sleeping bag and into his arms, settling her against him. One large palm lay flat against the small of her back, pressing so that her chest and then her face lifted to him. She inhaled the clean soap-and-shampoo scent of him, and slid her hands around him across the strong blades of his shoulders.

He released the two buttons on her stand-up collar and pressed a kiss to the base of her throat. Lexy's sweater-covered breasts pressed against his chest.

Maybe if they got some other stuff going first before the kissing, he wouldn't notice her lack of oral expertise so much.

His gaze narrowed on her mouth. "Whatever you're thinking," he said, "stop."

Lexy thought he must be doing a Jedi mind trick, because she started to answer, then leaned into him instead. His mouth caught hers, open, hot and sure. *Oh*, she thought and forgot all her past kissing failures. He tasted like toothpaste and oranges, and she kind of lost track of what was happening. All was heat and the press of his mouth. She felt him tug her shirt free of her skirt and place his hot palm against her naked waist. Just that hand, and her skin warmed everywhere.

He broke their kiss, his thumbs tracing sizzling arcs along her ribs. She brushed her palms across his chest and paused to feel his heart pounding. It popped into her head to calculate maximum heart rates, thinking they had reached the target zone much quicker than possible, when he said, "Time to lose the clothes, Laura Ashley." Then he pulled back and stepped onto his sleeping bag.

Lexy froze, resisting the tug of his hands. She sneaked a peek at the front of his jeans. He was definitely turned on. She, Lexy Clark, was having this effect on him, Sam Worth. Then she pictured him confronted by her pink-flowered underwear. Her hips and bottom, which required a whole rose bush, and each of her breasts that needed only a single bud.

"You first."

He pulled the T-shirt up over his head and

dropped it on the floor, and then he shed his jeans and boxers with a quick flick of buttons and a downward shove. Lexy got a little dizzy when he stepped out of the crumpled denim. She clasped her hands together to keep from touching him.

"I can't go on calling you Ms. Clark."

"Alexandra, then," she said. He was cocky for a naked guy, but Lexy supposed that being gorgeous would do that for you. For a moment she thought he might question the name.

He didn't. "Your turn, Alexandra."

"Could you close your eyes?"

"Worried that the tattoos and piercings will ruin your image?"

"How do you feel about flowers? Lots of flowers?"

His gaze didn't waver, not even a flicker. She had a feeling he was reading her mind. "Men are visual."

"Tactile was good. In the sleeping bag the other night." His gaze slid lazily from her to the sleeping bag and back. He seemed to sense her nervousness. "So let's do that again." He scooped up his discarded T-shirt, flung the sleeping bag wider, and dropped down on it. "Come here."

Lexy stepped to the edge of the bag. She watched him pick up his T-shirt, hook a finger into a tiny hole near the collar and rip.

"Shoes off."

She undid the laces and slipped out of her running shoes and socks.

He put a warm hand around one ankle and urged her closer. "Right here." He pressed a condom packet into Lexy's palm. Then he reached up and tied the torn strip of T-shirt around his eyes, and leaned back on his side, propped on one elbow. His free hand found her ankle again.

Lexy had taken Art History 101 at Pacifica; she had been to Rome, but this was better. She looked down at her very own living fresco—Adam, waiting for his Eve. He was absolutely still, absolutely intent, absolutely turned on by her. The fire cast dark gold shadows on his chest and groin. She swayed a bit on her feet, fumbled out of her sweater and shirt, and unhooked her skirt and let it fall. Sam's chest rose with a quick intake of breath when the soft fabric landed. She skimmed off her slip and stood in her flowered underwear, all her pink cabbage roses in full bloom.

She jiggled her foot free of his hold and knelt beside him, running the flat of her palm down the full length of his chest and abdomen, letting the heat consume her.

He said, "Alexandra," in a low warning voice, so she leaned over and kissed him. He pulled her down and rolled her over. His hands cupped her bottom and brought her close to him. "I've been waiting for this," he said.

For a blind guy, he sure knew his way around. Lexy did not have to direct him at all. She tried to take in the feeling of his weight against her, surprised at the way their bodies conformed. She wanted to tell him that they would need to trade places to do her complete workout. But his beautiful arms made effortless pumps, and he was moving against her in all the best ways and she was lost in the press and stretch and slide of her body's seeking, not worrying about her breathing or her heart rate at all.

She meant to tell him about varying their positions to use all the muscle groups, but he was way ahead of her on that one, and her body kept arching and opening to his touch in ways she hadn't expected, reaching for more. Whenever she opened her mouth, pleased sounds emerged.

Her mind tried to catch and hold on to thoughts like lubricant and contraception, but the thoughts threatened to fly up and burn out like sparks in a bonfire . . . until Sam uttered her name on a desperate rasp. Dizzy with heat, Lexy reached for the little packet. Their hands met briefly in a fumbling cooperation. Then there was only the glad rhythm of his body sinking into her and the pleasure building, faster and faster.

In one dazzling moment all the birthday candles on all the cakes she'd ever had were lit, their little flames dancing, begging for her to make a wish and blow them out.

And then she heard Obi Wan saying, *Use the force, Luke.*

She let go, mindless and soaring.

Sam shuddered his release in answer to hers—not a few brief jerks but long, deep notes, sweet and sustained, reaching places in her that had never been reached before and filling them.

"This blindfold is coming off," Sam warned Alexandra. He still needed time to recover. That had been one intense sexual encounter.

She pulled the sleeping bag up over her chest and lay back, staring at the ceiling, her cheeks flushed, her dark hair down and curling a little around her face from heat and sweat. He could see the creamy straps of her bra still looped over her shoulders. Next time, the bra was coming off.

For awhile they lay there, spent, looking at the ceiling, listening to the fire, her hip resting against his. She was smiling, and her body gave a little spasm of aftershock. His own body clenched in reaction, totally attuned to hers.

Now he understood her determination to keep her body covered. The thick sweaters and yards of skirts made sense—not because of some figure flaw, but because of the passion they concealed.

What you see is not what you get. That was a rule of life that fit her as much as it did him. She wasn't the church lady who would lie back and simply do her duty for God and country. He wasn't the friendly local handyman. Maybe they should leave it at that.

Their lovemaking, with him blindfolded, no less, was probably the most modest Worth House had ever seen, but Sam was usually careful and detached, and he hadn't been either. And he was pretty sure she'd been just as mindless as he had.

He liked the noises she'd made, the little gasps and sweet astonished cries as if she hadn't known so much pleasure before. And he liked her subtle demands, too.

She stirred a little. "The library was built once before," she said. "What happened to it?"

He kept his gaze on the ceiling. Trust her to go

right to the heart of his secrets. "It burned down."

She didn't say anything. He might have made her mindless for an hour, but she was back to thinking things through again. That was another of his surprising responses to her: He had let her handle his paperwork. Had even wanted her to handle it. Everything was there in one way or another: the story of his past, his reasons for coming back to Drake's Point, everything.

"And you're just now rebuilding?"

"Before the use permit expires. Like I said."

"So the Ladies Book Club must have held a lot of bake sales."

"There's some outside funding," he admitted. Her curiosity was palpable. As soon as he got some energy back, he would deflect it. "It's a green building. There's a lot of interest in that sort of thing right now."

"From the media?" He could feel her get tense again.

"Some."

"Is that why there are so many changes? So many as-builts?" she asked.

"Yeah."

"So . . . are the ladies the ones behind the library?"

"Vernon doesn't want it at all, if that's what you mean. A library won't line his pockets."

Alexandra was silent, thinking in that determined way of hers, probably reviewing what she knew of Vernon.

Sam finally said, "But people in Drake's Point want it. Those books on Sullivan's shelf get read by everybody sooner or later."

For some reason that gave her pause. Alexandra didn't move or speak. A log split in the fire.

"Are you a great reader?" she asked. He heard the change in her tone, the hesitation that said there was something more to the question. And he felt the intensity of her interest in his answer.

"I've been known to crack a book." It was as noncommital as he could make it and yet still a fraud. It seemed to startle her. She sat up abruptly, reaching for her clothes, shrugging into her shirt and sweater, all haste and furious energy. She groped frantically in the sleeping bag, and he fished out her underwear. *Pink. Flowered*. She sure had a thing about flowers.

She snatched her underwear from him. "Thanks."

"Was it something I said?"

She wriggled into her panties in the sleeping bag. "I just need to get back to the inn."

"Thanks for your help with the paperwork." He gave her a pleased grin.

She ignored it. "That was our deal, right?"

In another minute she had slipped into her skirt and shoes, finger-combed her hair, twisted it into a knot, and scrambled to her feet. She wasn't looking at him. "That was great. Thank you."

He waited for her to say *Let's do it again some time*, but she simply headed for the door.

He wasn't going to let her off that easy. "No blindfold next time," he said.

That made her pause. Then she was out the door, her steps light on the porch stairs as she fled.

Chapter 8
Cool Down

The next phase in a successful sexual workout is continuous activity at a lowered intensity that permits talking.

—*Workout Sex*, Lexy Clark

On Tuesday, to Lexy's dismay, nothing at the Tooth and Nail needed fixing. A three-hundred-year-old inn dismantled, transported from England, reassembled in California, and not a door on it squeaked, not a faucet dripped. Lexy couldn't find a missing roof tile, a loose floor board, or a cracked window pane. And she looked. Polite guests came and went, slept in lovely unbroken beds, praised Ernesto's food, admired Charlie Beaton's paintings, and left tips for Violeta. And that was all good because Lexy did not intend to call Sam Worth again.

She settled down with her tea in the inn office and pulled the rubber band off her stack of Spanish flash cards. She needed to practice her verb conjugations. It was Flo's day off, the inn's bookings looked good, and Lexy had a lot of thinking to do. She should feel bad. She had just had sex outside of a relationship; she should feel that dieter's post-cheesecake remorse and self-loathing. But she didn't. She wasn't sure what she felt, or more realistically, which feeling was uppermost. There were elusive layers.

She was pretty clear how she felt about the sex. Ironically, sex with Sam Worth had been a first in Lexy's career as a sex expert, the first time that she had had serious major sex. It had been great sex—high-octane, Pentium-processor, V-8-under-the-hood kind of sex. And she hadn't even used any of her moves. What if they had actually followed the *Workout Sex* program? They might have sent their heart rates out of control. They might even be dead! She had based her book on Colin, which meant her research was woefully inadequate.

Lexy knew about orgasms, those little feel-good moments that made the rest of sex worthwhile. She had researched the difference between superficial and deep contractions and how long, technically, one could make them last. All that was outdated data. Writing a book on sex based on Colin was like writing a barbecue book based on tofu, a dessert book based on aspartame, a gardening book based on artificial flowers.

Okay. The sex had been good. The relationship was the problem. She supposed they had progressed from banter to a kind of respect and appreciation. They had helped each other out. He wasn't the sort of scum she had met on her book tour. But they both had secrets. She knew she wanted to keep hers, and apparently he wanted to keep his, a good reason to avoid his sleeping bag.

He was a private person. If he found the publicity surrounding his engagement to a socialite distasteful, he would find the publicity that followed Lexy Clark outrageous—like dating a former Washington intern or Martha Stewart or J-Lo, women whom the media liked to catch in ugly moments for the pleasure of shoppers glancing at the supermarket tabloids. Lexy had not reached that status yet, but after the *Stanley Skoff Show* disaster, she had been conscious of strange men lurking with cameras whenever she went out.

And Sam had a history he wasn't sharing, too. She hadn't missed the way his sentences shrank to Cro-Magnon-like grunts when she asked certain simple questions, or the way he didn't look at her when she asked about the library. That easy manner of his was all a front. The signs around his heart all read, TRESPASSERS WILL BE SHOT. The walls were topped with barbed wire, the guard dogs were pit bulls, and Lexy wasn't a dog person.

And he was no Colin. Sam and Lexy were not a matched set. He was beautiful and dangerous, and Lexy was at best cute. He was *Star Wars*; she was *Space Balls*. He was the bull tule elk with a full herd already, and she was just a stray cow. He would keep her in the herd and maybe throw her the occasional scrap of attention. Maybe her book had changed her image, but she didn't want that. She wanted to be herself. But wouldn't he need her? She might easily come to need him, big time. And there would be no substitutes for his brand of sex—not a run, not a novel, not even chocolate, which as a rule Lexy only took in small doses, not intravenously.

So, they had yielded to their mutual attraction. That was okay. It was like finding that small out-of-the-way restaurant in Florence where they drizzled the white truffle oil on the thin slices of asiago and zucchini and tart arugula leaves. You went and enjoyed the food and the evening, and the memory stayed with you, but you didn't *have* to go back. It was a lucky one-time occurrence.

It was a good thing that he had his library to build and she had an inn to run.

She picked up the office phone on the first ring.

"Lexy?" Her agent Tess's unmistakable upbeat voice greeted her.

"Yes."

"It's really you!" Tess sounded excited.

"It's me."

"I've been calling and calling since you disappeared, and no one in Tooth Point has heard of you."

"Drake's Point. The Tooth and Nail Inn."

"Whatever. The video deal is getting so hot!"

Trust Tess to put a positive spin on disaster. "I thought that deal would be sort of dead after the Stanley Skoff disaster."

"Disaster?" It was a concept Tess did not understand. "Not at all. It was a memorable moment in TV history. I think Skoff would like to get you back. Listen, can you get down to L.A. tomorrow?"

"No." She was never going back to Skoff land.

Lexy could hear the tap of Tess's computer keys.

Her agent was no doubt multi-tasking. "Okay, we'll just shift things around a bit. Next week could work. Next week is good."

"Tess, I'm not coming to L.A. I don't want to do the video anymore."

"The producer wants to see a short demo. Just a formality. Same old, same old routine. The limo will pick you up. I've got an amazing hair person. We'll get someone for makeup. They've got a super director lined up. And casting has dozens of guys who want to be the *Workout Sex* Hunk. Did you look over the pictures I sent?"

Lexy pulled open her bottom desk drawer where the big Star Media manila envelope lay. "Nobody seemed right."

"Maybe I should send somebody up there to Drake's Point." Tess's voice started fading.

"No!" Lexy heard the keys tapping again over the quick beating of her own heart. "Tess, I said 'No.' Did you hear me?"

"So you can't make it this week or next?" Tess's voice sounded close again. "Well, I've got another call. We'll talk later, Lexy."

Lexy put down the phone and willed her heart rate back to normal. If her agent remembered her next week—and that was a big if—she would never come as far north as Drake's Point. Lexy would be safe.

"Are you okay?" Flo was standing in the office doorway wearing a T-shirt and jeans and a white hard hat with a redwood tree logo in green on the front.

Lexy nodded.

"Well, I'm off. I'll be at the library if you need me. Sam needs everyone's help today. We're painting."

"Oh." It was a good thing he didn't need *her* help, Lexy thought.

Flo was still standing there. She suggested, "You could get Nigel to cover for you and come along."

"No thanks." Lexy waved Flo off and turned back to her flash cards. *Hablo, hablas, habla, hablamos, hablais, hablan.* But she couldn't get her mind off the thought: Maybe ordinary life just paled next to mindless, orgasmic sex.

Thanks to Dawn Russell, Sam had the information that Vernon was in Monterey playing golf, and he was taking advantage of it. The library site swarmed with out-of-town sub-contractors, a few Drake's Point men who would dare stand up to Vernon, and the Ladies Book Club.

The club had formed in a time when respectable married women still called themselves ladies, and his mother had wanted to be a lady. She had joined for the title alone, and for all it suggested of small town propriety. Her dream of building a library had come later.

Now her dream was almost a reality. Sam was approaching that point in the project when all the systems that gave the building life had to come together—water, heat and air, and electricity. The sub-contractors were working around each other in an elaborate dance, and it took all of Sam's attention to keep them from bumping into one another. His volunteers moved to their own rhythm. Dawn and Flo and Meg were old hands at finding things that needed doing. They broke open rolls of blue masking tape and began taping the window frames. Forest, Leaf, and Meadow were taking care of distracting Chief Brock's deputy, Guidry, who had standing orders from Vernon to ticket the trucks of anyone who worked on the site. More Drake's Point men than Sam expected had been willing to come out, but he had no trouble putting them to work. Charlie Beaton was notably absent, but not every man could switch sides on a dime.

Keeping the book club and the professionals busy on the project meant he couldn't do much physical work himself, but he was probably useless anyway. He had Alexandra Clark on the brain. He had not asked her to the work day. She would show up in one of her long flowered skirts and absurdly bulky sweaters, and he would be thinking that underneath those layers were the two rosebuds he had not removed from her body.

He had let her walk out of his living room the night before because he and she were square. No harm, no foul. He didn't want to embroil her in his problems the way he'd wrapped her in his arms. If she came back even one more time, she was going to figure out secrets he didn't want to tell. And if she came back, Vernon was going to find out. Vernon didn't hate her now, but he would if he found her sleeping with the enemy. Sam was leaving, but Alexandra Clark was staying in Vernon's little kingdom, and Vernon could be nasty to anyone who crossed him.

Sam congratulated himself on his smart handling

171

of the Alexandra Clark situation, and promptly walked into a beam.

Lexy left the inn after tea started. Spanish verb conjugations were not the distraction she needed. She would not interfere where Sam Worth didn't want her; she would just stroll by the library and see how things were going.

She saw the first flyer on a telephone pole in front of Charlie Beaton's house. It announced a meeting on "The Future of Drake's Point," and urged citizens to take back their town from greedy outside corporate interests. After the first one there came another flyer on every pole, every fence, every available wall along Beach Street: Mayor Vernon striking back.

The city hall was deserted, but the library site swarmed with people. Dawn Russell waved to Lexy from the new building's porch as she put foil over some dishes on a cloth-covered table. The three blonde clones were there wearing jeans, T-shirts, closed-toed shoes and hard hats over their long tresses—a remarkable degree of body coverage for them. One skipped across the street.

"Hi, Ms. Clark." The girl was bouncing with energy. "We've been moving trucks so Chief Brock can't ticket them. Isn't that cool?"

Lexy nodded, trying to figure out which of the three this one was.

"Sam is so grateful."

"I'm sure he is. Leaf?"

The girl rolled her eyes. "Forest," she said. "I'm

172

sure you can help, too. It's not too late. Ms. Russell can find something for you."

"Oh, no. Looks like you've got it covered," Lexy responded. The herd was apparently turning out in force to help the head elk.

She kept walking past dozens more of Vernon's signs, as far as Sullivan's at the end of Beach Street. The feed store was empty. Meg Sullivan wasn't even there. Instead, Charlie Beaton lounged behind the register, unshaven and sullen. He didn't look up when Lexy came in. She wandered back to the recycled book shelf.

"Not you, too." Charlie muttered a familiar term of disgust. "Everyone in this stinking town is checking that shelf twice a day. The fire crew was in here this morning. You'd think they were all great readers or something."

Lexy gave the shelf a quick glance. The usual suspects were there, but no sign of *Workout Sex*. Who had it? Charlie came out of his slacker pose and sauntered over to stand beside her.

"What are they all looking for?" He picked up *The 10,000 Most Common Misspelled Words*. "Like some hot novel is going to show up in Drake's Point?"

"People in Drake's Point do seem to like books," she said. "Look at the way everyone's turned out to help with the new library."

"Yeah, well, that's dumb."

"Why?"

"Because Vernon doesn't want it."

"I know." There were flyers in all the front windows of Sullivan's. "It seems pretty obvious."

"Good," he said. He gave her a rare direct look with his angry dark eyes. "Because you've got to take sides in this town, and Vernon's side always wins. That's how it is."

"You're on Vernon's side?" Lexy couldn't keep the surprise out of her tone. Charlie Beaton seemed like a complete rebel, a man on his own side against the world.

"Damn right."

"No one else seems to be on Vernon's side," she ventured. There was nothing like a cheery conversation with Charlie to lift a girl's mood.

He leaned toward Lexy. "Maybe they don't remember what happened to the library last time, but I do. The thing went up in fucking smoke. And Sam Worth ought to remember, because his parents died that night."

Lexy was shocked. She had not put the two events together. "In the fire?"

"On the mountain. Car accident. She took off, and he chased her. They both went off the road." Charlie Beaton made a hand gesture simulating a long dive. "Moral of the story—don't cross a Vernon. Then or now." He slouched back to his place at the register. "And don't side with Sam Worth."

Lexy tried to sort it out in her mind. The beautiful woman in the portrait had driven to her death over a library? Lexy was sure she did not have the whole story, but Flo would know. She determined to find out.

But Flo didn't return to the inn that night. Lexy was left waiting, picturing Flo in a happy crowd of adoring females offering Sam Worth pumpkin seeds and oysters and bountiful boobs to admire.

Three hard-hat-wearing workers stopped by and filled the pub briefly with their laughter and talk. Then they were off, and Lexy was left with Nigel the silent. He spoke even less now than before Grindstone. Lexy gathered up the few glasses left behind on the pub tables and put them on the bar.

She almost dropped them when she found Nigel looking at her. "What?"

"Do you know what you're doing with Sam Worth?" he asked.

"Helping him with his paperwork?"

Nigel gave her a don't-try-that-one-on-me look. "After hours?"

Lexy lifted her chin. She was suddenly overcome with annoyance. Who was Nigel to lecture her? "At least I'm seizing my moment."

"It's not missing the moment that will get you in trouble. It's not escaping the past." Nigel was dead serious, his gray eyes bleak. Lexy was pretty sure his remark had nothing to do with her.

She suggested, "Flo showed you her past. Isn't it time you showed her yours?"

He snorted, and a brief pained look crossed his face. "A few tattoos and some leather pants? Tame stuff our Flo was into." For a minute he sounded exactly like one of the Grindstone band members. This Brigadoon had apparently attracted another expatriate Brit.

Lexy took a deep breath, summoned her courage, and leaned across the bar. "Did you kill someone?" she asked.

Kate Moore

His head came up. "No."

"Go to jail?"

He wiped the bar with excessive force.

Oh. Lexy did not pretend to know how bad jail could be, but she knew how generous Flo was. "That's all? Just tell Flo the bad stuff and get on with it."

Nigel looked like she'd asked him to kill himself.

Lexy found herself thinking of the night before. "You know what you need, Nigel? Sex. It would be good for your disposition." She headed for the door. "And sex in a committed relationship is healthier than sitting and sulking all the time."

"Well, sex with the mayor's enemy is plain daft!" he retorted.

The crack spoiled Lexy's perfect exit, even if the mayor was the least of her worries. Her agent had called, and her book was out there somewhere going from bedroom to bedroom in Drake's Point. Sexy Lexy could be exposed any day, and for the first time in her life her body craved sex. With Sam Worth. He had given her that end-of-movie moment with Ewoks dancing in the trees, with Obi Wan, Yoda, and even Darth Vader smiling at Luke and Han and Leia. And Lexy's Ewoks wanted to dance again. Lexy could fight it as she had been doing all day, or she could give in. At the moment, giving in seemed like the better idea. And she knew only one way to attract Sam without swallowing her pride.

It was time for some property damage to the inn. Lexy went looking for a rock.

* * *

Ajax Worth had always encouraged his son to take a direct approach to getting what he wanted. Standing in the darkness outside Alexandra Clark's inn with a thermos of brandy-laced, killer coffee, a flashlight, and a sleeping bag was as direct as Sam knew how to be. But he wasn't prepared to see the object of his desire rock back on her heels and hurl a stone at her own inn. Her shot bounced off a black shutter next to an upper story window.

"Hey, Alexandra! What are you up to?"

She gave a little yelp and spun toward him.

"I'm . . . I'm . . . testing the inn alarm system?"

He stepped a little closer. "I don't think so."

Naturally she was wearing an ankle-length skirt and a thick sweater. This one probably weighed five pounds and would easily fit Sam. It had a weave like chain mail made for a giant, and it hung below her waist to mid thigh. She had turned the cuffs up into thick rolls above her wrists.

"You don't think so?"

"Nope. I think you're making an excuse to call your favorite handyman."

"You'd like to think that, wouldn't you? What are you doing here?"

He answered her with a piece of wisdom his father would have liked. *"You miss a hundred percent of the shots you never take.* Wayne Gretsky."

She brushed her hands together, moving into the shadows where he waited. He saw her eyes take in his rolled-up sleeping bag. "Are we going back to the beach?"

He grinned, liking how quick she was to catch on. He tilted his head toward the trail behind the inn and offered her the handle of his big yellow flashlight. "Up the hill. You lead."

The warm October day had turned into a cool clear night. They were ahead of the moon's rising, but the flashlight illuminated the rough switchback trail through trees and brush. The rustle of her skirts and the exertion of her breathing sounded like sex. But Lexy's long, flowing skirts, high-necked blouses, and big sweaters were at odds with the few glimpses he'd had of her in shorts or running gear. She *was* sexy. He didn't get it. The most athletic and desirable woman he knew dressed for a British sitcom every day. The clothes might fit her idea of the inn, but somehow they didn't fit her.

They came to a series of high stone steps, and she stumbled. He reached for her, but she righted herself before he could help.

"Sorry, stepped on my skirt."

"Why do you wear those long skirts?" he asked.

She took another of the steep steps. "I love them. I love flowers."

Sam took a moment, then made a joke. "Er, I don't want to blow your cover here, Alexandra, if you're in witness protection or law enforcement or something, but the skirts, like your name, are too long for you. You should be an 'Al,' or 'Allie,' or 'Alex,' or . . ."

He was just rambling, keeping his voice teasing, but she spun so fast she nearly clobbered him with the flashlight. The big circle of light caught him square in the chest. They stood for a moment, breathless from the climb. She reached out a shaky hand and flattened it against his chest. Maybe she meant to hold him back, but he leaned in slightly to her touch.

"No nickname," she said in a little puff of air. "Just Alexandra."

The glow of the flashlight showed the intensity of her gaze. He had pushed a hot button he hadn't intended to push. "Alexandra, it is," he said.

Then he leaned forward and kissed her, and she responded fiercely, opening to him and letting him plunge his tongue deep into her mouth. He held on briefly to the idea that she was deliberately distracting him, then the heat of the kiss incinerated all thought.

They were twice as breathless when they resumed the climb. At the crest Sam managed to say "left," and direct her along the point toward the ocean. It was easier going in the open on top of the narrow ridge, and in minutes they reached the headland where tourists could pull off by day into a small parking lot to gaze at the vastness of the Pacific. Wind-bent cypress trees surrounded the place, and the hillside crumbled down to the sea below. The air smelled of ocean and sweet dried grasses. "Drake's Point," he said lovingly.

He took the flashlight from her and directed the beam to the cement roof of a bunker set in the hillside. Lexy stopped dead beside him and said, "I'm not into public displays of affection, but this looks like we're going into hiding."

"We are," he joked. "From Vernon," he said more seriously.

"People have told me not to cross him."

"Sound advice." He led her to the bunker entrance.

"I'm missing parts of the story here."

"You've got the main plot. I'm leaving Drake's Point, you're staying, and Vernon can be nasty to folks who go against him."

"Why does sex with you put me on Vernon's list of people to be nasty to?"

She was stalling. He could sense it. And . . . was she digging? "You keep digging for my secrets, but you don't share yours, Alexandra."

"Is Sam your full name?"

He would give her this. "Samson. My father was Ajax. He believed men should have strong names."

"Interesting. Samson didn't do so well against Delilah, you know."

"My father's sense of humor. As he saw it, women were the great weakness of Worth men. But Samson brought his enemies' roof down on top of them, too." He laughed. "That was definitely a move my father admired." He took her hand and tugged her toward the bunker.

Despite Sam's warm grip, Lexy didn't move. She had visions of snakes writhing around Indiana Jones's ankles and spiders clinging to his girlfriend's back. "We are *not* going in there."

"It's a lookout bunker. After Pearl Harbor, folks on the west coast thought an invasion was coming, so they put up bunkers to watch for enemy subs."

"Snakes and spiders live in places like this," she mentioned. None of Lexy's sexual fantasies involved things with multiple legs.

"This is a palace of a bunker, and tourists keep the critters away."

"No tourists now."

"That's the point."

"Indiana Jones always finds snakes in places like this."

"Well, I'll let you use the whip." He handed her the flashlight again, ducked down and led the way inside. She resisted a few seconds longer, then yielded to the pull of his hand, of her desire, swinging the light around every corner while he spread the sleeping bag on the floor against one wall. The flashlight's powerful beam revealed a few dead leaves, but no cobwebs and no bugs. The walls and floor of the bunker met in clean seams of cement.

"Give me your sweater," he said.

She didn't argue, just pulled it off, shuddering once in the night air.

"This thing weighs five pounds," he said, taking the bulky garment and making a pillow of it against the wall.

"It's an Irish fisherman sweater. I come from a long line of Irish fishermen. The weave helps the family identify the fisherman if his boat goes down in the North Sea."

Sam refrained from commenting that the sweater weighed as much as an anchor and probably took the drowned sailor straight to the bottom. He dropped down on the sleeping bag, shed his shoes, and leaned back against the wall. "Come here."

Lexy knelt down beside him, and he took the flashlight from her, setting it aside and flicking it off.

She held her breath, expecting the skitter of insect feet in the total darkness, then her eyes adjusted, and she could see Sam Worth looking at her from a bright rectangle on the back wall of the bunker where the view-slit let in the moonlight.

"The perfect place for the woman who likes things tactile, not visual," he said. He took her by the waist, coaxing and lifting until she straddled him. He pushed his hands up under her shirt and filled his palms with her breasts, and made a sound of pleasure deep in his throat. Lexy's nipples pebbled and she arched forward with a moan. His fingers circled and tugged, the smallest touch sending dizzying waves of sensation all through her. His absorbed attention fascinated her.

She gripped his shoulders. "You've been thinking about this," she said in wonder. It hadn't just been her.

"All day. There are spots I missed last time." He kissed her, taking time to enjoy filling her hot sweet mouth. He broke the kiss to undo her shirt and trace the dip of her bra over the tops of her breasts. He unhooked the clasp, spreading the soft bits of fabric, finding the softer swells of woman underneath. He liked the small, neat mounds, athletic like the rest of her, and so sensitive. He took one then the other in his mouth, driving her to gasps and moans.

She reached for him, running her thumbs up the length of him through the denim of his jeans, fanning her hands across his abdomen and drawing them back down, rocking him in swells of sensation that lifted him with each touch.

He sat up, away from the wall, and stripped off his

shirt and T-shirt, and lying back, he hooked his fingers in the leg openings of her panties, stretching them, sliding his fingers along the crevice toward her center, her heat, until she squirmed and pressed down against his erection. He slipped his hands out of her panties and ran them the length of her smooth thighs to her knees, pushing lightly to straighten her legs so that she lay on top of him, soft breasts pressed against his chest. He brought his arms around her, squeezing tight. Then he slid his hands down her back, over her bottom and down her thighs, catching the folds of her skirt, drawing it up, and reaching under it to strip her off her panties. He stroked and kneaded that soft roundness that he had first seen in the headlights of her car as she faced the bull elk, and a word flashed in his mind. *Mine.*

She sat up again and tugged at his fly, and he reached down and freed his sex. Before her stroking could drive him over the edge, he dug the small packet from his hip pocket. She rose up on her knees, and he lifted his hips and let her pull away his jeans.

They were face to face, heat to heat in the dark, her skirts falling softly around them. She caressed him, and some hole in space and time opened and sucked him right in.

Lexy struggled for control briefly, but he held her hips and met her movements with his own, and they slipped into a mutual rhythm. And the word *mine* beat faster in Sam's head with each press of their bodies.

Lexy caught the fierce, glad beat from Sam and felt it take hold of her breath, her heart, and the flex of her hips. The first peak of sensation rocked her and jarred her senses free of gravity, lifting her out of herself. And then there were peaks upon peaks, a whole vast Sierra Nevada of mountaintops, and Lexy touched them all.

Later, she rested her forehead against his shoulder, drifting down from the high—feather light, leaf light. Sometime during her long weightless descent it occurred to her that she really did need to rethink *Workout Sex* based on Sam Worth. Maybe there would be a second edition. Maybe she should add a chapter on the benefits of good sex in treating drug addiction, substituting a natural high for a chemically-induced altered state. She couldn't imagine anything that compared to this.

The cool night air dried the perspiration on her back and shoulders, but she wasn't cold. Everywhere their bodies touched was a warm and slick reminder of their experience together. Lexy shifted just to feel her skin sliding against his, and to evoke the clean scent of him.

He turned her in his arms, pulling her to him, her back against his chest, him wrapping one of his strong arms around her, a man enjoying her breasts again. Lexy settled into his warmth. Her skirt was the only garment between the two of them. It bunched around her hips and covered her lap and the tops of her legs. Her bottom was bare and pressed against him, and he seemed to be enjoying that contact, too. His other hand rested, warm and heavy, on her thigh. Moonlight made a bright bar across their outstretched legs.

"Cold?" he asked.

She shivered in response to the low rumble of his voice and the gust of his breath at her ear. *Hot.*

"I have coffee."

"Coffee might be good." But neither of them stirred.

A little of Lexy's brain function returned. She had had sex in a sleeping bag in a bunker! She'd had sex in a sleeping bag twice! Discretion was clearly a good idea, given the size of Drake's Point and the warnings she'd heard about Vernon, but sleeping-bag sex had a temporary feel to it. She wasn't sure she wanted that.

"You don't have a bed in Worth House?"

She felt him come alert and wary at the question. "Bunker sex is good for a person." There was that cocky bull-elk tone of his.

"Why?"

"Trust me, it's good for you. You have 'good girl' stamped in the middle of your forehead. You haven't done this before."

"*You* obviously know the territory," she snapped.

"I grew up here. Want to tell me where you grew up?"

He was doing things to the insides of Lexy's thighs with the rough pads of his fingers that probably weren't legal. They certainly weren't fair.

"Pacifica College, on the coast, near L.A. I grew up on campus actually. My mother is a classics professor. My dad's the basketball coach. My three older brothers played under him."

"Not bad for your first effort at self-revelation. And actually I do have a bed in Worth House."

Bad answer. He had a bed, and he obviously didn't

185

want her in it. Lexy felt crushed. She was just a bunker-sex girl. But that shouldn't bother her. The bunker sex had been like no other sex she'd ever had and it was depressing to think how temporary it might be.

Sam went on, "The sleeping bag is for the library. I spend most nights there."

"Because the first library burned down?"

She felt him nod. "Arson. Never proved though. No one prosecuted."

"It was insured, wasn't it?"

"Minimally. The Ladies Book Club started over with the settlement."

She didn't need to ask if he feared another fire. Whatever the history was between him and Mayor Vernon, it was still alive. And Charlie Beaton had intimated that Vernon had been the one responsible. "So . . . being here with me takes you away from the library."

"If you're trying to worm an invitation to my bed, you've got to cough up some more details about Alexandra Clark."

"Who says I want to get into your bed?" she retorted.

His warm hand closed over her breast, and she arched into the perfect fit of his palm. "Nobody wants to get pulled out in a riptide, but the rip grabs hold and pulls you out anyway."

"So we shouldn't go near the water."

"As long as we're both in Drake's Point, we're going to get sucked in." He suckled on her earlobe.

"You aren't exactly Mr. Open Book."

"It's my bed we're talking about. My rules. If you

want in, you've got to say something more about your family."

She paused and gave it some thought. The dark and the warmth of his arms around her invited honesty. Maybe she couldn't tell him about Sexy Lexy, the queen of sexual fitness, but she could trust him with a bit of Alexandra Clark's past. "My parents are brilliant. My mom quotes Greek epigrams at dinner. My dad quotes John Wooden. My brothers are athletic."

"All brothers? No sisters?"

"Just three older brothers."

"Do they quote epigrams, too?"

"Mostly movies. *Star Wars, Indiana Jones, Blues Brothers, The Godfather*. There's sort of a Clark family canon."

"*Star Wars*, huh? You know your Wookiees from your Ewoks?"

"Try me."

"Give me your favorite line."

"There are too many."

"Just one."

"*Let the Wookiee win*. My dad always used to say that to me when I tried to take on my brothers."

His hand paused in its lazy stroking. "So, you tried to hold your own with your brothers?"

"I wasn't very successful—not when they ganged up on me. Do *you* have siblings?"

He didn't answer right away. A single earnest cricket made faint intermittent chirps in the cool night. The heat of their lovemaking had faded, and Lexy pressed back against Sam's chest for warmth.

187

And she found it. He rubbed her arms slowly with his warm hands, and when she thought no answer was going to come, he spoke again.

"Charlie Beaton and Meg Sullivan. They're my siblings or close to it. The three of us went through school together. Kindergarten to high school."

It was more reassuring than Lexy cared to admit that Sam thought of Meg as a sibling. And Lexy savored the companionable silence between the two of them created by their revelations. But then he turned the conversation back to her.

"So, your brothers aren't academic?"

"They're smart, not intellectual. There's a difference. They're goal-oriented. They get stuff fast, but they like knowledge because it makes money or a deal or a difference. They're sort of a mix of my dad's coaching and my mom's insights."

"What about you? What are you a mix of?"

Nobody had asked Lexy that before. She wasn't sure she had an answer. She had a feeling she got the leftover parts of her parents' legacy, the recessive genes.

Sam nuzzled her neck. "Come on."

"Well. I can lose myself in a book like my mother. I get her sudden inspirations. I like routine and practice like my dad. He shoots a hundred baskets a day, every day. I don't have their obsessions, though. The college is their real pride. They love it. And they are its biggest boosters. Whenever the development office wants to get money out of someone, they call on Mom and Dad."

"Maybe the inn will be that something special for you. Did you win the lottery, save up to buy it, or inherit the money from a rich aunt?"

Lexy twisted in his arms. "What about that coffee?"

Chapter 9
Recovery

"Recovery is an essential phase of any workout. Recovery time will vary depending on the length and intensity of each workout, but partners who want the full benefits of the program should not ignore this step."

—*Workout Sex*, Lexy Clark

Sam didn't need the flashlight; the setting moon made bright white squares of the windows along Beach Street. He could hear the muted slap of small waves hitting the cove shore. After making love to her, this time he had been unable to let Alexandra Clark go so easily. Tonight they had talked, and he had coaxed the smallest of revelations out of her. He could imagine her struggle to compete with three athletic older brothers, and even though she hadn't said it, how often she'd been the loser in the games they played. It was clear she didn't go down easily and she didn't quit. But she had shut up fast when he asked about how she'd got to the Tooth and Nail.

Maybe next time he could focus on that question when he wasn't so distracted by sex.

Lord, how he liked her shyness. She didn't seem to know her own power. She gave pleasure freely, without trying to exact any control in return. And there was lots of pleasure. They were both pretty helpless in its tide. Just when he thought he might recover some normal brain function, her softness pressed against him and heated up his non-thinking parts again.

He didn't need a psychology degree to understand why he liked her small breasts and lush bottom, either. He had grown up hating other guys' centerfold fantasies, their casual talk of knobs, knockers, melons, and jugs. His mother had come to Drake's Point to live down the reputation her breasts had earned in San Francisco's notorious O'Farrell Street theaters.

His father had regarded those breasts as trophies, monuments to his masculinity. *Your mother thinks that because she has the world's best tits, I'll do anything for her.* "Anything" had not included building a library, though, and Ajax Worth hadn't liked it when his topless-dancer wife set off on her own to direct the building project from fund-raising and design to construction. The usual shouting and door-slamming that ruled the Worth household had escalated during Sam's senior year in high school to a pitch that often drove him out of the house. He had needed his two friends more than ever that year.

He reached the library steps before he recognized that something was wrong. The place was too dark. No windows reflected the moonlight. He flung his sleeping bag over the porch rail and bounded up the stairs. His boots crunched on broken glass. Swearing, he walked the length of the porch, putting his hands through the smashed windows. The vandals hadn't missed one.

All he could think was Vernon—Vernon, who was conveniently out of town. Vernon had probably black-mailed someone who owed rent or a favor into doing the actual dirty work. But Vernon wouldn't have to blackmail Charlie Beaton. Charlie would smash any-thing of Sam's just for the pleasure of it.

Sam had been a little stupid. He knew Vernon and Charlie. He knew Drake's Point. Until he'd started sharing his sleeping bag with Alexandra Clark, he had slept in the library every night. Here was the cost of letting desire make his decisions.

He reached through the broken entry window and wrenched open the main library door. A truth that he had always tried to avoid reared its ugly head. He was his father's son. His sexual appetites were just as strong as Ajax's had been. He had tried to control them by choosing a passionless fiancée and burying himself in work, but Alexandra Clark had undone those efforts. His footsteps on the bare boards echoed in the unfinished room.

His father would laugh at his situation. It would confirm Ajax Worth's view that Cherry and Sam could do nothing without him. The night before the first library's dedication, Sam finally confessed to his parents the secret he had been hiding through twelve years of school—his terrible difficulty with reading. His mother had been struck with shock and dismay, her face full of concern. They would get testing, help, whatever he needed. His father had been disgusted, disbelieving. *How did you get to be a senior in high school without learning to read? Are you stupid?*

Now he had a name for the different wiring in his brain that made school a nightmare—*dyslexia*. Now he could appreciate and use the advantages it gave him when it came to seeing the big picture. Then he could not have explained to Ajax how elusive the words were or how he could get more lost in a sentence than he ever could on the mountain above Drake's Point. That night he had refused to explain the ways he had beaten the system. He wouldn't rat on the friends who had helped him, or the friend who in the end had made Sam promise to confess. His father immediately gave up trying to understand and exploded with rage against his defective son and stupid wife. *How stupid do you feel now, trying to be somebody, building a library when your own kid can't read?* Ajax had called them a pair of incompetents who could do nothing without him. He'd flung buckets, waves, oceans of blame at Cherry Popp. It was her fault Sam was stupid. Sam had turned on his father in an attempt to protect his mother, but she'd refused to let him come between them. She'd said they would deal with it in the morning and walked out.

Ajax had gone on shouting for hours, it seemed to Sam, until he'd finally gone off in search of Cherry, unable to let it go. The tragedy had taken its final toll when someone put up the old sign from her topless days across the street from the library. Cherry fled over the mountain, and Ajax chased after her. By the next morning the library had burned to the ground, and both Sam's parents were dead.

There were things he would probably never know about that night, but he had long since accepted that at seventeen his had been the least share of the blame for the disaster. He also accepted that, as the only one who remained, it was his job to put things right. He had to finish this library, and if he had to give up sleeping with Alexandra Clark to do it, he would. And if he cared about her future in Drake's Point, it meant the same thing.

The fire alarm sounded at the other end of town. Sam heard the station doors rattle open and the guys shouting. The big engine and the smaller paramedics truck came rumbling out, lights flashing, and he waited for the siren. The first wail came, and the trucks turned out of Drake's Point headed north over the hill. Sam let out the breath he didn't know he had been holding, and he turned back to his own minor emergency.

Nigel stared at the serene faces of the four Tibetan monks in the pub. They were irritatingly cheerful for a bunch of temporarily homeless celibates. He knew about being celibate and living in a cell, and he wouldn't recommend the lifestyle to anyone.

The monks had arrived with the firemen sometime after three. The fire in their borrowed house had been extinguished, but smoke and water damage had made the place unlivable. Nigel had roused himself from his nighttime post at the reception desk to make tea and stir the fire in the hearth. The monks had nothing with them except their maroon robes, but they seemed impervious to cold and lack of sleep.

Alexandra Clark appeared from somewhere—obviously not her bed in the inn—and asked the monks to wait while she made some rooms ready for them. The head monk, the one who spoke some English, indicated that one room would do for all.

The fire crew ordered their usual post-call round of beer and talk. In between bouts of reliving the fire, they took turns reading from a small red paperback.

" 'When partners are ready to end their workout, the man should increase the speed and depth of thrusting.' Hey, I like this workout."

"Beats lifting. My turn." Tim tossed the little red book across the table.

Mike caught it and flipped through the pages. "Hey, where's the chapter on going down?"

"There isn't one, moron. It's a *fitness* book. Nobody's worried about a fat tongue." The book flew across the room again.

"Reread the chapter on positions." Another toss.

"He doesn't need to. He's got that one memorized."

The monks seemed oblivious, and Nigel hoped their knowledge of English didn't include those words every teenager knew. He had sex on the brain after Alexandra Clark recommended that he get some. Ever since he had drifted into Drake's Point and Flo Locke interviewed him for the bartending job at the Tooth and Nail, celibacy sucked. He had a job that allowed him to see Flo every day because he spoke Spanish. But he would never tumble Flo Locke because he had learned Spanish in the hardest school of all, the Sinaloa State Correctional Facility. Maybe Flo Locke had once been Roger Fripp's "Tyne River Girl," but in her neat cottage with her casual elegance, she was not for a drifter who had failed to make anything out of himself. So he slept away his days in his narrow rooming house bed and took care of his own needs.

The firemen finished their rounds of beer and hilarity and headed back to the station. The monks sipped their tea with no apparent need for conversation. Nigel wasn't a talkative guy, but he was a flaming talk-show host compared to these boys in maroon. They chanted briefly. Then, on a signal that Nigel missed, they got up and began to gather glasses, tea cups, and napkins, returning them silently to Nigel.

He nodded, acknowledging each one. The last monk, the head guy, extended his hands palms up with the final offering: the red paperback book.

Nigel bowed. It was the book that the firemen had been passing around the pub. Nigel could see the title now. *Workout Sex, A Girl's Guide to Home Fitness.* The book slid from the monk's hand into Nigel's palm, and he had an instant image of Flo Locke's deep red hair falling forward around her face as she looked down at him, her magnificent breasts bared. Opening the little book, he started to read—and had a feeling his karma was about to change.

Lexy was at her desk by eight in the morning, trying to make sense of the plans for the Lovejoy-Blackhart wedding party. They had booked the entire inn for the coming weekend of wedding festivities, but had given her two conflicting lists of plans for sleeping arrangements, catering needs, and ceremony details. No one from either family was answering her calls.

Between Sam Worth and the rescued monks, Lexy hadn't had any sleep. She should be exhausted, but she felt exhilarated. She had learned something quite unexpected about sex from Sam Worth. There was the euphoria, of course, at a far different level than she had experienced before, but there was also closeness. She'd actually felt connected to him when they were making love, as if his full attention had been concentrated on her. And it hadn't ended when their bodies slid apart. She had sensed him listening as they talked. And the effect lingered. Sex with Sam made her feel remarkably alive, energized, aware of every joyous thing around her.

Now her senses were wide awake. Ernesto's cooking was a symphony of flavors. The morning light picked up a blue she hadn't noticed in her favorite chair. She could make out the Spanish words in the love song Violeta was singing. Sex was not like flossing after all, and she did not want to skip it—not a single opportunity that was left while Sam Worth remained in Drake's Point working on the library.

On that happy thought, she stretched, feeling the places where her muscles were particularly relaxed. She was mid-stretch when Flo stormed in, waving a fistful of torn flyers for Mayor Vernon's town meeting. Lexy had never seen the hotel manager so unsettled.

"What's wrong?" she asked.

"The library's been vandalized, all the windows on

the first story broken!" Flo dropped the pile of flyers on the desk.

Lexy's stomach knotted. Because Sam Worth had been with her having bunker sex, his library had been damaged. "Did anyone see who did it?"

"No." Flo picked up a handful of flyers and began tearing them in half. "But Vernon's behind it."

Lexy frowned. Charlie and Nigel had both warned her about Vernon, but this seemed so awful she could hardly believe it. "Are you sure? Is Vernon really that bad?"

"Yes." Flo dropped the first of the torn flyers in the waste basket.

"Then why doesn't anyone stand up to him?"

"Besides Sam, you mean?" Flo started in on another bunch of flyers. "He raises your rent or blocks your farm from something you need—like water," she explained. More shredded flyers hit the trash, and Flo paused for breath. "Sam Worth is doing something right and good and healing for this town, and Vernon will not get away with sabotaging our library this time."

Now was the moment for Lexy to question Flo about the library's past, but a clapping sound made her turn to the office door. Nigel stood there, clean-shaven, his pony tail gone, his gaze fixed on Flo. His face without the gray beard was harshly, unexpectedly handsome. "Can I see you?" he asked.

"Me?" Flo glanced at Lexy. The flyers slipped from her hands.

"Now."

There was no mistaking the intent in Nigel's gaze.

He extended his hand, and Flo went, just like that, like a match igniting dry brush on the mountain.

"Bye," Lexy called after them, amused. She doubted they heard. She took one of the remaining flyers, swept the rest into the trash, and went looking for Violeta. She needed a broom, a dustpan, and someone to watch the inn while she met with Mayor Vernon.

Except for Tuesday meetings, Lexy usually walked right past the Drake's Point city offices in their rambling one-story gray-shingled building. Today she marched through the double glass doors into the brown-carpeted foyer, carrying a broom and dustpan. Opposite the wall of P.O. boxes, a half wall enclosed a reception area with a couple of desks and computers. Dawn Russell sat at the far desk, her head cocked toward an opaque glass inner door inscribed with Mayor Vernon's name and impressive term in office. Angry male voices came from behind the door. Lexy stopped. The door burst open, and she was face to face with a furious Sam Worth, his eyes cold, his jaw clenched.

From behind him came the mayor's voice. "Your mother is not going to have a library named after her in my town. And get your dog under control. Drake's Point has a leash law."

"Worry about your own dogs, Vernon. Damage the library again and I bring the law into it."

"If I see that dog of yours, I'll shoot him."

Sam gave Lexy a curt nod and kept moving. Lexy had no time for the little stab of pain his dismissal caused her; Mayor Vernon was leaning over a limo-sized desk, his mouth still open, his face flushed and contorted. His hair was mussed, his tie loose. Lexy felt as if she were seeing him naked. Not pretty. He saw Lexy and automatically began to straighten his tie and hair.

"Alexandra, how are you?" He came out from behind his desk, all smiles.

"I'm distressed, and naturally I wanted to talk to you, Walt." Lexy parked her broom and dustpan in one of the two spindly chairs on the visitor side of the desk. They appeared more decorative than practical.

Vernon eyed her broom, and his smooth face sort of twisted, as if he didn't know whether she was friend or foe. "Distressed?"

Lexy nodded. "Did you know that the new building across the street was vandalized last night?"

Vernon frowned. "I heard."

"As a businessperson, I was wondering what steps the city was taking to protect commercial property in town."

He turned away from her and moved back behind the big desk. Along the wall was a low bookcase topped by dozens of golf trophies.

"As you know, there's some dispute about the use of that building. It hasn't been designated for commercial use yet."

Lexy nodded. "Nevertheless," she said, "that building is a valuable piece of property. I'm sure you understand how important it is to everyone who runs a business in Drake's Point to be reassured that the city can protect us from vandalism."

"Oh I assure you, your inn is perfectly safe."

"Thank you, Walt. But I'm still concerned about the new building. If we want to attract businesses, as you plan, we won't want them worried about property damage, will we?"

"Of course not."

"That's why I think you should put an extra officer on duty at night while the building remains under construction." Lexy smiled as she made the suggestion, at the same time telling herself there was absolutely no self-interest in her request.

"I hadn't . . ." Vernon shuffled the two papers on his desk.

"If you can't spare a police officer, how much do you think it would cost to hire a security guard?" If she couldn't get him to hire somebody, Lexy thought the monks might provide protection for the library. Maybe she could work out a trade for staying at the inn.

"I don't . . ."

Tired of his waffling, Lexy made a decision. "You know, don't even worry about it, Walt. I'm prepared to supply whatever security is needed to ensure that there is no further damage to the new building. Especially before your big meeting." She dropped his flyer on his desk. For a moment Lexy thought she'd gone too far, that he could see whose side she was on. But then he caved.

"I'll see what I can do."

"Oh." She smiled. "Well, I'm glad I came to you. See you at tea?"

"Of course."

* * *

Lexy stopped at Dawn's desk on her way out, to get a copy of the mayor's petition. He had over three hundred signatures now—three hundred people she wanted to talk to about the future of that building. Then she took her broom and dustpan across the street. Tiny bits of glass glittered sharply on the porch floor. She put her dustpan on the rail and began to sweep.

Sam Worth emerged from the building, his jaw clenched tight. Clearly, he did not want to see her.

"What do you think you're doing?" He snatched the broom from her hands.

"Sweeping."

"I got that part. And the trip to Vernon's office?"

"As a businesswoman"—she poked him in the chest—"I had to ask Vernon to pay attention to an episode of serious vandalism in town. I asked him to hire extra security for your building from now on."

She'd obviously stunned him; the look on his face was comical. "And he *agreed?*"

She grabbed her broom back. She did not tell him she had offered to pay.

"You're living dangerously."

She shook her head. "I'm . . . sorry the library was damaged last night."

"It's not your fault." He looked away.

"Except that I kept you from being here when you needed to be."

"I knew what I was doing."

"Yes. I thought so. You seemed perfectly competent to me." She waited for him to get the joke and laugh. He turned back to her, but his smile was only a brief quirk of his lips. The silence that followed was awful.

"We . . . can't do it again."

Just like that. He could stop just like that, when Lexy had decided she wanted it to go on and on. Her whole body wanted to protest, but she tried not to let her reaction show by so much as a flinch. Sam's face was too sober, too sad. She thought back to his words of the previous night, about the tide of their passion. "You think the riptide is done with us? It's spit us out somewhere beyond the breakers? We just have to swim back on our own?"

He shook his head. "Our meeting was an accident. This"—his gesture took in the whole library—"is what I came to Drake's Point to do. Now I have to finish. That's all."

She knew she should smile and wave good-bye, but she couldn't move. He was choosing the library over her. It made sense. Isn't that what she would advise any friend of hers in a similar spot? *Stay on your life path.* Only several days ago she had been thinking that way, too. But she couldn't stop herself from saying, "I can help."

"Not necessary."

She managed to pick up her dustpan and broom. "When's the inspector coming back?"

"Tomorrow."

"You introduced me as your assistant, remember? So it makes sense for me to be helping you."

His serious glance came back to hers. It was a staring match, but she refused to back down.

"Okay, but no sex."

"No problem." She could be just as tough as he was.

* * *

Lexy wasn't sure how she got back to the inn, but she did. At her desk she found a note from Flo saying she and Nigel would not be in. Ruth, another member of the Ladies Book Club, would take the reception desk for a few days, and Charlie Beaton of all people had agreed to substitute bartend for Nigel. The longing between Nigel and Flo had been palpable, so Lexy was glad for them.

She dropped into her favorite chair and considered her new agreement with Sam Worth. No more sex. That was smart. It was fair. It had been inevitable from the beginning. She hadn't made any life plans based on him. She had no visions of rings and white dresses or sprays of roses and baby's breath. She told herself that she had probably gained as much as she could from the relationship. Sex with Sam Worth had expanded her research, except for the committed relationship part, and her new realizations would be invaluable if she ever wanted to go back to her career as Sexy Lexy. So why had she felt so gut-punched when he said no more? She had her inn. He had his library.

Of course, maybe he didn't have his library. Maybe Vernon was going to do something mean and underhanded that would cost Sam Worth the library. Whatever his reasons for wanting it built, they were strong ones. And old Walt was not looking so nice at the moment. She had already seen how he tended to browbeat the members of the committee. She had heard him threaten to shoot Winston. Sam and Flo both believed Vernon was behind the obstacles to getting the library built.

She took out the copy of the mayor's petition and

began to look it over again. Maybe she ought to talk to some of the people who had signed, about three hundred of them.

By Thursday, Lexy was convinced that everyone in Drake's Point was having ecstatic, mind-altering sex, except her and Sam Worth and possibly Charlie Beaton, whose disposition was mid-root-canal surly. Walking into town with a thermos of the inn's best coffee and a basket of Ernesto's buttery scones for the building inspector, Lexy passed the old white-haired Italian man with his twinkling eyes. A truck from Macy's was parked outside a house two doors from Charlie Beaton's, and two men were wrestling a plastic-covered mattress out of the back.

She told herself it was not because of her book. Even if *Workout Sex* had passed through a few Drake's Point bedrooms, it could not have reached the whole population. There had to be something else going on—too many of Meg Sullivan's roasted pumpkin seeds or some natural cycle related to tule elk mating, maybe.

On the city hall porch she caught Dawn Russell in the arms of a tall, fit-looking gentleman of seventy or so whose sun-browned hand had a firm grasp on Dawn's bottom. Resolutely, she turned her gaze away.

She had been a little uneasy about her plan to help Sam with the building inspector, but really, it looked as if she had worried over nothing. No one in Drake's Point would notice that she had changed out of her usual Laura Ashley clothes.

She did not have her signature Sexy Lexy things,

but she did have the cropped top she had worn while driving up I-5, and she had one pair of black Spandex leggings for her morning workout routine. Recreating Sexy Lexy's cleavage had required a bit of invention, but she had taken the shoulder pads out of an old blouse and arranged them to get a little lift where she needed it most.

Sam knew it was stupid to feel sex-deprived after two days without Alexandra Clark, but he recognized the surly, disgruntled feeling. He was supposed to be focused on his building, keeping his wits about him to fend off Vernon's attacks and finish the library. From the beginning he had ordered backups for things like windows that he felt were vulnerable to Vernon's methods of getting his way. This morning he had called in a few favors from builders in the area, so today a second set of windows would be in place, but he was conscious of being closed off from the other guys. He was not offering the good humor that was essential to the last phase of a project when everyone was feeling the pinch of their deadlines and trying to work around each other.

He couldn't stop thinking about Alexandra Clark's confrontation with Vernon. From the moment they met, she had been standing up to something bigger and nastier than she was, including himself. Now she was taking on his enemy. It was about as smart as trying to chase off a bull elk.

Jay Johnson was one more of Vernon's tactics. Without Johnson's sign-off on the plumbing, the building could not get a certificate of occupancy. It was time for Sam to focus on that.

Johnson showed up just before noon to reinspect the plumbing fixtures. They had waited all morning for him, and the tile guys were already at work. Johnson was going to be pissed. He pulled his truck up in front of the library where Vernon would ticket anyone else, a sure sign of whose side Johnson was on.

"So, Worth, am I just wasting my time here? You can't have made those corrections yet." Johnson was just starting to heave his bulk up the porch steps when Alexandra Clark showed up. She had left off her flowered skirts and heavy sweaters in favor of a tank top and leg-baring shorts and some form of EPA-banned assistance to nature's bounty that created serious cleavage instead of the soft sweet mounds he knew from tactile experience.

"Sorry to be late, Mr. Worth," she said. The words were directed at Sam, but the high voltage smile and the tilt of Alexandra's chest hit Johnson full on. His clipboard slipped in his loose grasp.

She offered Johnson her free hand. "I'm sure you don't remember me—Alexandra Clark, Mr. Worth's assistant. I've brought you some coffee and a scone."

Shit, Sam thought. That was his thermos she had her hand wrapped around.

Johnson had to put down his clipboard to take the coffee she poured for him. While he was still breathing in the rich brew and the warm scone, and eyeing the bosom under his nose, Alexandra was explaining how pleased people like herself would be to have his approval so that the library could be completed on time.

All her concentration was on Johnson. She picked up the clipboard and led him from bathroom to bathroom, keeping his eyes more focused on her than on the fixtures.

Sam followed silently. Alexandra's ponytail bounced with each of her light steps. Every guy on the job site checked out her legs and bottom while Sam kept thinking the unreasonable thought: *Back off, she's mine.*

When she handed back the clipboard that had been pressed against her chest, Johnson made quick work of initialing the documents he carried. Alexandra saw him all the way to his truck. She waved from the porch as he drove off.

"Anytime," she said, turning, as if Sam had managed the polite thank-you she deserved.

"Pleased with yourself, are you?" He backed her across the porch and up against the building in the narrow space between the south turret and the main wall, then let himself look down at the view she'd been offering the plumbing inspector.

"I brought your thermos back. You probably need it."

"Has anyone ever commented on your split personality? Are you Miss Church Lady or ... Miss Sexy?"

She swallowed and her gaze shifted away from his. After a moment she said, "Just wearing the right clothes for the job."

He didn't know whether he was more angry or disappointed. In her or in himself. He wanted her to confess whatever it was she was hiding, but he had no right to her secrets. He certainly wasn't sharing his own. And he had ended their thing or fling or whatever it had been.

"I have to come up with something to call you, innkeeper—something that suits you. Alexandra is too long, too formal."

Her face didn't look cocky anymore.

"Yes, well, it's my name." She ducked under his arm and backed down the porch. "Bye now." She didn't look back. He watched the sway of her hips and the bounce of her ponytail disappear down Beach Street.

Had she won that round? Not quite. *What's in a name, Alexandra?*

Flo and Nigel had not come up for air in three days, so Charlie got stuck with the reception desk again. He watched the monks string lines of colorful prayer flags across the beams of the inn dining room. Sam Worth was working away on the library like an idiot, hoping Vernon wouldn't stop him. Vernon was in his office plotting the next dirty trick for Charlie to play. And Alexandra Clark was running around town talking to people, as if that could make a difference. As if Vernon wouldn't find out.

She was a little too trusting for Charlie's taste, and he didn't get her whole over-dressing thing. He didn't know any woman who hid her body quite as much as Alexandra Clark.

The monks started chanting. Charlie yelled at them

to shut up, but the chanting only grew louder. He thought a guest would be good, any guest, so the monks would stop.

Charlie got his wish when a bodybuilder walked in. The guy looked twenty-five, blond and buff with a sprayed-on tan, designer sunglasses, and flawless teeth. Charlie's first impulse was to rearrange his looks some, but even he recognized that as seriously antisocial.

"So, I'm looking for Lexy."

"Lexy?"

"Sexy Lexy, the *Workout Sex* girl."

"Not here. You want a room?"

"Is this Tooth Point?"

"Drake's Point. The Tooth and Nail Inn."

"Whatever. Is it?"

"Yeah."

"So, you don't know Lexy?" He sounded incredulous.

Charlie fought back irritation. "She's not here, dude. Try in town."

It was one of those days, and it occurred to Meg Sullivan that pumpkins ripening in the fields of Drake's Point led more exciting lives than she did. Right now they filled the big bins at the front of the feed store, and everyone was checking them out, looking for the best one to carve. In another week, she would be scraping out slime-covered seeds for roasting, another season come and gone. She opened the box with people's requests for the feed store's weekly order and began to make her list.

Something odd was going on in Drake's Point. Five people wanted a book called *Workout Sex, A Girl's Guide to Home Fitness*. Nobody knew the author or publisher, but they'd all heard great things about the book. Meg made a note to call a bookseller over the mountain in San Rafael who would know. More people than she cared to think about had requested Durex Gold Seal condoms and a coconut-scented, oil-based lubricant that had never appeared on the feed store shelves before. Apparently everyone in Drake's Point was caught in an end-of-summer heat wave, except for Meg and Charlie Beaton. Just the usual nuclear winter for them.

Back when the pumpkin bins had been filled with bunches of daffodils and lilies, Meg had thought things were changing. Charlie had begun to paint again, canvases full of light, full of the beauty of Drake's Point. He had teased that maybe he would paint her. Then in May Sam had come back. Meg couldn't blame him. No one knew better than she why her old friend needed to rebuild that library, but there was no denying that Sam brought out the worst in Charlie. All the old jealousies and angers that had plagued their friendship came back. Charlie, Meg, and Sam, the threesome that had started kindergarten together, riding to school over the mountain on those old yellow breakdown-prone buses with the cracked green vinyl seats. Twelve years later they had ended high school together, riding in Charlie's first truck, Meg in the middle. Friends forever.

Except that Charlie still believed that she had chosen Sam the terrible night of the fire all those years

212

ago. He didn't trust her, and he didn't trust Sam. But he was the one who didn't believe in himself or anybody else, who always had to smash things first.

Taking a blunt instrument to Charlie Beaton's hard head seemed the best option for dealing with her one and only beau. She probably would, too—except that knocking sense into people had been her father's way of dealing with the world. Charlie Beaton deserved a knock for this latest stunt. If no one else in Drake's Point figured it out, she knew Charlie had broken those windows. Sam probably knew it, too.

Maybe things would never change. Maybe she and Charlie were frozen in position, like the arm wrestlers on the Tooth and Nail sign or like two old tule elk with their horns locked, starving to death together up on the mountain. But she wasn't going to stop being Sam's friend now. She wasn't going to change the rules she lived by for a man who'd sold himself to Vernon for years. Before she did that, she would stop waiting for Charlie Beaton. Before she did that, she would leave Drake's Point.

The shop bell tinkled and a stranger walked in.

He had perfect teeth, TV-commercial teeth, dazzling teeth. And he had spent more on his designer sunglasses than most folks in Drake's Point would spend on a car.

"Where are your waters?"

Polite, too! Meg directed him to the drink section of the store. "Not a wide selection."

He came back to the counter a few minutes later with a bottled water and a package of the feed store's best-selling condom.

213

"This all you've got?" He held up a box of twelve. Meg made a mental note that supplies were low.

"So, you're local, right?" he continued.

"Lived here all my life."

The man pulled out a hundred dollar bill. "I'm looking for Sexy Lexy. Do you know where she is?"

"I don't know *who* she is. Do you have a twenty?"

He put his big money back and handed her the smaller bill. "Sexy Lexy, the *Workout Sex* girl?"

"Like the book?" She glanced at her order list. How had everyone but her discovered that book?

"And the video. You're looking at the future *Workout Sex* guy." He paused, obviously waiting for Meg to be impressed.

"Are the producers casting in Drake's Point?"

"That's the word. Fifty guys want this gig, but it's all mine. Once I find Lexy and make that first impression. In the flesh, if you know what I mean." He glanced at the box of condoms Meg was bagging.

She held out his change, careful not to touch him. The guy oozed slime. "You think Sexy Lexy is here? In Drake's Point?"

"Tip from my agent. He's on the inside track."

"Did you try the inn?"

"They sent me here."

Meg shrugged her shoulders. "Then you've pretty much covered the town."

"You mean I drove all the way up the I-5 for *nada?*"

Meg stifled a chuckle. "There's a gas station as you leave if you need to fuel up."

He pulled out his cell phone and stared at its panel, pushing buttons frantically.

"There's no service here," Meg explained.

The guy was more fluent in expletives than in ordinary English, abusing his agent and his misfortune equally. "He's trying to sabotage my career. He sent me here and they're choosing the *Workout Sex* guy in Santa Monica!" And with that thought, he was gone.

Meg went back to her thrilling life.

Lexy came back renewed from her walk to town. She had talked to fifty people on Vernon's list so far, and her message was the same for everybody: Be sure to check out the new building. See what you think. Come to Vernon's meeting. The citizens of Drake's Point had to decide for themselves.

On the way back, the warm October sun, the fresh breeze, and the view of the waves had lifted her spirits. She had let her mind dwell on pelicans skimming along above the sparkling crests, gulls crying, and shore birds darting along the lacy foam where the waves broke. She needed Flo back, and she missed the whole Sam Worth sex experience, but she was holding up, carrying on. Now she just had to straighten out the Lovejoy-Blackhart wedding confusion.

"About time you showed up." Charlie Beaton's usual snarl greeted her. "There's a bird trapped in the dining room."

"Oh dear. A sparrow? A hummingbird?" Lexy pictured the frantic wild thing, beating itself helplessly against the windows. It would be good to help the bird escape before they began lunch service.

But when she stepped into the dining room entry, she got confused. Tables and chairs were overturned.

Flatware, linens, and roses littered the floor. Little rivers of water trickled from spilled vases. Ernesto and the kitchen staff were squared off on one side of the room against the monks on the other. Ernesto shouted in Spanish and waved his cleaver at the monks. Violeta and Paula watched from the doorway, laughing and holding their sides.

Lexy strode into the space between the glaring adversaries. Each side had reverted to its native language, so there was no meeting of the minds. Yesterday, the monks had been teaching Ernesto to make butter sculptures. How had a trapped bird caused such animosity?

And Lexy didn't see a bird anywhere in the chaos until Charlie strolled up beside her.

"Wild turkey," he said, pointing. Lexy followed his gesture. In the deep window ledge beside the fireplace was a swollen mass of brown and buff feathers surrounding a naked red and blue head with a lethal-looking beak and one hostile eye. This was no sparrow, no hummingbird. This was twenty pounds or more of angry birdlife. Lexy had never considered her Thanksgiving dinner as having killer instincts, but this avian obviously did.

The bird fanned its tail and gobbled, a loud raucous protest. Ernesto switched to English. "I'm going to roast that cursed bird for wrecking my dining room."

"No. We must respect the sacredness of all life," said Thruong, the head monk.

"Shoot it," said Charlie.

Lexy studied the bird. Wild turkeys were supposed

216

to be smarter than domestic birds, so how had this genius found himself trapped in her inn's dining room?

The bird made a low coo and deposited a soft plop of bird poop. Ernesto snarled and charged, cleaver raised. The monks locked arms and swung into a line in front of the bird. The bird took off to the left, and Ernesto gave pursuit, veering around fallen chairs. He nearly caught up to it, and slammed his cleaver into the paneling. While the cook worked his cleaver out of the wall, the bird circled the room, dipping low then rising again. Everyone ducked. The bird crashed into walls, tangled itself in the lines of prayer flags, and scrabbled for a perch on the mantel, sending a half-dozen brass candlesticks clattering to the floor.

When the ringing stopped, everyone started shouting.

"Stop! Stop!" Lexy shouted, silencing them, looking around at everyone. "Tom there wants to go back to the wild, and we'll just help him."

Thruong bowed to Lexy. "If we put food in the doorway, the bird will eventually find its way out."

"No time," said Ernesto. "Customers will be coming for lunch and tea soon."

Ernesto was right, but Lexy wanted to give the monks and the turkey a chance. "We'll seat people on the patio and give Tom one hour. Everyone out." She turned to Ernesto and asked him to bring some corn from the kitchen. He headed off, mumbling.

Lexy turned to the turkey. "Seize the moment, bird. Go now. You only get one chance to escape."

* * *

By late afternoon Sam's helpers had gone on to other jobs. Once they left, he could think his own thoughts without interruption. Ordinarily that might be a good thing, but today his thoughts were all centered on Alexandra Clark and the way she had shown up to help him. He didn't think she had any idea how big a deal it was that Johnson had signed off on the plumbing, but she knew whose side she was on and she wasn't afraid to go against Vernon.

And it astonished him that she had come to help him even after he had said they were through.

His plan was to keep working while the light lasted. He liked building. It made him feel different from his father. His father had been a taker, a grabber, a man who had wrested wealth out the earth. Sam liked to feel that his strength was steadier, quieter, more enduring. He liked to put himself into buildings, and he liked the honesty a building ultimately required. You couldn't fudge it or fake it and have the thing stand up for very long. His brain couldn't sort out the squiggles on the printed page, but it could easily see the struts and beams, the lines and angles of a sturdy building.

He had always liked the feel of tools in his hands—the familiar weight, the smooth worn handles, the rhythm of swinging a hammer, its sweet, sharp contact with the nail head, the brief yielding as the nail sank into wood, and quick finish. The thought stopped him cold. He smiled grimly to himself and started unstrapping his tool belt. Who was he kidding? He was thinking of filling his hands with Alexandra Clark's sweet flesh, of lifting her, turning her, sliding against her and into her. Like father, like son.

He put down the tool belt, and Winston lifted his head and trotted over to his side.

"Stick with me, dog. I don't want you shot."

The monks' offering of food did not tempt the turkey. An hour later Lexy and the others were still at a standoff with the bird. They had directed more than a dozen guests to the patio, and Ernesto had sharpened his cleaver. The guys at the fire station had got word of the excitement and come to offer suggestions and watch.

The staff and the monks gathered back in the dining room, looking to Lexy for guidance. As trapped insects always moved toward light, Lexy reasoned the turkey might do the same. She took a deep breath. "Okay, new plan. We will herd the turkey out onto the patio." How hard could that be?

No one showed signs of enthusiasm, but Lexy explained her plan anyhow. "Here's how it works." They would close all the curtains to darken the room, then turn the tables on their ends and line them up to make a chute. The monks and Ernesto would stand behind the turkey making noise. Only the patio door would be open. At the signal, someone would shoo the turkey off its perch, and it would fly through the chute to daylight.

Slowly, quietly, the group moved furniture to create a long path from the bird's perch to the patio door. Tables, benches, stacks of chairs, draped tablecloths all contributed to the structure. The curtains were drawn, the prayer lines came down. Lexy didn't trust Ernesto to shoo the turkey, but everyone else got into place, and Thruong inched his robed way toward the wary bird.

They were poised, ready to act. At Lexy's signal, Thruong stood up next to the bird and banged an antique brass bed-warming pan with a candlestick. At the clang, the turkey exploded into motion. Swooping down, it headed for the chute, picking up speed, a bird with a direction. The plan was working!

Then the front door opened. A stranger stood silhouetted in the burst of light. Lexy shouted, but the bird veered left, plowed into the stranger, knocking him flat on the slate-tiled entry floor, and ascended to a roost at the top of the stairwell.

The firemen rushed to the stranger's aid while everyone else followed the bird. Lexy stared at the unconscious victim in her entry. His dark glasses and the brown paper bag in his hand had gone flying. He looked like he was in his mid-twenties, with model-perfect features marred only by a bloody cut over his left eyebrow. He had a sculpted chest, and the waist of guy with seven percent body fat and low testosterone levels. He looked vaguely familiar. He had an L.A. face, the kind of face that had looked back at her from the audience of the *Stanley Skoff Show*.

He started to come around, but the firemen kept him down, pressing an ice pack to his brow.

"Take it easy, guy," Tim advised.

Behind Lexy, Ernesto, the monks, Paula, and Violeta were arguing about the bird in two languages again. She quieted the babble and turned back. The injured man was staring at his damaged face in the entry mirror, expressing himself in expletives.

Tim clapped him on the back. "Just a few stitches. You'll have a black eye, but probably no concussion," he said cheerily.

"Stitches? Black eye?" The man peered closer.

"We can take you up the road to the clinic. They'll sew you right up."

He shook his head and winced. "I've got gigs, man. I can't have a black eye. Where's the nearest plastic surgeon?"

At least his ego was intact, Lexy thought.

The firemen just stared at the man. The bird gobbled and shifted its perch, making a fresh deposit on the carpet. Paula shrieked.

"Get me outta here," the injured man said.

Charlie Beaton stepped forward and handed the guy his dark glasses and brown paper bag, and the man stalked off, firemen in pursuit.

Lexy glared at the evil bird perched above her entry.

"I told you," Charlie said. "Shoot it."

Lexy was tempted. But for all the chaos, she realized the bird had done her a favor and she couldn't let Ernesto cook it. She had just been visited by one of her agent's *Workout Sex* wannabes.

The inn door opened again, and Sam Worth strolled in. He was his usual competent, cocky, beautiful self, and Lexy's insides somersaulted happily.

He and Charlie Beaton exchanged a pointedly hostile look, and Charlie shrugged and wandered off.

Sam glanced up at the bird. "Communing with the local wildlife again, Ms. Clark?"

Violeta said, *"Es un maldito parajo."*

Sam Worth laughed. "A cursed bird, huh." He turned to Lexy. "Need some help, innkeeper?"

They were right back where they'd started. "It's true that dealing with local wildlife is not my forte, but just because you can handle a bull tule elk doesn't mean you can handle a turkey," she challenged.

He leaned forward and tucked a straggling lock of her hair behind her ear. "You doubt me, innkeeper? I've got a secret weapon."

He stepped back, pushed open the inn door, and whistled.

Winston came bounding in.

The dog came to a halt at the foot of the stairs and froze. Not a hair moved. He seemed not to breathe as he and the turkey made eye contact.

Lexy's gaze shifted from the dog to the bird. She swore old Tom was reassessing his options under Winston's intense scrutiny. She motioned everyone back and signaled Sam to prop open the front door.

The silence grew tense.

Then the turkey squawked, and Winston erupted with a leaping lunge that nearly reached its perch. The bird stretched out its neck, wattles wobbling, flapped its wings wildly, and took off in a lurching flight. It crashed first into the ceiling and then into the wall above the reception desk. Winston seemed to be everywhere at once, barking and leaping, and blocking the frantic bird's return to the dining room, until on a low swoop it found the open door and escaped.

Winston bounded after it, giving a few last triumphant barks.

It was all over but the clean-up. Ernesto shook his head and took himself off to his kitchen, muttering. Charlie returned to his post at the reception desk. Lexy, Violeta, Sam, and the monks turned to put the dining room back together.

Thruong, the head monk, bowed. "It is good. Life has been respected."

Chapter 10
Safe Workout Sex

"With a few simple steps, partners can maintain
contraceptive effectiveness during their exercise."
— *Workout Sex*, Lexy Clark

"Come on." Sam took Lexy's hand in the darkness
outside the inn.

"I thought we weren't going to do this anymore,"
she said.

"Me, too, but apparently there's no choice for us."

"Inevitable, huh?" She owed him that jibe.

"Inevitable."

"No sleeping bag?"

"Nope. Not this time." He was striding along toward town.

Lexy grabbed her long skirt, skipping to keep up.
"You're not worried about the library?"

"Not while you've got Charlie Beaton working
nights."

Lexy stopped short. "You think *Charlie Beaton*
broke the library windows? Why?"

Sam tugged her hand. "We go way back. Also, Vernon holds the mortgage on Charlie's grandfather's farm."

Lexy gave in to the pull of that warm, firm grip. "Did you confront Charlie?"

"A long time ago. I broke his nose once. I'm not breaking it again for Vernon's sake."

They were moving at a fast pace through the early darkness of the last days before the fall time change. Lexy was a little breathless by the time they turned up the path to Worth House. "Are you going to explain any of this to me?"

This time Sam stopped, and Lexy crashed into him. He turned so that they touched each other front to front. "Is tonight going to be visual as well as tactile?" he asked.

"Could be." She leaned into the long hard strength of him. But tactile was good. And he seemed to think so, too. He shifted, his arms came around her, strong and tight, and he kissed her, a mind-melting, time-expanding contact.

He drew back. "Men," he said on a rasp of breath, "like to look as well as touch. I want you totally naked, lights on."

His rough voice brushed her skin, raising gooseflesh all over her. Then they were moving through the night again.

His big house was dark and empty. No warm lived-in smells greeted them, just the ashy smell of their fire from a few nights before.

A thought occurred to her. "How long have you been back in Drake's Point?"

"Since May."

It seemed a long time to be in a place without disturbing its profound loneliness. But maybe she was reacting to the grand scale of these rooms, so much larger than any she had ever inhabited. He was leading her through the living room into the soaring marble entry that she'd glimpsed on the day of her run. They made their way up its wide sweeping staircase to the open landing above.

At the top of the stairs Sam turned left and led her to a door at the end of the landing. He found a switch, and a wall lamp cast a warm circle of light into a turret room, like the ones he had built for the library. It was furnished with masculine simplicity—rich dark woods in big pieces of clean-lined furniture. He dropped into a chocolate-brown leather chair, removing his shoes while she looked around. There was a mahogany bed worthy of her inn with a tall paneled headboard and a spread of deep burgundies, golds, and blues like the colors in the Persian rug underfoot. Next to his chair was a table with a stack of books-on-CD and a small CD player. An unused fireplace with a stone mantel dominated one wall. French doors opened to a balcony overlooking the sea, and in one corner a spiral staircase led through the ceiling to an upper story.

She picked up a CD, curious about his tastes, but he took it from her and rose, and he coaxed her toward the bed.

She halted, suddenly conscious, in the face of his unexpected openness, of the truths she was still holding back. They had joked in the bunker that he would only let her in his bed if she revealed herself, but this room was a revelation. It showed plainly how privileged he had once been, growing up the only child of the richest man in town. And it wasn't that Ajax Worth had merely been richer than his neighbors in Drake's Point. Lexy suspected that Ajax had made millions, amassed an old-style California fortune from land or railroads or oil. That was another clue she and Sam did not belong together.

"Worried about your secrets?" He was waiting for her beside the bed, free of his shoes and shirt, which meant that Lexy was distracted by his arms. Those arms. "Come here." He flicked open the fastenings on his fly.

Lexy's doubts demanded attention, but she ignored them and crossed the room to stand before him. "What did your father do?" *To get so rich*, she didn't say.

He reached for her, making quick work of getting her out of her sweater and shirt. But when he spoke, it was clear that he understood her unasked question. "He took oil out of the ground and turned it into cash. 'Cash is king' he used to say. Although, mostly he took that cash to the racetrack. And he would have left it all there, except that he invented a couple of improvements to the electronic totalizer that updates the racetrack's changing odds and results. It was big before computers."

"And your mother?" Lexy wanted to know who the beautiful woman in the portrait downstairs really was; why she had come to Drake's Point and why she had died. She knew it was all connected to the library

Sam was building with such energy of purpose. For a moment his hands stilled. Then he seemed to come to a decision.

"We'll get to her. First, the naked part." His hands went back to their efficient work. "Did I tell you my innkeeper fantasy?"

Lexy shook her head.

"There's this innkeeper, all buttoned up from her chin to her laced-up running shoes." He was unlacing them fast enough, though, lifting her feet, pulling off her socks. "She wears sweaters as thick as her favorite Wookiee's fur."

"The Irish fishermen are going to get you for that crack," she retorted in amusement.

Lexy's skirt and slip dropped into a crumpled heap.

"But when I get her naked, she moves . . ."

There was nothing between her and Sam Worth's gaze except the roses on her bra and panties. He pulled her into the angle of his legs, up against the place where his erection tented his boxers. His big warm hands slid up her hips and ribs and cupped her breasts. "This is so much better." His eyes drifted closed briefly, long straight dark lashes against golden skin. "This is what I remember. Not what you flashed at Johnson."

Lexy couldn't speak. Sam dipped his head and dragged his teeth across the fine fabric of her bra, breathing heat into the valley between her breasts. She held his shoulders for balance as her knees gave way. She wanted out of her bra, but her arms felt too heavy to lift.

He raised his head and slid her straps down her arms. Lexy let out a long, shuddering breath, and her bra slipped down her rib cage. She stood, incapable of movement, her arms still trapped, her breasts under his gaze.

His throat worked, and a word came out low and dry. "Perfect."

Then he was kissing her again. His hands slid down, working the hooks and releasing her dangling bra, stripping away her panties. He pulled back to look, letting his hands drift over her, the backs of his knuckles grazing the curls at the apex of her thighs. The blue of his eyes was deep and dark as the ocean, the pull just as powerful.

Abruptly he stood, drew back the covers on the bed, and swung Lexy up onto it. She bounced and fell back against a pile of pillows, and he froze again, that stunned watchful look tightening the lines of his face. Lexy had never been the object of such a look. Here she was—unwrapped, her flaws and imperfections clear for him to see. And he wanted her. The dazed desire in his eyes made her feel powerful. She didn't need Obi Wan telling her how to use this kind of force. She felt that look burn into her, releasing her limbs of all their awkward tightness. She slid down the pillows in a slow lazy stretch.

Sam's feet tangled in her cast-off clothes as he lurched toward her, and he frowned down, considering them. With sudden resolution he scooped up the pile of clothes and strode to the balcony and tossed them off.

Lexy made a squeak of protest.

"It's not your look, innkeeper." Then he was back, stripping off his jeans and boxers, drawing Lexy's gaze. It was her turn to admire his rugged, clean-limbed strength, to grow dizzy and mindless with wanting. He slid into bed beside her, pulling her under him, looking down into her face. "I like you better naked."

Lexy reached up, taking his face in her hands. He gave her one quick, heated kiss, and drew back to gaze at everything, at her face and breasts, at her body open beneath him, at the dark place where they then joined. All the talking and touching that had gone before seemed to burn up in that look. They started moving, gazes locked, Sam holding himself above her on strong arms, pushing into her with slow, teasing dips until she arched against him. Then they were pressed against each other everywhere, heat fusing them together.

Little atoms of pleasure collided in the hot core of Lexy's sex, their wildly pulsing electrons leaping from orbit to orbit, giving off heat and energy, building a chain reaction to steal thought and breath, and when the consummation came, Lexy was sure it registered on the Richter scale.

After, she lay back in bed. Sometime she would move again. Sometime she would regain control of her body. Messages from her brain would again reach her distant limbs. Sometime she would remember her name and where she lived and what day it was. But there was no hurry. This century or the next.

It occurred to her that she had not been uncomfortable in the sleeping bag or in the bunker; there had been too much newness and heat for her to truly notice her surroundings. But now everything was different. Sam's bed was special territory. They had bounded across it like moon explorers planting their national flag. Their bodies had warmed the sheets and covers and made the mattress and pillows conform to the shape of their lovemaking. And their heated joining had scented even the air.

Sam had stopped moving. He had disposed of the condom and pulled the covers up. Now he lay beside her on his belly, his face turned her way. Lexy studied his lean, strong features. He claimed to have broken Charlie's nose, but it looked as if Charlie might also have broken his. His left brow had a gap where a faint scar disturbed its perfect symmetry. One fine, muscled arm was within her reach, and she traced its veins with her fingertips.

He stirred and shifted onto his side, and lifted one hand to cup her breast. "I really like you naked."

"A good thing. You threw away my clothes."

His fingers zeroed in on the peak of her left breast. "Was that outfit recommended in your witness protection handbook?"

She shifted her gaze to the ceiling, a nice ceiling high above them. "I told you, I like flowers."

"But you didn't wear them in L.A." His fingertips went on doing wonderful things to her nipple. "What were you doing there?"

All of Lexy's previous doubts had their moment of satisfaction. *We told you so. You thought you could pretend Sexy Lexy never existed. That you could kill her as easily as you made her up. Hah!*

"What makes you think I was so different in L.A.?"

His answer came after a thoughtful pause. "That's a tough question. But . . . the way you make love. It's like it's all new to you—like you've just been released from a locked cell somewhere."

She swallowed her fear of discovery and laughed. "Nice! You think I was an inmate at Camarillo or something." She pushed at Sam's hand, which was still coaxing sensations from the tip of her breast.

He laughed, too, and gave her nude body a pointed look. "I've pretty much uncovered everything about you. Can't you tell me what brought you to Drake's Point?"

She realized the trap she had fallen into. Her disguise had freed her to become this genuinely sexy woman. He had never seen her in the charade of Sexy Lexy. Right here, right now, Sam Worth had seen *her*. If she told him the truth now, it would make this naked, vulnerable woman in his bed—the woman she really was—seem the lie. She wanted the moment to last; she wanted him to go on thinking of her as Alexandra Clark in flowers, the woman he so obviously liked. "I can't."

He stirred a little beside her, withdrawing his hand. His eyes drifted closed, and the silence stretched between them, not angry, just a moving apart, a shifting back from shared space to separate spheres.

Lexy's throat ached, and she squeezed her eyes tight for a moment against a brief stinging.

Sometime later she realized she had dozed, and the sweat had dried, and the house was cold. She was hungry—tummy-growlingly hungry—and she wanted to put something on, maybe a T-shirt of his. Anything to cover herself. She pulled the covers up to her chin, and he stirred beside her.

"If you want something to put on, try my mother's room down the hall. But no long skirts or heavy sweaters," he joked.

Was he testing her? She grinned. At least he wasn't so angry at her refusal to tell him her past that he wouldn't tease her. She thought about his suggestion. It meant walking naked in front of him. Clearly, he didn't think she would do it. *Hah!* She flung back the covers and stood. His eyes popped open, and he made a grab for her, but she slipped past. It felt liberating, being naked like this, and knowing he was watching her walk away. She felt his undivided attention on the sway of her hips and the vibration in her breasts when her heels made contact with the rich rug.

"Which room?" she called back from the doorway.

"Last one at the other end." She liked the choked sound of his voice. *Got to you, didn't I?* she thought to herself.

In the hall the house felt really cold, so she didn't linger. She felt her way along the wall, wondering where the light switches were. Light would banish some of the ghosts and dispel the loneliness.

She pushed open the last door and found a switch, and miraculously a light came on. It was a pretty room, all faded pinks and creams, with chintz cushions and valences and ruffles enough to make Lexy's favorite designer proud. Sam's mother had obviously loved light and flowers and books. There were botanical prints on the pale pink walls, and flowers on the cream-colored curtains, rug, and spread. White recessed bookcases, decorated with grooves and topped with cornices, dominated one side of the room. It fit the lovely woman in the dining room portrait.

Two pairs of double doors filled the wall opposite the bookcases. Lexy was contemplating them when she heard Sam's footsteps in the hall. She pulled open the first doors and froze, a sudden chill washing over her. Her mind struggled to connect the closet's tawdry contents with the sweet elegance of the bedroom.

A cluttered backstage dressing table filled the darkened space. Its base was surmounted by a cracked and foggy mirror framed by a border of dust-and-cobweb-shrouded lights. The mirror gave back a blurry image of Lexy's pale nakedness. Stale smells of old cigarettes and mildew and dead perfume drifted over Lexy. On one side of the dressing table hung a white uniform and cap. To the other side was a street vendor's old-fashioned white ice-cream pushcart with a handle and wheels. Flowing candy-apple red script on the cart's side read:

GET YOUR CHERRY POPP-SICLES HERE

Lexy didn't move. All the bits and pieces she had heard coalesced in a flash of understanding, and Sam Worth suddenly made sense to her, his caution, his silences. This was Cherry Popp's dirty little secret. It was her little red book. She had not had her past tattooed into her skin as Flo had, but it had been inextri-

235

cably linked to her life in Drake's Point. Like Lexy, Cherry had tried to escape, but it had been there all the time in the midst of her beautiful life, ready to be exposed with the opening of one door.

"Shocked?" Sam's voice was grim and flat behind her.

Lexy was shivering. "Not in the way you think."

"You're cold." His arms closed around her from behind and he buried his face in her hair. He was naked, and his heated skin warmed her.

"Why did she keep it?" Lexy needed to know. It made no sense. In Cherry's place, Lexy would have left this stuff behind in whatever theater it had come from, or burned it. Why had Cherry Popp kept the evidence of the performer she had been?

Sam's laugh was clipped and bitter. "My father saw her act and wanted her to do it for him exclusively. He was obsessive about it, the way he was about most things. He bought out her contract, bought her props, even bought the neon sign that featured her act. Then he brought her here. She made him put the sign away in a shed."

Lexy slipped from his arms and closed the doors on his mother's past. She turned and pressed herself against him, offering her warmth to him this time. He rested his chin on the top of her head. Deep inside, she was shaking. She would let him think it was from the cold. The moment to tell him who she was had passed. Cherry Popp's son and Sexy Lexy did not belong together. She might have told him the truth about herself any time until now. Now she couldn't. Their relationship had an expiration date. Like coupons and cereal boxes. *Best If Used by November 1.*

It was Sam who opened the second closet. It held a complete wardrobe for the wealthy, beautiful woman of the dining room portrait. Rows of shoes and sweaters, tailored shirts, skirts, and slacks, each on the appropriate hangers and coordinated by color, zippered plastic bags with formal beaded gowns winking inside them. Cashmere coats and furs. Filmy negligees in creamy shades hung on padded hangers.

Lexy was mystified by the two closets. One made perfect sense, but the other seemed some kind of scarlet letter, like the one Hester Prynne wore in the book they'd all read in high school, or Demi Moore in the movie for the non-scholars in her class. She picked a wrapper with a few strategic lace flowers and turned to Sam. "Tell me about her."

They took themselves back to his bed, the pillows piled against the headboard, Lexy nestled in Sam's lap. She was learning that he liked her where he could touch her but she couldn't see his face. Oh, their secrets. She took his beautiful, corded hands and played with them while he told her the story.

"My mother was a reader. She read hundreds of books. All the time she had that act in the city, she read about English lords and ladies. She wanted to live in the country with a garden and dogs and good furniture. She wanted a kid."

He paused for a moment, and Lexy thought again about the disjointed halves of Cherry Popp's life. Lexy couldn't help a shudder, imagining Cherry Popp stepping from that dressing room night after night onto a stage where men had expected her to be hot, hot, hot—a seductress cheerfully ready for action. Lexy imagined the avid male faces in the crowd, the hoots and catcalls, the voices yelling to hose her down, and the propositions that came after each show. *The Stanley Skoff Show* was nothing. Lexy's own brief brush with notoriety, however embarrassing, had been tame and still it had made her distrustful of men. The real mystery was how Cherry Popp had managed to become the elegant woman in the portrait.

"She must have been very disillusioned with men." She did not say anything about Sam's father.

He seemed sad as he answered. "My parents had a bargain. He gave her what she wanted, and she did her act for him." He paused again, a man who didn't often talk about himself, telling a hard story, and Lexy wondered when he had first seen the inside of his mother's closet.

He went on. "Whatever was strange in their marriage, they did feel strongly about each other. But I think as she changed, it baffled him. He wanted her to be the stripper forever, always in need of rescue. Instead she became more and more independent, more and more a part of Drake's Point. She found friends."

Lexy knew who they had been. The Ladies Book Club—earthy, unshockable, and loyal to each other. They were still that way.

"Their marriage might have worked. I don't know. But then Vernon's father made a fool of himself over her, and the library made things worse. Finally, my father's obsession and her old reputation caught up with them. Someone put her old neon sign up in front of city hall, across from the new library the night before it was supposed to be dedicated. She took off in her car over the mountain. He went after her."

He sounded so weary telling the story. Lexy did not let go of his hand, did not let on what she was feeling. The ache of it filled her chest with a heavy pain. He had been eighteen. At eighteen, her own life had been a comparative breeze. She had escaped the humiliations of high school and moved on to Pacifica where the world was familiar and endlessly supportive. Sam had been plunged, grieving, into all that was unfamiliar and difficult.

"You must have been a great joy to her."

He didn't say anything. It wasn't a good sign. Lexy had a moment of perfect clarity. The best thing that could happen would be for him to leave Drake's Point without ever knowing he'd been to bed with a woman who, like his mother, had gained a hot public reputation.

In the meantime she would make Sam Worth laugh, and they would make love until he couldn't remember one sad thing that had happened in his life. She twisted in his arms and pressed her face into the middle of his chest, drawing a breath and filling her senses with him.

"Hey," he said.

She started dragging her mouth down his abdomen. "The Irish fishermen asked me to get you for that Wookiee crack," she joked. Then she slipped lower.

* * *

Lexy returned to her inn the next morning and found Flo back in the little office, hunched over the computer.

"Flo, am I glad to see you!" she cried. "Have you got the Lovejoy-Blackhart wedding tangle worked out?"

Flo looked up, but her smile faded instantly as she took in Lexy's outfit. "*Cherry's* clothes?"

Lexy looked down at her borrowed garments. She hadn't realized they'd be recognizable. "Yes."

"So, you and Sam . . . ?" Flo's expression was distinctly worried.

Lexy nodded. "I know it can't last. I'm just going to be a good memory for him, his recovery girl. He's still going to leave November first and get on with his life."

Flo turned off the computer and handed Lexy a paper bag from the desk. "This is you, isn't it?" she asked.

Lexy peeked inside. It was her book. She sank into the old chintz chair and hugged the bag to her chest. "Yes. Thank heaven *you* found it." Maybe now, Sam Worth would never know.

"It's made quite the rounds in Drake's Point. Nigel got it from the monks, who got it from the boys at the fire station."

Lexy's breath caught. "Do they know *I* wrote it? Does everyone?" If she had to leave, she would. She tried to remember where her car keys were and whether she had gas in the thing. She hadn't driven anywhere in weeks.

"What matters is, does Sam know?"

Lexy shook her head.

Flo's gaze held hers. "You should tell him the truth."

"It's too late!" Lexy smoothed her borrowed wool skirt over her knees. "I know about his mother now. That's why his engagement broke up, isn't it?"

"Cherry's past didn't help, but I think he was lucky to get out of it. Julia Flood Stoddard wasn't right for him."

"Well, I'm not either."

"You're sure?" Flo gave her a penetrating stare.

"You're the one who told me how much he hates publicity. If he's with me, the publicity will come, and my past will come back. If he's with me and any reporter gets word of us, it will make a splash. He'll hate that. He's leaving soon, and I just need to keep my secret till then."

Flo didn't say anything for a minute. "It's quite a book. Nigel and I owe you, Lexy."

"Oh, don't call me that. I truly am Alexandra Clark now."

"Do you think so?" Flo shook her head. "Haven't you learned anything by living in Drake's Point?"

Winston showed up just as Sam retrieved Alexandra's clothes from the garden. They were damp from contact with the weedy grass and night air, and he spread them over the backs of a pair of chairs in his mother's sunny kitchen. Hanging them over the porch rail would not be smart. No need to further advertise that Alexandra Clark had spent the night at his house. Walking out of the inn together under

241

Charlie Beaton's nose meant the news would get to Vernon soon enough, but the rest of Drake's Point didn't need to know.

He took his coffee out on the porch. Winston collapsed at his feet, a tired happy dog, a satisfied dog. Sam laughed, nudging the beast with his toe. What a pair they were, helpless in pursuit of their women.

He was still astonished at Alexandra's reaction to his mother's closet. She had not turned away, but toward him. If anything, she had given herself more freely after she'd opened that door. He had sent her off for clothes in a moment of stupidity, not thinking about what she would find. Then it had come back to him. He had been up and after her in a heartbeat, but of course, he had been too late.

He had been seven and too curious for his own good the first time he opened that closet. Nothing had seemed too alarming about it at first, except the guilty feeling that he'd stumbled onto a secret. It was the look on his mother's face that told him he had violated her privacy. It took years for what he had seen to make sense in the picture he built of his parents' marriage from seeing them together, from hearing things in town, and from fighting endlessly with anyone at school who called his mother a name. This morning, the closet's secrets didn't seem so ugly. Maybe because there was no one left to fight except Vernon. Maybe because the library was nearly finished. Maybe because Alexandra Clark had understood.

Winston snored lightly at Sam's feet, the exhausted canine Romeo. Vernon was going to be so pissed. Sam let himself laugh again. Winston opened a sleepy eye.

"You're a dead dog, if Vernon sees you, buddy," he advised.

This return to Drake's Point had taken an unexpected turn. Maybe he would stay a few weeks after the library opened, just to make sure that all the systems were working properly.

Winston regarded him narrowly.

"You don't want to leave, do you? There's nothing for you back in the city. Maybe Alexandra will take you at the inn. She'll need a good watchdog when Vernon finds out where she's been sleeping."

Winston did not deign to reply.

Charlie did not appreciate Vernon's early morning summons, but it did not surprise him. He would give Vernon his due; the guy always knew what was going down in Drake's Point. Charlie refused to sit in either of Vernon's stupid stick chairs, so he took a sofa cushion from the reception area and dropped down on it, leaning his back against the wall. His low seat gave him a funny perspective on Vernon, the mayor's small head stuck onto his big over-sized coffin of a desk. Charlie thought maybe there was a painting in that somewhere.

"What's up, Vernon?"

"Are you ready with our next project?"

"That would be *your* next project, Vernon."

"Don't try sarcasm with me, Beaton. I've carried Amadeo's mortgage for over a year."

Yeah. Ever since you shut down his ability to farm. "You're a true gentleman, Vernon."

"Is it ready?"

Charlie rolled to his feet and grunted. "I'm working on it today. It'll be finished in time."

"Good. I've made my arrangements." Vernon frowned. "The security will be gone. How much help do you need getting it in place?"

Charlie studied the view out Vernon's window. It was funny; Vernon had the best view in town, but Charlie didn't think the mayor ever looked at the cove or the point. "A couple of guys is all. I've got ropes and tackle."

"One more thing, Beaton."

Charlie was at the door. He didn't look back. "I'm not going to shoot the dog, Vernon. You've got to do that yourself."

Lexy decided that if Miss Manners ever wanted to sponsor pro-wrestling, the Lovejoy-Blackhart wedding would be her idea of a match. By Saturday noon, just hours before the ceremony, Mrs. Lovejoy and Mrs. Blackhart each had a win, and the deciding third bout was under way. The issue was the proper place for the bride and groom to say their vows. Mrs. Blackhart wanted the happy couple in front of the red-bronze brilliance of the inn's Boston ivy-covered west wall. Mrs. Lovejoy preferred a site nearer the creek, backed by the florist's white rose-covered trellis.

The bride lay in her darkened room with a migraine. The two fathers hovered in the background, occasionally responding to their wives with a "Yes, dear." And Nigel, to his credit, was doing his best to keep the other males of the wedding party relatively cheerful and oblivious in the pub. He was, however, taking staff bets that the event would never actually happen.

Lexy listened to the mothers' argument, fading in and out of awareness without the energy to intervene, thinking that as long as the women had no access to boutonniere pins or salad forks, actual bloodshed might be avoided. She was ready to take Nigel's odds. Margaret Lovejoy and Chuck Blackhart, the unfortunate offspring of the two families, were mad to think they could make a match of it.

The Blackharts were thin, dark-haired, and quiet. The Lovejoys were big, raw-boned, carroty redheads with carrying voices. They thundered up and down the stairs, shouted to each other from room to room, and slammed doors, while the Blackharts slipped in and out of their rooms, as silent as fog. The bride- and groom-to-be bore an uncanny resemblance to Charlie Beaton and Meg Sullivan, another doomed couple as far as Lexy could tell. This particular Brigadoon seemed full of them—Charlie and Meg, Sam and Lexy, and now Chuck and Margaret. Lexy was thinking the bride and groom had come to the right place, when their resemblance to Charlie and Meg gave her an inspiration. Maybe she could break the wedding impasse and show Charlie and Meg they were meant for each other.

She sat up in the white wrought iron chair as Francisco and Oscar moved the rose trellis to yet another position on the patio and the photographer trotted after them.

"I know what we need." Everyone turned her way. "Stunt doubles. Like in Hollywood." She stood up and stepped between the two mothers. Mrs. Black-hart had a dainty fist clenched around her pearls. Mrs. Lovejoy's carroty strands were escaping her chignon. They didn't seem convinced.

Before either woman could speak, Lexy went on, "We have two people in Drake's Point who would be perfect to stand in for Margaret and Chuck. We'll bring them here, and you can see which site works best."

"We will need to see the dress," Mrs. Lovejoy insisted.

"And the tux," Mrs. Blackhart chimed in.

Lexy smiled. "No problem."

Charlie Beaton had to be dragged from some welding project in his workshop and bribed with a chance to sell his art to Mr. Blackhart before he was willing to shower and shave and don the groom's tux, but he eventually did so. Meg was cheerfully ready to help and got Ruth to cover the feed store counter. Lexy thought it prudent not to mention Charlie as the stand-in groom.

The gown was every little girl's dream wedding dress, with a satin bodice that tapered to a narrow waist and a long skirt of layers of fluffy tulle. Flo took Meg's hair out of its customary long braid and placed the dainty shoulder-length veil on her head.

Even Lexy was unprepared for the effect of Charlie and Meg transformed. Charlie came out to the patio with his usual edgy, angry strides, but, cleaned up and standing under the warm brilliance of the ivy wall, his dark elegance was striking.

Then Meg emerged from the back of the inn.

Everyone stilled. Charlie plainly couldn't breathe or speak. Meg looked for a moment as if she might retreat, but came resolutely forward.

"You clean up nice, cowgirl," Charlie said, offering her his hand.

"You're not bad, yourself, paint boy."

"What do you want us to do?" Charlie called, not taking his eyes off Meg. The photographer stepped up and started directing everyone. He quickly shot a few rounds of photos, exclaiming to the mothers how right this was going to be. It looked like a clear win for Mrs. Blackhart—and more problems for the wedding. Then the photographer saved the day with a diplomatic stroke, suggesting that they move the trellis behind the cake for the cake-cutting shots.

There was a moment of tense silence, then agreement. The two mothers did not exactly shake hands, but it seemed to Lexy that they put down their weapons. They snapped orders to the fathers and went off to change. "Bring the clothes up as soon as you get those people out of them," Mrs. Blackhart ordered, and Lexy didn't even mind. Two workers immediately set the dais in place for the minister and began to arrange the chairs.

When Lexy turned back, Charlie and Meg were engaged in a furious exchange of whispers. It ended when Charlie ripped off his silk bow tie and stomped across the patio. Meg called his name, and he stopped at the inn door and turned back to her.

"Charlie, I'm warning you, stop doing Vernon's dirty work."

"I can't, cowgirl," he said. He pointed at Lexy. "And

don't think you won't pay for screwing Sam Worth, Alexandra Clark."

He banged through the door. Meg burst into tears and ran after him. When Lexy followed, she found the tux draped over a chair and Meg locked in the bathroom with the dress. Great chest-wracking, breath-stealing sobs came from behind the closed door, as if Meg had put years of sorrow into one category-five cry. It couldn't be because Charlie Beaton had blurted out that Lexy was sleeping with Sam, could it? Charlie and Meg burned for each other. Lexy would bet all her royalties she was right about that, that Meg did not have a single lover's feeling for Sam. But maybe she did. Maybe Charlie had hurt her so much, she'd focused on Sam.

The ceremony was less than an hour away. Lexy knocked and called and pleaded, but she doubted Meg could hear her. Flo had the only suggestion that seemed to offer hope: "Send for Sam."

Of course he came. When did Sam Worth ever refuse a damsel in distress?

He took in the situation quickly. "Meg, it's Sam. Open up, cowgirl."

There was a break in the storm of sobs, and the lock turned.

"I'm coming in," Sam said. He glanced at Lexy. "Give me a few minutes," he told her.

He opened the door and disappeared, Lexy's lover who was tied to Drake's Point by secrets and history that she couldn't share.

Lexy slid down the wall and hunched over her

knees. She would not let herself be jealous of his closeness to Meg, of their friendship. That would be dumb. But she couldn't help thinking that she and Sam were just going to have a brief time as lovers, no time to develop the kind of open trust Sam had with this other woman. He would always come for Meg Sullivan. Lexy did not even expect him to come for her about certain things, and certainly not always. Their relationship was simply about sex. And she had discovered that she *was* sexy. So how could she be disappointed to see it end in a natural and painless way, like those summer loves in the old songs? She and Sam certainly hadn't been calling it love, only a riptide. Love had never entered their teasing conversations.

Still, she found herself wanting to make the most of his last days in Drake's Point. They had a week or more of mindless nights ahead, as long as no one revealed her as Sexy Lexy. Just a while longer, she pleaded with the powers of the universe. Just a week.

The doorknob turned again, and Sam Worth came out holding Meg up with one arm, the frothy dress lying across his other. He handed Lexy the dress, and she rushed it upstairs as he led Meg Sullivan away.

So Nigel lost his bet, and Lexy never saw a man happier about it. There was a tense moment when both mothers appeared in the same olive silk dupioni suits, but once Chuck and Margaret appeared, the wedding party actually became fun. The families gradually began to mix, the Blackharts growing livelier under the Lovejoys' influence, the Lovejoys occasionally falling silent in admiration of the happy couple. And Lexy was proud of her inn. It glowed in the warm candlelight, with brilliant sprays of fall color against the ancient oak paneling, and the tables groaning with Ernesto's tasty delicacies.

Very late, just as Lexy prepared to sleep on the couch in her office, thinking that the extra hour from the time change would do her good, Sam Worth showed up. He leaned over her in the dark of the room, pulling off her quilt.

"I don't think this is a good idea," she said, suddenly doubting. The truth was out there, in Drake's Point, where her book had made the rounds—and her conversation with Flo made her want to warn Sam somehow.

"Because Vernon knows?" He pulled her into his arms, holding her and letting her come fully awake.

"I meant for us."

"*Us?*"

"I know 'us' is a word men don't use often. I didn't mean that there is an '*us*' except in the sense that both could be . . . let down." He moved against her so that she would know he was not let down.

"The riptide is still pulling us out, innkeeper," he said. "You can't strike for the shore yet." He was kissing her neck, and her hair was falling out of its loose knot.

And she was yielding to the pull of the tide in every way. "You're not angry with me for hurting Meg?"

"You may have *freed* Meg. She's thinking about leaving Drake's Point."

Lexy pulled back. "With you?"

He looked surprised. "It was never me for Meg."

"I don't understand that, you know." Lexy pressed back against him. She needed shoes and a sweater if they were going somewhere, but she wasn't prepared to think about that yet. He caught her chin and lifted her face to his, and she had one last fleeting thought before the kiss took over. The time change didn't mean an extra hour of sleep. It meant an extra hour with Sam Worth. Sleep was vastly overrated.

But after the kiss, when Lexy was catching her breath, Sam said, "There are no condoms left in Drake's Point."

"Oh." Lexy tried to fight back her disappointment.

"Meg sold her last box this morning, and apparently placed a big order for some oil-based lubricant." Sam shook his head. "You have to wonder what's going on in our little town."

Lexy was afraid she knew. "So, what are we going to do?"

"Move on through the senses."

Lexy was puzzling that one out when he stuck his tongue in her ear and drew his hands up to cup her breasts. He whispered, "Touch, sight . . . taste."

Chapter 11
How Long? How Often?
Tailoring the Workout Sex
Program to Your Lifestyle

"Ideally, partners will combine regular Workout Sex with other aerobic exercise to maintain cardio-respiratory endurance, muscle strength, and flexibility, and to burn fat. Weekly sessions are necessary to keep muscles toned."
—*Workout Sex*, Lexy Clark

By Monday, it was clear Lexy was no longer even close to being on Mayor Vernon's good side. To be fair, she had always believed that Monday was a perfectly good day of the week, if one took the right attitude. But attitude was not helping this particular day. The county health inspectors had come to the inn and brought their own rat droppings. Ernesto and the inn cats were highly and vocally offended by the lie, but fortunately for the inn license, the inspectors did not speak Spanish or cat. Considering how much territory the health men had to cover and the inn's past reputation for spotlessness, their appearance was a testament to Vernon's power.

Lexy scooped up the planted rat pellets and shoved them under the inspectors' noses, bagged in a sachet tied with a piece of lavender ribbon, with an attached note for Vernon: "We'll miss you at tea, but under the circumstances, no more scones and clotted cream for you." If she had to choose sides publicly, she wanted there to be no doubt. But the inspectors' visit tied her up most of the morning and kept her from continuing her visits to the people on Vernon's petition. She sent Francisco to deliver Vernon's present, and picked up her ringing office phone. It was Tess on her cell, announcing that she was on the road and would be in Drake's Point soon.

"It's the off-season, now, right?"

It was. Rates and occupancy had dropped for the time being. Rain was predicted for the end of the week, and the reservations calendar had some noticeable gaps.

"A good reason to stay in L.A., Tess," she told her agent. "I'll try to get down soon." She would, too—after Sam Worth left Drake's Point.

"This deal is too hot."

Lexy tried to pin down Tess's actual whereabouts in the five hundred miles between L.A. and Drake's Point, but the sound of passing trucks from Tess's end convinced her that prolonging the conversation would only endanger her agent's life. "Hang up and drive, Tess," Lexy advised.

She put the phone down. Tess's timing was really bad. For the first time in their brief acquaintance, Lexy and Sam had real plans. She had left his house in the gray light of a clear morning with that happy thought to sustain her.

She didn't expect to see him during the day. It would be one of his busiest at the library. She was amazed at the thousands of details about the building that he kept in his head. In his place she would have made endless lists, but he preferred images and models to paper. The library existed in his head in some three-dimensional way, and he was creating that image in the real world, the way he had made her inn appear out of napkins and pretzels on the pub table. She knew he was still worried about Vernon's making trouble. At least her idea of using the monks for building security had worked. Their presence had deterred further nighttime vandalism.

But now her dinner plans looked doubtful. She had arranged to take something from Ernesto's kitchen up to Worth House, and afterward she and Sam planned to wander Drake's Point, enjoying the costumed trick-or-treaters. Lexy had intended they spend some time at the inn welcoming kids there. She had punched Sam in his ribs when he suggested that they go as Han Solo and the Wookiee, as she already had the costume.

Somehow she would have to get word to him that they would have to cancel the early part of their evening. She wanted to be sure Tess did not encounter him.

She checked her bottom desk drawer. Her book was still there, tucked in its concealing paper bag, right on top of the manila envelope full of photos of potential *Workout Sex* hunks. If Tess made it to

Drake's Point, Lexy would keep her at the inn, away from town. She had handled Grindstone; she could handle Tess. Sam Worth deserved to finish his library and leave Drake's Point without ever knowing he'd been to bed with Sexy Lexy.

Meg Sullivan had known worse Mondays, she supposed. Like after her mother left, when her dad made poor choices on a weekend. Those had been bad Mondays. She had gone to school hungry and dressed funny, and she had needed Sam and Charlie to make her laugh and to give her food from their lunch bags. But she didn't think she'd ever had a Monday when she'd given up on someone. Someone she believed in. Someone she had always loved. That was a new low for a Monday. She was glad Charlie wasn't around, actually, that whatever he was doing for Vernon was taking all his time.

She was crying again. She hadn't cried over Charlie Beaton in the fifteen years they had been on-and-off lovers, but since that pretend wedding she couldn't stop. She wiped her flannel sleeve across her wet cheeks and dripping nose, and opened the week's delivery.

There were some late-arriving Halloween items from an earlier order—Spider Man costumes and Shrek masks, and the usual boxes of candy lips and fangs, fake fingers, and glo-sticks. Those she put out right away on the big table in the front of the store. There were plenty of condoms, thank goodness, because everyone in Drake's Point seemed to need them these days. And then there was a supply of the oil-based lubricant a half dozen people had requested. Meg pulled one of the tubes out of its narrow box and untwisted the cap. It smelled like coconuts, like pina coladas. Somebody was going to have fun. Then she came to the books.

There were the five copies of the red paperback, *Workout Sex, A Girl's Guide to Home Fitness,* by Lexy Clark. On the cover a couple embraced lightly, their bare torsos just enough apart to show the guy's perfect abs. The male model had the kind of body Meg liked—a body like Charlie's. Of course, the model probably worked out religiously to get those cut abs. Charlie was hard and lean because he never took time to eat, and he used up so much energy being mad at the world, hauling heavy sacks of coffee, doing work for Amadeo, flinging paint at his canvases, or welding some piece of metal sculpture.

She opened the little book and skimmed the table of contents and laughed. Somebody had certainly found a better way to get fit than the treadmill and the stairmaster! No wonder people were ordering copies. She wondered who was getting rich on the idea, and opened the inside back cover to check out the author. There was a black and white picture of a fit-looking blonde in a cropped top that bared her abdomen, and sleek black lycra exercise pants that hugged her curves. The blurb below the picture read:

Lexy is a fitness instructor and nutrition specialist at Pacifica College in Los Angeles. She developed her Workout Sex program for couples in response to the needs of active women everywhere trying to balance the demands of career and family with no time for exercise.

Meg looked at the blonde. So this was Sexy Lexy. She looked hip and hot, a babe. And she looked like a woman who would take charge and go after what she wanted, not wait for it for fifteen years. The picture explained why that hunk had tried to track her down. Then Meg looked again. Something about the face seemed vaguely familiar. She flipped to the front of the book to check the copyright. Alexandra Clark?

For a minute Meg couldn't believe it. The blonde could *not* be their new innkeeper, could not be the woman sleeping with Sam Worth, the woman who was making her friend Sam happy because she was so real and ordinary. This was not good. Meg was sure Sam didn't know. And Lexy Clark probably didn't know about Cherry. Lexy Clark, sexual fitness guru, and Sam Worth, son of Cherry Popp, topless dancer? That was a train wreck waiting to happen.

The bell on the front door tinkled with the arrival of a customer. It was Dawn Russell's niece, with two small children in tow. With a quick glance at the clock Meg tended to their Halloween buying. But as soon as she took care of their order, she would head for the inn.

After the health inspectors left, Lexy suggested that Ernesto restore his injured pride by baking. By eleven the inn was filled with the rich warm smells of pumpkin, cinnamon, and cloves. Lexy restored her own spirits by arranging bright fall leaves and tiny pumpkins on the dining room tables. She was filling the inn entry with larger displays of ottoman-sized pumpkins and fall foliage, and feeling good about the inn's festive look, when Jayne Silver and Jackie Gold strolled in and dropped their designer bags on the slate floor.

Lexy noted that they both had the Halloween spirit in a cashmere and silk sort of way, like black cats with orange jewels. Jayne had added a wristful of orange-beaded bangles, and Jackie had switched to burnt-orange rimmed glasses.

"We knew you'd have rooms now that it's the off season. And we had to come back."

Lexy tried not to be too insulted by their tactlessness. She knew self-absorption was tough to overcome.

Jackie held up a cellophane-wrapped basket of pancake mix, jams, syrup, and fancy coffee, tied with orange ribbon. "We never did thank the firemen adequately for rescuing us."

Jayne pulled a clipping out of her handbag. "And I was right about Sam Worth. I *had* seen an article about him. He was engaged to Julia Flood Stoddard." She handed the clipping to Lexy.

There was Sam in a tuxedo, looking movie-star glamorous, next to a haughty-nosed woman with a big rock on her finger. Lexy would never recommend weights to a woman who already had a ring that size to heft. To be fair, the woman was lovely in a ten percent body fat sort of way, but Sam didn't look like himself. He looked powerful and distant, like somebody she didn't know at all.

Jayne tapped the article with a long, beautiful nail.

"He's that millionaire builder that's won awards for his buildings. He's got to be one of the most eligible men in the city. He's still here, right?"

"Right," Lexy said. *Millionaire builder*. The new information was another jolt. Of course he didn't need to charge her for his work at the inn. And all those bills on his big table had not been paid by the Ladies Book Club of Drake's Point. He had funded the library himself. The day had a sudden bleak emptiness to it, and she had a sinking feeling that she had already seen him for the last time. She called Flo to help see Jayne and Jackie to their rooms.

Monday deteriorated rapidly after that. By noon Tess arrived, punching the buttons on her tiny phone.

"My cell won't work." She looked at Lexy, distraught.

"We don't get service here, Tess."

"Are we in Area 51 or something?" Her agent hurried back out the inn door, still pushing those buttons.

"No, Brigadoon," Lexy muttered to herself.

Tess was back. "So I'll just have to use the phone in my room. Okay, I can deal."

"We don't have phones in the rooms," Lexy explained. "It's a genuine English inn."

To her credit Tess did not faint, but it did take the woman a moment to recover from the shock of being back in the technological dark ages.

"You can use the phone in my office, or the phone right here at the reception desk." It was fairly modern and cordless, but SUV-sized compared to Tess's tiny cellular. Tess looked at it with disdain.

"Okay, okay. The important thing is the deal." She leaned toward Lexy with a big grin. "We are a French nail away from this. We just need the right *Workout Sex* hunk."

"You want me to choose one from those shots you sent. I will get right on it. I can pick somebody in half an hour, and you can be on your way before dark."

Tess was staring at her, plainly not listening. "What are you wearing?"

"Laura Ashley, vintage."

Tess wrinkled her nose. "Well we've got to get you out of that. That's not your look at all."

Flo came down the stairs in one of her silk jackets and drew Tess's gaze. "I have the two princesses settled in their rooms," she said.

Lexy made the introductions.

Tess looked at Flo with total approval. "You're her hotel manager?"

Flo nodded.

"Super. You are just what she needs."

Lexy rolled her eyes and handed Tess's bag to Flo, then let Flo lead her agent away from the entry toward the office.

"You aren't going to give me a room?" Tess called back over her shoulder.

"Tess, chances are you can be done here in an hour. We'll give you a great tea and send you right back to the land of working cell phones."

Tess had the look of someone who suspected she was being conned, but she followed Flo.

When Lexy turned back to the entry, Meg was wait-

261

ing for her, holding a small brown paper bag. "Lexy." She paused, and Lexy's heart sank. "We need to talk."

Lexy led Meg to the blue-and-white room where the staff took their morning coffee. Ernesto had just put out baskets of warm scones wrapped in linen. Meg and Lexy sat at the table, smelled the scones but didn't make a move toward them.

"You have to see this." Meg pushed the paper bag over to Lexy. "This is your book, isn't it?"

Lexy lifted the bag edge and peeked in. There it was, the rise and fall of Sexy Lexy. "Did you find it on the recycle shelf?"

Meg shook her head. "Five people ordered it through the store, and the books arrived today."

"You didn't give them out to anyone!"

"Not yet. But, Alexandra . . . Lexy?"

"Alexandra."

"You have to tell Sam. You can't let him find out from someone else."

"I know. But he's going to hate me."

Meg didn't deny it. "Do you know about Cherry?"

"He told me."

"That's bad. He really trusts you."

"I tried to stay away from him when Flo said he didn't like publicity."

"Doesn't like publicity? That's an understatement."

"I wanted to stay anonymous," Lexy cried. "I didn't *want* anyone in Drake's Point to know about *Workout Sex*."

Meg looked unmoved. "It's too late now. Someone is going to tell him if you don't."

Lexy took a deep breath. "No. He never has to

know. We just have to keep it from him for two more days. You can tell your customers that the order was delayed. He can leave Drake's Point without any more losses."

Meg shook her head. "It's a big risk. Anyone could say something to him. Think about it. If he finds out now—"

"He'll feel completely betrayed." Lexy didn't know which was worse; having him find out, or telling him herself. How could she do it and watch his eyes lose those teasing lights, have him look at her with cold disgust?

Meg stood with a shaky laugh. "Who am I to advise anyone on relationships?"

Then Flo popped into the room with bad news. "Alexandra, I think you should know your agent and your guests have headed for town."

Sam was having a good Monday. All his plans were coming together, personal and professional. The bake-out phase had gone well, and the final punch list was shorter than he had expected. He had completed the building before the permit expired. Today the place actually looked like a library. There were no books yet, but the shelves and furnishings were in place. The computer people were checking hardware and software, and the library's hook-up to the main county database. It was a first for Drake's Point, this public Internet access. Sam suspected it would change the town, but not all at once. The fog would still roll in and isolate them from the rest of California, but they would have a link to the outside world.

Getting the occupancy certificate was tomorrow's task. The dedication was planned for the following Monday. Flo and Dawn and the other Ladies Book Club members were working on it, and the inn would help cater. The sign with his mother's real name was ready, carved by Amadeo: THE HARRIET POPSON WORTH LIBRARY. The past was dead.

Vernon was still a problem. The mayor would fight till the end. He would have his town meeting. But Sam believed that most of the town would choose the library over Vernon's retail fantasy. To his surprise, people had been stopping by all day, walking around, exclaiming over the computers, the light airy space, the water system, the comfortable arrangements of tables and chairs.

In case Vernon was planning petty revenge, Sam figured it was wise to keep a close eye on Winston, to make sure the dog did not wander off. Winston's girlfriend might feel abandoned, but Sam wasn't going to see his dog shot.

But what was really making him feel happy was that tonight he had plans with Alexandra Clark. Maybe she was still holding out on him, not revealing all her secrets, but he hadn't told her about his dyslexia either, or his real business, so they were even. And maybe with a little more time they would let down those last barriers. That was an interesting thought—that there would be more time for him and Alexandra, though he still had to find something else to call her, something suited to her plucky personality.

Sam stopped to talk to the guys doing the finish work in the main room on the library's first floor, thanking them for bailing him out whenever Vernon threw a curve his way. Today he didn't have any trouble laughing with them.

He was talking with one of the electricians when three women dressed in black came up the porch steps. He was so used to seeing Alexandra Clark's flowers, he did a double take. Then he recognized the magazine reporters: Jayne, and the tall one with the camera around her neck, Jackie. He was instantly wary, remembering Jayne's intention to look up that article on him. He didn't like to think what she might have found if she had done any real searching. He didn't know the third woman, a short, intense-looking blonde. They clearly recognized him. None of them looked at the building.

He moved to head them off before any of the guys noticed. The three women walked right up to him, and he heard the work stop around him and knew that he wasn't going to keep the guys from taking a look at these visitors.

"Do we deliver, or what!" Jayne nudged the short blonde who was checking Sam out.

"Oh my, yes," she said. She stuck out her hand. "Tess Gibson, with Star Media. Do you have a minute?" Her voice was a sultry purr, and the guys let out hoots and whistles.

"Go for it, Sam," was the general consensus. Jackie was looking around through the viewfinder of her camera, making Sam nervous.

"This is a hard hat area," he warned. "Maybe you ladies would like to step out on the porch."

"Let 'em look, Sam," someone yelled.

Someone else called out "Take me, babe." Tess
fished in a large gold bag with its designer logo of
linked letters repeated in a dizzying overall pattern.
She pulled out a red paperback book and handed it to
Sam. "Take a look at this."

He turned the small red book over in his hands. He
didn't like being put on the spot to read in public, but
he got the gist of the subject matter from the illustra-
tion. Sex. He gave the title and the author's name a
quick sliding glance. Sometimes he could catch more
from a general impression than he could from trying
to focus directly on the words. This time he felt a dis-
tinct jolt, like the first instant of an earthquake hitting, no major rolling yet, just that first shake that
roused the instinct to brace yourself. *Lexy.* His own
words came back to him: *What's in your name, Alexandra?* He went straight for the inside back cover, and
the name Pacifica College leapt out at him from the
dense block of print below a picture that was both familiar and unfamiliar. He knew that ponytail and
those legs. The earthquake was rolling under him
now, screwing up his sense of balance.

One of the guys came up beside him and looked
over his shoulder.

"Hey, that's the book everyone in town is reading!
My wife ordered it from Sullivan's."

Sam was still trying to take it in. Lexy Clark. This
was what she had been hiding. This was who she really was: some sex expert. He had been what—making love, having sex, whatever—while she had
been—doing research, keeping herself in shape? He
was back in one of those moments in school when

everyone else was reading along, and he was adrift in the conversation, looking desperately to Meg or Charlie for some clue, some scrap he could cling to that would get him to the next place that made sense. But Meg or Charlie could not help with this one. More guys came over to stand around and join in.

"Everyone in Drake's Point is reading this book?" Little blonde Tess grinned.

"All the guys at the fire station," someone confirmed. "And I think Sullivan's ordered a bunch more."

"Perfect! That is killer publicity." The agent reached for her cell phone, then seemed to realize it wouldn't work.

"Looks like you have a winner, Tess." Sam kept his tone even. He handed the little book back to her. He had to get out of the center of attention.

She held up her hand. "No, keep it. Read it."

"Hey." The guy next to Sam snatched it from his hand and stuck it up on a shelf. "Just what the new library needs, some great literature!"

Everyone laughed, and a couple of things happened fast. Jackie snapped a picture of the little red book alone on the shelf, and when Sam stepped in front of the camera, Jackie shot his picture, too.

He closed a hand over the end of her lens before she could get another shot. "Look, the library isn't open yet. Let's save the picture-taking for the dedication. Back to work, guys." He snatched the red book off the shelf and waited for the workmen to turn away.

"Ladies, let me show you out."

267

Tess, Jayne, and Jackie didn't move. "Listen," the agent said. Even Winston didn't look at his supper dish as intently as she was looking at Sam. She lowered her voice. "Sam, the real reason I wanted to bring you the book is that we are looking for the *Workout Sex* hunk for the video version of the program. And you would be perfect."

We. Her and Lexy. He had always known the long name didn't fit.

"You've got our vote," Jayne and Jackie added.

"Thanks, ladies," Sam managed to say, *but no thanks.* So the whole thing was a try-out. She'd been looking for her video hunk.

"Think it over. We're at the inn. You can reach me there anytime." Tess slipped her card into the book he was still holding, then turned and walked away.

Sam didn't often get angry—not steamed up, reactor melt-down angry, the way he felt now. He was surprised the heat of it didn't incinerate the little book in his hand. His thoughts came too fast to sort them out or make sense of them. Every encounter with Lexy Clark rushed through his mind, a squeaking, garbled flash of images like hitting rewind on a VCR. He couldn't sort out the real from the false, but it didn't matter.

He forced himself to wait for the three women to disappear across the street. They stopped next to Vernon's silver Mercedes, and Vernon came out of his office to talk to them. A few minutes later, their car pulled out and drove away. Then Sam took off.

He was so angry he was almost blind with it, so he

didn't see her at first, hurrying toward him along Beach Street, in one of those long, flowered skirts and her big bulky sweater. The phoniness of it almost stopped him cold.

They met in front of Charlie Beaton's house—perfect, another false friend.

She knew he knew, those big brown eyes of hers wide with fear. *Good.* He held up her little book. "Now I know what to call you, Lexy."

"I'm sorry I didn't tell you. I'm sorry you had to find out this way." She looked horrified.

"So, how famous are you? Three million in print. Pretty impressive." His throat felt tight, and he was surprised he could read that bit of cover copy.

"Those are mostly overseas sales. The book did especially well in China."

He said a very rude word. "And it's doing pretty well in Drake's Point, too, apparently."

"I tried to keep the book out of Drake's Point. I thought I succeeded."

"And yet somehow everyone ended up reading it. I hear you made the Drake's Point bestseller list." He raked her with a disgusted look. "Makes the modest innkeeper outfit a little ridiculous, doesn't it?"

Her chin came up, but he thought he detected a tremor in it. "I came here to run an inn, so I can wear what I please."

"But this sexless, buttoned-up stuff—it's all part of the act, isn't it? In fact, your life is an act, an elaborate striptease. And I was your best audience."

He expected her to cringe, but she fought back. "If I was acting, so were you. You didn't tell me you were a millionaire builder. You let me think you were a handyman."

"At least I was honest in bed."

"You were a bull tule elk, adding another cow to the herd. Like that inspires a woman to confide."

"But you aren't a *woman* in bed, are you? You're some kind of sex expert."

This time she flinched. "It's a fitness book, not a sex manual."

"Know your stuff, do you?"

"Sex is healthy and natural and good for you." Her voice was not so steady anymore. He should stop, but he couldn't.

"So what were you after—the exercise? Was I your Thigh Master? Or was this all just an audition for the chance to be your *Workout Sex* hunk?"

"That video deal was going on before I ever planned to come to Drake's Point, before I ever met you. And I didn't want to do it. That's why I left L.A." She wrapped her arms tight across her chest.

"I'm supposed to believe that, when your agent tracked me down to offer me the video part?"

He watched her shrink in her heavy sweater. "You guessed right that first day when you said I was running away. I *was*."

"I bet. L.A. must have been too hot for you."

He saw a spark of her usual sass flare in her dark eyes. "Stop it. Stop it. I thought you were . . . kind. But you sound like every stupid, leering male who ever came on to me since I wrote that book."

"Do I? Then why do *I* feel like the prize idiot? Why

270

were we in the dark, like you were some shy flower that had to be coaxed open?"

A car went by along Beach Street, its radio blaring Spanish news.

"You don't know anything about me," she said quietly.

"Except that you lied to me." That was the painful thing. He shouldn't be saying it, shouldn't be letting her know how much she'd got to him.

"I never meant to. I came here to get away. I thought I could be myself here. I thought you liked . . . me—just me, no hype."

It was a plea, but it only made him feel more savage. He *had* liked her, damn it. He felt suckered by how much.

"I never thought my book would end up here."

"Don't worry, your little book won't be shelved in this library." He stung her with that; those too-revealing eyes of hers were big with hurt, oceans of it. Funny that it didn't give him the satisfaction he thought he'd get.

He tossed her little red book to the pavement at her feet. "Lose the flowers, Lexy. They're not you."

Lexy stood shivering in the gathering dark, in spite of her heavy sweater. One of Drake's Point's few streetlights sputtered on overhead. In Charlie Beaton's garden everything else faded into the darkness, except those white porcelain bowls. Fitting.

Lexy didn't move. She tried to think back, to find the time when she should have told him, when she

should have trusted him, but before they had gotten
in too deep. She might have told him before she
opened that closet, but she had not known Cherry
Popp's secret was there waiting.

A group of kids came along Beach Street in costumes, the first trick-or-treaters of the evening. She
looked down at *Workout Sex*; the book that wrecked
her life had struck again. She gave it a push with her
foot, shoving it under the blackberries tumbling
down from Charlie Beaton's yard.

The riptide had finally spit Sam and Lexy out.
There was nothing to do but swim for shore. Or
drown.

Tess, Jayne, and Jackie had taken over the inn pub
when Lexy returned. She could hear the laughter as
she went up the stairs to her room at the back of the
inn. Apparently, guys were lined up vying for the
role of *Workout Sex* hunk, taking off their shirts for
Jackie's camera. Flo came to the door, but Lexy didn't
answer. Tess came up twice to report that she had
managed to connect with the outside world and
spread the word of Sexy Lexy's whereabouts. Because
of the library opening the local press was in town,
and she had networked with several reporters in the
pub. There were interview requests from local TV
news folks, the Marin papers, and even the *San Francisco Chronicle*. Tess was loving it. A writer couldn't
buy publicity like that.

The babble from below grew louder and louder as
Lexy thought about how long she could remain in her
room and how far away she could go this time as

soon as she had the energy to move. Then abruptly it stopped. There was some shouting, some excitement over something, car engines started up and faded, and the inn fell dead silent. She should feel relieved, but instead she felt uneasy. The next minute Nigel pounded on her door.

"Alexandra, there's something you should know."

She dragged herself up off of the bed and opened her door.

"They've all headed for the middle of town. There's a neon sign up over the library." He tossed her the keys to the inn Suburban.

Neon sign? The only neon sign in the history of Drake's Point had been the one across from the library that had driven Cherry Popp to her death. Lexy tore past Nigel, down the stairs, and out the front door. In the distance above Drake's Point she could see an unfamiliar red and gold glow.

It was less than a mile to the center of Drake's Point, but it seemed to take Lexy forever to drive there. She didn't pass any trick-or-treaters, though it was early enough for the older kids to still be making rounds. She saw the crowd milling in the street in front of the new library, like a Halloween block party. She pulled the Suburban over and hopped out. Then she saw the sign. It hung from the second story of the north turret of the new library, seven or eight feet tall. Red, white, and golden neon lines formed the image of a woman pushing an ice cream cart. For a few seconds she was clothed in a white jacket; then the color changed and a different neon squiggle outlined her generous bosom, and her nipples flashed red.

Like everyone else, Lexy watched, enthralled by the sign's clever shift in perspective. It was tacky. It was exploitive. It was jaunty and playful. It was Cherry Popp exaggerated, made larger than life.

The woman in neon teased and played with her audience. She was all sexual confidence. Lexy knew how exhausting it was to be that woman. Lexy realized Cherry had come to Drake's Point to find herself again, the woman not the icon. Like Flo, like Lexy. But Cherry had refused to deny who she'd been. She had not kept that closet just for her husband's entertainment. She had kept it because she didn't want to forget who she was and where she had come from, even as she grew and changed.

Lexy wanted to find Sam and tell him what she understood about his mother now, but she couldn't. And he would never see the sign as she was seeing it.

Where *was* Sam? Was he watching from Worth House? The crowd was between her and the library. There were TV cameras going. They were there because of *Workout Sex*. Lexy's book had brought them to Drake's Point, but they had caught Cherry Popp in a glare of publicity that Sam would hate. It wasn't fair to him and to what he was trying to do, and she had to stop it. The sign had to have a power source, had to be plugged in somewhere. She moved around the outside of the crowd, trying to think. She had walked every inch of the building with Johnson. Where was that sign plugged in?

By the time she reached the library porch, Lexy was sweaty-palmed. Her knees were shaking, her heart was racing. She pulled herself up over the porch railing and crawled along the base of the wall in the building's shadow, watching for where the sign was plugged in whenever it went white and gold. She came around the wide base of the turret and saw a big orange extension cord sticking out of an outside socket and snaking up the wall.

She grabbed hold of the plug just as two quick, short notes of a police siren sounded and the doors to the city hall opened.

Sam levered himself up out of the chair he'd borrowed from Dawn's desk in the reception area. He refused to sit in one of Vernon's spindly chairs for supplicants. There was a noise outside of city hall like Halloween was getting a bit out of hand, and he wondered if Brock knew what was happening. He didn't know how long he had been sitting in Vernon's office, but he wasn't meeting Lexy Clark ever again, so it didn't matter.

"Have your town meeting, Vernon. We're done." The mayor's last-minute compromise was insulting. No surprise. Vernon only knew how to suck up, manipulate, or kick you when you were down.

Vernon rose slowly. "Worth, I know we haven't always seen eye to eye, but we both want what's best for Drake's Point. That's why I suggested this arrangement."

"Nice try, Vernon, but remember, I have known you for a long time. See you at tomorrow's meeting."

Sam shoved the borrowed chair rolling back toward Dawn Russell's corner of the reception area, and he headed for the double doors. The crowd noise had grown louder, and he realized he hadn't heard it clearly from Vernon's office at the back of city hall. Through the double glass doors he could see people's backs and a flicker of neon light pass over the crowd.

The light flicker sent an icy prickle of awareness through him. He shoved the doors open, scattering a handful of people on the porch, hardly hearing their protests. His full attention was on the glowing neon sign on his library. It changed from white and gold to red, and he plunged into the crowd, elbowing people aside. There were TV cameras going. He was going to kill Vernon. There was a plug somewhere. First the plug, then the people who betrayed him—Vernon, Charlie Beaton, and Lexy Clark.

He heard two short notes of Chief Brock's siren, and the sign went black. He spun around in the darkness, shoving his way back through the milling, muttering crowd. He bounded up the city hall porch steps and rattled the doors. Looked. Too late. He pounded on the glass.

"Vernon! Vernon, you fucking coward!" He hauled back and punched his fist through the glass.

Chapter 12
End Results

"The point of this book is that sexual activity in a committed relationship, especially when it culminates in orgasm, is good for you. Sex burns fat, causes the brain to release endorphins, reduces anxiety, and strengthens bones, muscles and immune systems. A vigorous sex life is the second most important determinant of how young a person looks. And how alive they feel."

—*Workout Sex*, Lexy Clark

Lexy watched her agent spread newspapers across the floor of her bedroom. Tess had already calculated the column inches devoted to the story—a depressing number in Lexy's view. Now she was picking out her favorite headlines.

SEXPERT, LEXY CLRK, SURFACES IN DRAKE'S POINT.

SEX GURU, LEXY CLARK, SPURS INTIMATE FITNESS CRAZE

HUNK WANNABES LINE UP FOR CHANCE TO BE IN
WORKOUT SEX, THE VIDEO

"It's that sign that did it," Tess said. "Pushed this
story right over the top. Image is so important."

Oh that sign. It had definitely pushed something
right over the top: Sam Worth's pain and rage. Lexy
had heard his fist go through the glass door on city
hall. Fortunately, Chief Brock had been there, so she
knew Sam's damaged hand must have received care.
She kept seeing his face, stark in the glare of the neon
when he'd burst out of city hall and seen the sign. She
had helped to cause that moment of searing pain.
And in that moment she had realized she loved him.

Her timing was not great. Romantic realizations
were meant to happen by candlelight in intimate set-
tings, on balconies under new moons, at sunset on a
Maui beach. She knew how he felt. She had been
there on the *Stanley Skoff Show*, betrayed, humiliated,
helplessly enraged. And Sam had felt a double dose
of it all because her betrayal had brought back his
mother's tragedy.

The news at eleven had shown footage of the sign
before Lexy got to the plug. And each of the morning
papers had a shot of Cherry Popp's ice cream cart, a
paragraph about her past fame and mention of who
her son was.

Today, Sam would face the whole town at Vernon's
meeting. And Lexy's past had played into Vernon's
hands in the battle between the two men. Vernon
would be so smug. Lexy tried to console herself that
she had personally talked to half the signers of Ver-

non's petition, urging them all to visit the new library and think about what it might mean for the town.

Tess was fondling the newspapers again, rustling them. "We've heard from *People* and *Entertainment Tonight*, and I think NPR is going to do a spot."

"NPR?" Lexy could not imagine that the high-toned public radio network was interested in *Workout Sex*.

"Yeah. Get this." Tess bounced a little on Lexy's bed. "They want to do a spot on how everyone in Drake's Point is reading your book—sort of a hot twist on the 'One Book, One City' initiative. You know, like some cities do *Grapes of Wrath*. Drake's Point is doing *Workout Sex*."

Lexy thought about Alaska, Antarctica, and Fiji. There had to be some escape. What was that river in her mother's Greek myths where you took a little dip and found forgetfulness? Lexy could use a major soak in oblivion. She would submerge herself in its waters until she was a mass of wrinkles. She wondered whether bath salts were permitted.

"What we want is to keep the buzz going until the video release. I've got copies of your book for everyone down at city hall, and we'll get good coverage of the town meeting today."

"There will be media coverage of the town meeting?"

"Mayor Vernon was all over that." Tess looked up from the papers.

"Mayor Vernon?"

"Yesterday, after we met your Sam Worth. And by the way, he still remains my top pick for the *Workout Sex* hunk—you should help convince him to do it.

Anyway, we went over to the town hall. Sam mentioned that there was going to be a library dedication, and I was thinking maybe the town had scheduled some press coverage for that. Well, the mayor was right there. He's a bit clueless, but he said he could arrange all the coverage we needed."

Lexy realized that no river of forgetfulness was deep enough. She needed an ocean. She needed one of those submersibles that could take her down to the *Titanic*. She would just park there for awhile until *Workout Sex* went out of print and no one remembered Sexy Lexy.

Tess was carrying on about her plans. "We'll have a bunch of *Workout Sex* hunk candidates right there. Jayne and Jackie have all kinds of local contacts."

Lexy wondered briefly if she could stop Tess or stop the meeting, head off the media, send the would-be hunks home to L.A. An earthquake or a landslide would be nice. Lex Luthor could arrange it. Where was Darth Vader when you needed him?

"I know we won't be able to do you as a blonde, but I brought workout clothes for your signature look."

Lexy managed to lever herself out of the chair. "Tess, I'm not going to that meeting. I like Sam Worth. I respect him. He's trying to do something good for Drake's Point. He doesn't need a media circus, and he doesn't deserve to have his mother's past brought up as part of the joke. Most of all, we should not use his situation to hype the video."

She walked out on Tess's protests, and took the service stairs down to the blue-and-white coffee room.

She could at least warn Flo what to expect at the meeting. And Flo could warn Sam.

There was no one in the little coffee room. The morning staff gathering was over. Lexy retreated to an armchair in the corner and curled herself into a ball under her long skirts and heavy sweater. She tried to picture Antarctica, but all she could think of was the *X-Files* movie: Mulder pulling a naked Scully out of that watery pod.

The door opened. Violeta bustled in and stopped short, studying Lexy.

"I want to be alone," Lexy said. It took a lot of energy to muster that phrase.

"*Solo?*"

"*Solo.*" Definitely. That Spanish word was clear, at least.

Violeta disappeared, but she was back in a moment, with a steaming cup of tea. She pulled a little table up next to Lexy's chair and placed the tea cup within reach, talking all the time in Spanish.

Lexy couldn't understand a word. How had she imagined she was learning Spanish? The steam curled up from the pretty flowered cup, and Lexy wondered if a person could live on steam. Maybe there was a book in that—the Steam Diet, sort of like aromatherapy.

Violeta stopped talking and stood over her with her hands on her hips. She shook her head and reached down and put the cup directly into Lexy's hands, and this time Lexy understood the words, or least the gesture. She was supposed to drink the tea.

She took a sip and was rewarded with one of Violeta's radiant smiles.

Violeta squared her shoulders and looked straight at Lexy. "Is good book," she said in English. "You write a good book." She blushed a deep rose.

"Thank you, Violeta."

The hot tea was working its restorative magic when the door opened again, and Meg Sullivan came in. Meg wore a tailored gray suit, pantyhose and charcoal pumps, her cowgirl self erased, her flaming hair contained in a smooth coil at her nape.

Lexy had to stare. "You're leaving Drake's Point."

Meg nodded. "You helped me decide. I've spent fifteen years waiting for Charlie, being patient with him, trying to show him that he was wrong about me and Sam, wrong about himself, wrong about life. But I can't convince him. I can't make him happy. Worst of all, he keeps choosing Vernon's side. After what he did last night, I can't stay."

"He's the one who put up Cherry's old sign, isn't he?"

Meg hung her head. "You must wonder how I can love the guy."

"I saw the sign in his studio weeks ago. I didn't realize what it was."

Meg pulled a chair up next to Lexy's corner and settled in. "All part of Vernon's plan," she said with some heat.

Lexy nodded and let some more steam waft her way.

Meg took a deep breath. "Alexandra, you've got to let me tell you a few things, or you're going to miss a good thing here."

"You mean Sam and me? Too late."

Meg shook her head. "You don't know the history. Me and Sam and Charlie, we go way back. Sticking together in school on the other side of the hill, helping each other out through the bad times. Charlie's dad and my mom ran away together. It made things complicated."

Lexy took a sip of tea. No wonder Charlie and Meg struggled.

"In some ways Sam had it worse than me or Charlie. His parents stayed together, but they fought all the time. Sam didn't have any illusions about his dad. That's why he kept his secret for so long. The secret that he probably thinks caused a lot of this. Charlie and I knew, but we didn't tell." Meg gave Lexy a long, earnest gaze, full of intention that woke Lexy out of her daze.

"Oh, no." Lexy put her cup down and held up her hands. "You can't tell me any more secrets of his."

"You have to help him."

Lexy shook her head. "I'm the last person who can help him."

"You have to go to Vernon's meeting."

"He doesn't want me there. In fact, I should hold a media conference here to draw people away from city hall." Lexy uncurled her legs and put her feet on the floor. The tingling sensation of circulation-deprived limbs took over. "And Sam doesn't want you to tell me anything, Meg."

"You need to know."

"I've done enough harm in his life."

"And you're the only one who can undo it."

"Exactly. I can go to Antarctica. I've been thinking about it. I know a woman who went and came back renewed and fired up to take charge of her life." She had a fleeting thought that there were no flowers in Antarctica.

Meg waited until Lexy stopped. "He loves you," she said.

Lexy knew she was gaping at Meg. She shook her head, trying to quell the little spurt of hope that sprang up with Meg's words. It couldn't be true. Lexy could remember every meeting, every word. She couldn't think of a time or place where he had been any different with her than he'd been from the beginning. Meg went on while Lexy struggled to get her mind around the possibility.

"Sam is dyslexic, severely dyslexic. Before that night, before his parents died, Sam could barely read."

"What?" Dyslexic? Lexy certainly knew the word. It meant letters reversed themselves or dropped out entirely. It meant you couldn't spell and had trouble reading. Famous people were dyslexic. "He couldn't read?"

Meg shook her head. "Not the way school required. Not the pages of dense stuff in a textbook, and not aloud on the spot. He hated that."

Lexy tried to match the idea of Sam Worth struggling with anything. Everything he did seemed so effortless and competent. But certain details flashed in her mind—the untouched piles of paper on his dining room table, the books-on-CD by his chair, the tone of his voice telling her his mother was a great reader and that he had disappointed her.

"He didn't tell anyone except you and Charlie? He

didn't get, what, tested? Or diagnosed?" How had he kept such a secret for so long? She thought of all the deceptions that would require.

"No. He didn't want his dad to blame his mom for his deficiency." Meg went on. "He reads now. It was the first thing he did when he left Drake's Point—learned to read. Once he could admit the difficulty, he got help, and it was easier to learn because he could draw from a wide knowledge base. But when we were young, we helped him, Charlie and I." She grinned. "We probably got better grades because we always had to do our homework in order to help Sam. We couldn't let our friend down."

"And his mom was building a library?"

"It drove him crazy. I made him promise to tell them, and he finally did, the night of the accident. It was all predictable. His dad blew up, blamed his mom. She went out, and his dad yelled at him for hours. Then Sam came to me. We tried to make a plan to deal with them. He was still with me the next morning when the news of their deaths came. It turned out that she had gone down to the library and seen the sign. No one knows what she thought, but she took off in her car. Everyone was looking for Sam all night, and when they found him with me, Charlie thought Sam and I had become lovers."

Lexy was reeling, staggered by the knowledge of all his easy manner concealed. She had not known him after all.

Meg was leaning toward her, pleading. "Go. Make this better for him. I have one more person to see before I leave Drake's Point."

* * *

Mayor Vernon's town meeting was scheduled for four in the afternoon. The sky was heavy, with low, pewter-colored clouds. Lexy wore a parka against the wind and the hint of dampness in the air. She could hear the crowd in front of the city hall before she could see them. As Beach Street curved around the cove, she could see two vans with local TV network logos on their sides, long poles raised with microwave dishes to catch a signal. Reporters were taking turns doing segments in front of the library, and people shifted to watch. The Cherry Popp sign was down, but missing shingles marked where it had been.

"Here in Drake's Point, the hottest little town in northern California, the five-member town council will vote today to renew or deny a use-permit that allows the Ladies Book Club of Drake's Point to operate a library in the building behind me. What a group of ladies they are! The main controversy stems from the club's intention to name the library after its founder, former topless dancer, Cherry Popp . . ."

While everyone watched the reporter, Lexy worked her way through the crowd, excusing herself and moving forward. She reached the city hall steps before anyone recognized her. Chief Brock had a couple of deputies standing on either side of the door. One of them held out a copy of *Workout Sex*.

"Hey, Lexy, will you sign my copy?"

Heads turned. People started whispering and jostling. Murmurs turned to shouts, and the crowd swung around to move in on her.

Lexy turned on the top step and looked out over the group. Five microphones waved in her face, close enough to get lipstick smudges. Flash bulbs popped. And the questions started coming.

She thought about Cherry Popp on that sign and in the portrait. The woman in the painting had gained strength from the experience of the woman on the sign. Lexy took a deep breath and handed her parka to the stunned deputy, and started answering.

"How did you end up in Drake's Point?"

"I followed Mapquest."

"Is it true that Cherry Popp's son will be the Workout Sex *hunk?"*

"Not likely. He has a multi-million-dollar construction business."

"Have you started the videos yet?"

"We are casting, gentlemen. Have you got what it takes?"

"What other connection do you have to Sam Worth?"

"We have worked together to build this beautiful new library for Drake's Point."

"How did you get everyone in town to read your book?"

"People want to change their lives. My book speaks to that need."

"Why is your book so popular here in Drake's Point?"

"People in Drake's Point have a zinc-rich diet. Check out the pumpkin seeds in Sullivan's Feed Store."

"Are the people of Drake's Point more sexually active than other Americans?"

"This week? You bet. They should be the envy of the rest of the nation. But you all can catch up."

A man in the back of the crowd held up a hand-lettered sign that read PICK ME. Lexy shook her head at him; she had already picked her *Workout Sex* hunk. If only she could get him back.

Lexy excused herself, and Brock's deputy allowed her to slip through the duct-taped door into city hall.

Inside, the tiny auditorium was packed and very warm. The five council members sat behind a long table on the small stage, with Mayor Vernon at one end. He reminded her of an older Stanley Skoff—a different style, but the same smirk. Lexy had met all the council members through Vernon's committee. They were the big employers in town, the people who could make a loan, find housing, or get someone hired or fired.

The capacity crowd squirmed on gray metal folding chairs. More people stood along the walls and filled the space in the back. The Ladies Book Club had a section in the front where Flo, Dawn, Ruth, and the blonde clones were sitting. Sam Worth stood to one side, dressed in a dark, well-cut business suit, looking remote and unapproachable, rich and powerful, nothing like the man with whom she had teased, joked, and made love. But she knew him better now. Halloween might be over, but Sam Worth was still wearing a mask.

One of Vernon's loyal underlings was speaking, saying everything she'd heard at committee meetings for weeks. He held the mayor's petition up for all to see.

"The turnout here today says the signers of this petition, the citizens of Drake's Point, want the council to make the right decision for the future of our town. What *is* the right decision?" He went on about jobs, and tax revenues, and retail sales.

The crowd was silent except for the creaking chairs.

The speaker came to a ringing conclusion. "The right decision is a *NO* on the library use permit. Now we will hear from concerned citizens."

At first, Vernon's lackey tried to limit speakers to signers of the petition, but people Lexy had spoken with turned the mike over to the book club ladies. Flo and Dawn and the others talked about the library as a gathering place for classes and groups, a support for young people, even a source of job opportunities: clerks and cleaning crews, and a librarian and her staff.

Lexy watched the council members doodle on pads, sip from bottled waters, and twist in their chairs without even a pretense of thinking it over. They had made up their minds and were just waiting for the formalities to end. The book club ladies could talk themselves hoarse, and the vote would go against the library. Lexy had to act.

Sam's hand throbbed, and the worst of it was he hadn't even hit Vernon. Brock had stopped him before he could get to the mayor. His throbbing hand had kept him awake all night. He'd had plenty of time to think about beating Vernon, and about Lexy Clark. The Vernon part was actually easy. A line from one of his favorite movies had proved true. *If you build it . . .* The people of Drake's Point had come to the library yesterday and to the meeting today. Vernon might orchestrate this meeting to shut the library down for a few weeks or months, but Sam had faith in the Ladies Book Club and his fellow citizens.

While they fought on, he watched Lexy Clark. He was acutely aware of her presence, though he tried not to look at her directly. She had come in late, in her fitness gear, the clothes she was wearing in the photograph in the back of her little red book. The look suited her, but he missed the flowers and the big sweater—which was crazy. He had set out a few weeks earlier to seduce the only single woman in Drake's Point with whom he did not have a prior history. He had intended to leave all along. He had succeeded on both counts. So why did he feel so hollow?

He watched her excuse herself to the people in front of her and start to move. She came straight up the center aisle with Vernon leering at her, and flashed a smile at the confused citizen holding the mike. He handed it over, despite the protests of Vernon's lackey. She turned to the crowd, glanced down briefly, gathering herself, and spoke.

"Hi. You might know me as Alexandra Clark, the proprietor of the Tooth and Nail. I've spoken with many of you about the new library."

There were some shouts of "Hey, Lexy," from the audience.

Lexy grinned at the crowd. "I'm also Lexy Clark, author of *Workout Sex, A Girl's Guide to Home Fitness.* I think some of you have read my book." She flashed Sam a direct look that said, *You still want me.*

You got that right, his body couldn't help responding.

She turned back to the crowd. "I'm a newcomer to

Drake's Point, but this fall I've learned a lot about our town on Mayor Vernon's committee. And I've watched the library take shape in front of us and heard the arguments for different uses of the new building."

Sam looked around. Everyone was listening.

"Now I'm ready to tell you why the city council should renew the library use permit." She held up one finger. "This library shows just how alive Drake's Point is. It's at the forefront of new building practices that are gaining followers all over the country. The Drake's Point Library is going to be a place where people come to study and train in new building techniques, and Drake's Point will feed, house, and entertain them while they're here."

She held up a second finger. Every eye was focused on her. "This library is a product of Drake's Point. It is the work of a group of dedicated women and of a master builder who grew up here and who has come back to enrich the community with the skills he's honed. And that's what any community needs to thrive."

A third finger came up. "Most of all, this library is the result of the vision, energy, and dedication of a remarkable woman who came here over thirty years ago. Last night, vandals reminded us of Cherry Popp's past as an exotic dancer. She, herself, never forgot it. She kept her name when she came here. Maybe that seems an odd choice for a woman who wanted to leave her notoriety behind. But it's not so odd if you think about it."

She paused to let them think about it. Sam was

stunned. He hadn't thought about why his mother had kept her name.

"No one is a better model for the young people of Drake's Point than a woman who refused to let other people's opinions of her character limit her dreams or her accomplishments. By her example, Cherry Popp teaches all of us to fulfill our dreams, and we should be proud to honor her by dedicating the Worth Library in her name."

Flo, Dawn, and Ruth gave Lexy thumbs up from the front row. The clones started clapping. Everyone was standing and clapping, and lots of folks were waving copies of *Workout Sex*. The five council members stopped doodling and exchanged glances.

Sam started to smile. He felt the grin grow, and made no effort to control it. Maybe this all was going to turn out okay.

Lexy put down the mike and stepped aside. She wanted to punch her fist in the air, but that would hardly be discreet. Vernon's underling banged his gavel to restore order. Once everyone was settled again, Vernon himself took the mike.

He waved a wad of newspapers at the crowd. "Drake's Point was in the news yesterday. There are cameras out front today. Why? Because of two notorious woman, two tabloid figures—Cherry Popp and Sexy Lexy Clark. These two women made themselves infamous with their sexual exploits. Is this what our town has come to? Are we so titillated by a few minutes of fame that we lose sight of our real economic needs? Do you want the council to choose a library built by a man who can barely read and name it after a topless dancer?"

A collective gasp sucked major air out of the room. The crowd fell silent. Lexy watched Sam Worth flex his bandaged hand. A noise at the back of the room shifted everyone's attention from the mayor. People made room for someone coming through, and Charlie Beaton strode up the aisle between the folding chairs. Meg Sullivan followed. Her long red hair hung loose down her back, and the buttons didn't meet on her gray suit. She grinned at Lexy and held up a copy of *Workout Sex*.

Charlie came up to Vernon. "Your tie's crooked, Vernon." When Vernon reached to straighten it, Charlie took the mike out of his hand and turned to the crowd.

"You know me and Amadeo." Charlie looked over at his tall, thin, white-haired grandfather. "Vernon holds the mortgage on Amadeo's farm, as he does on many farms around here."

He paused, and there were nods and murmurs.

"Vernon had the town pay for a water-use study that ended Amadeo's fifty years of growing flowers. It made things tough for my grandfather. He could no longer farm, so he could not pay his mortgage."

Charlie looked down at the floor. "Vernon told me I could help my grandfather and asked me to break the windows in the library. He asked me to repair the old Cherry Popp sign and put it up last night." Charlie waited for his words to sink in. The metal chairs didn't squeak. "And I did those things because Vernon could take away my grandfather's farm. I think you all might want to ask Vernon why he will threaten the farms and livelihoods of old men, and why he'll stoop to blackmail and vandalism to stop the library."

Vernon made a dive for the mike, but Charlie evaded him and tossed the mike to Dawn Russell. Dawn stood up, clutching the mike close. Vernon held out his hand, coaxing his secretary to turn it over to him, but she shook her head.

When she spoke, there was a screech of feedback, then her words came out loud and clear. "Vernon said he would shoot Sam's dog. It's just not right, Mayor Vernon."

A man in the second row stood and reached for the mike, then explained how he'd been coerced into signing the mayor's petition. The mike passed from him to another fellow, who asked if Vernon had a good lawyer and joked that he could recommend one. Pretty soon, people worked out a system of passing the mike down each row.

Vernon looked at the exits, but each speaker spoke so directly to the mayor that leaving was not an option. He signaled to his lackey, who again banged the gavel on the council table until the crowd fell silent.

"While the council encourages citizens to voice their opinions, we've lost sight of our purpose here today. I move to put the question to the council. Is there a second?"

There was a quick second. The question was called. Everyone looked at the council. Its members were no longer doodling or playing with their water bottles. They glanced from Vernon to the crowd of fired-up citizens in front of them. There was a moment of tense silence. Then four hands went up.

"The motion carries." Vernon's dumbfounded lackey could hardly speak. "The library use permit has been renewed. Meeting adjourned." And just like that, the library was saved.

Sam looked for Vernon, but the mayor was gone in an eye blink. Applause filled the room, and people shouted for him.

Someone handed him the mike, and the crowd grew quiet. Sam said, "Thank you for all your support of this project. I will save my speeches for next Monday, I expect to see everyone at the library dedication." He looked straight at Lexy Clark.

Meg came down the aisle, put her arms around Charlie Beaton and kissed him full on the lips.

Sam clapped Charlie on the back. "It's about time, you two."

Charlie turned to him, all seriousness. "I'll help repair any damage to the library."

"You'd better. And will you let us hang some of your works in the library?"

Charlie said a rude word. "Stop being such a nice guy."

Sam shook his head. Plucking the copy of *Workout Sex* out of Meg's hand, he said, "I need this." And he tucked it into his coat pocket for later.

Chapter 13
Tips for Starting Your Own Workout Sex Program

"Real, natural sexuality comes from energy and zest for life. Stretch out on that mattress, let yourself feel glad to be alive, warm those sheets, and reach out and touch your partner."
— *Workout Sex*, Lexy Clark

The first rain of the season started at six—heavy, cold, and impenetrable, like nothing Lexy had ever seen. All the vans, reporters, and cameramen fled. Jayne, Jackie and Tess returned to the city with some of the still-hopeful hunk wannabes. Drake's Point was left to the people of Drake's Point, Brigadoon without the strangers. They all gathered in the Tooth and Nail pub, except for Sam Worth. The happy mood was irresistible.

Lexy signed dozens of copies of *Workout Sex*. But she kept wondering: was she in or was she out?

Her fame was over. It had pretty much done its worst. It had made her rich, noticed, got her name and her face featured in the media, made her a joke, chewed her up and spit her out, left her like a splotch of used gum on the pavement. She was free. She could live as she wanted to in Drake's Point. She could wear her long skirts and sweaters or spandex and sneakers.

And Lexy was pretty happy about some good she'd done. She was pretty sure that everybody in Drake's Point right now, with the exception of Mayor Vernon and Sam Worth, was having *Workout Sex*. Her book had launched a revolution in town.

And of course, she was on the sidelines.

Violeta and Emiliano, Flo and Nigel, and now Meg and Charlie . . . The sneaking suspicion that Lexy had had all along was true. *Workout Sex* was better in a committed relationship. Her book was the biggest winner in the hands of couples who truly loved each other. And sometimes it even helped bring them together.

What did Lexy and Sam Worth have compared to those other couples? Meg had said Sam loved Lexy. She was sure he wanted her, but he hadn't come near her at the end of the meeting. Not even to say thanks. He had looked right at her when he invited everyone to the library dedication, but he knew she'd be there anyway. The inn was catering the dedication tea.

Maybe she should offer to take his dog when he left. Because he was obviously still leaving. Winston would want to stay in Drake's Point. After all, even he had found love here.

How pathetic was that! Lexy refused to be pathetic. She was *Sexy* Lexy. She had been willing to stand up and say she was Sexy Lexy and mean it, and to be proud of the book she had written and her professed knowledge of mattress moves. And she had even found the man who was the best partner for her, who had taught her to feel things on a deeper, more spontaneous level.

And he needed her. She still had things to tell him about who he was, about how he was not like his father, how he liked women and respected them, and about who his mother was. She would go to that library dedication, and she would let Sam Worth know that if he left Drake's Point without her, he would be passing up the best thing to come along in his life.

Sam waited in the dripping darkness under an old redwood at the edge of Worth House drive. Vernon expected him to be down in the pub celebrating his victory with the whole town, but Sam knew Vernon, knew Vernon had to come. He was the same kind of man his father had been, a man who couldn't accept defeat without lashing back.

The library was being watched by Chief Brock and the monks, but Vernon couldn't really hurt Sam through the library again—not even through Cherry. Lexy Clark's remarkable speech had seen to that. There was only one way left for Vernon to hurt Sam, and Winston was inside dozing by the fire.

He hoped Vernon would make his move soon, because he had a book to read, and it would probably take him all night. Then he heard Vernon's Mercedes roll to a quiet stop in the lane at the end of the drive. Of course Vernon wouldn't bring a light or come up the path from town; Vernon came quietly, only a soft brush of his expensive loafers on the paving stones. Sam watched him approach, holding a dripping white package, low and away from his body as he walked.

"Looking for me?" Sam stepped out of the shadows.

Vernon started and spun, and the package spattered dark drops. "Worth, you think you've won. You think you've got the town on your side and people are going to stop thinking Cherry Popp was a cheap tart who bared her tits for money."

"Yeah, Vernon, I have won. Today, my mother got the respect she earned a long time ago. It's hers now. Even you can't take it away."

"My mother was humiliated, embarrassed, afraid to walk around this town because of your mother."

Sam shook his head. "I doubt it. She was probably embarrassed because your father made a fool of himself—and because he was guilty of arson. Bringing that sign out again was a mistake, Vernon. It means there's a trail back to your father, back to that fire."

Vernon's gaze shifted, and Sam turned to see Winston come trotting over the lawn and up to his side.

Vernon fumbled with his white package, trying to tear it open while holding it away from his slacks. The white wrapping fell to the ground. Sam could smell it now under the rain freshened air. Vernon dangled a big bloody steak with one hand, shaking blood from his other hand.

Winston crouched at Sam's side, his neck hairs up and a low growl rumbling deep in his throat.

"Vernon, you never know when enough is enough."

"I'm going to kill your damn dog."

"No, you're not." Sam shifted slightly, shielding Winston from Vernon's sight.

"I'll shoot you if you get in my way." He shook the meat juice from his right hand again, brushing his jacket aside and reaching behind him, fumbling in the waistband of his slacks.

Winston lunged. Sam grabbed for him. Vernon jumped back. The pop of a single gunshot sounded.

"Vernon?"

The mayor drew a gun from behind him with a slack hand. He held the thing as if it puzzled him somehow, dropped it, staggered and collapsed, rolling back and forth on the ground, moaning. Sam ordered Winston to stay, and he went to Vernon's side.

"Vernon, you want me to call Chief Brock or the guys at the fire station?"

Vernon moaned and writhed and cursed. Winston growled.

"Vernon? You pulled that trigger a little prematurely, didn't you?"

"Shit. I just shot myself in the ass," the mayor yowled.

Sam choked back a laugh. "Even for you, that's excessive."

The dedication of the new library of Drake's Point was short and sweet. A crowd gathered on the library porch late on Monday afternoon, in spite of heavy rain. Most of the town had turned out to support the new building. Except the mayor, of course; Vernon was still recovering from his wound.

The Ladies Book Club members all wore corsages. Flo and Dawn made brief speeches and turned the makeshift podium over to Sam. Sam Worth thanked everyone for their work and their faith in the project. He pulled the cover off a beautifully carved wood sign.

"I got this sign wrong the first time," he said. "But Lexy Clark"—he looked at her, and her toes curled in her sneakers—"set me straight about my mother's name preference, and Amadeo worked all week to correct it." He hung it up for all to see:

THE CHERRY POPP WORTH MEMORIAL LIBRARY

After the brief ceremony, Sam invited everyone to enjoy the food provided by the inn, and to explore the new building. Lexy was stunned by the interior decorations. All day she had been checking on the inn's catering, and asking Ernesto if he needed help. All day he had reassured her that things were under control, and that there was no need for her to go to the library. Lexy hadn't honestly known whether she wanted to go early or not. What if she ran into Sam and he didn't want her? She hadn't heard from him. But now she wandered a library filled with banks of pink roses.

Sam had dozens of questions to answer and people to accept congratulations from. But he kept his eye on Lexy Clark, mingling with the Ladies Book Club and other Drake's Point folks. She wore one of her long flowered skirts, but all he saw was the sway in her hips that moved those flowers in a soft motion as she walked. Now that he'd read her book he understood that the flowers and Spandex *were* her—a sweet and sizzling mix of energy and joy in life that had shaken his world. He saw Amadeo flirt with her, and Meg give her a hug. He was pretty sure she couldn't miss his signal. With Amadeo's help he had filled the place with roses. Just like those on her underwear.

Lexy was looking for her coat when he finally grabbed her arm. He kept her by his side as the last people left the library. They stood on the porch and waved at people hurrying off in the rain. Winston showed up with Vernon's dog. With the mayor temporarily hospitalized, Winston and Sam had freed her from Vernon's backyard.

"It was a nice ceremony." His grip on her arm was pretty reassuring. He obviously wanted to talk. Finally.

"Thanks for the food."

"Glad to help. The library looks beautiful."

"Thanks. *Eco-Structure* magazine called. They want to do a feature on it."

"That's great. Are you leaving today?" The words just slipped out, fear and doubt making Lexy less smooth than she'd wanted to be. His words took her aback.

"Not today."

They were still watching people drift away down Beach Street. The sun was breaking through the clouds a little, sending down shafts of light on the cove. Lexy tried to make a recovery. "So, are you looking to find someone to take Winston?"

"No."

"Well, if you're—"

"Listen, there's something I want to show you. Do you have a minute?"

Lexy fought back the shivers that overwhelmed her. "Sure. It's off-season, and Flo's gone back to the desk." It was a cool reply, except of course, for her trembling. And she felt sure that he felt it.

He opened the library door, and their gazes collided and held. "Thank you for setting me straight about my mother," he said.

"You shouldn't thank me. I'm sorry I brought so much attention to her past just when you wanted to put it behind you."

"Better not to be afraid of secrets. I should have learned that already. You can't escape your past. Not even—or should I say especially—here in Drake's Point."

Lexy followed him back into the library, through the main room to the stacks. The shelves were empty, but it was a hopeful kind of emptiness—a readiness, a freshness of new beginnings.

He led her to one of the far rows. On a shelf about eye-level was a single familiar book: *Workout Sex, A Girl's Guide to Home Fitness.* Taped to the spine on a white strip of paper was the book's official call number.

631.96
Clark

"Dawn figured out the call number and put you in the card catalogue—the library's first acquisition."

Lexy turned to him, hope and uncertainty making her feel even more shaky.

"I read it. It's good. You know your stuff—although we didn't try much of it. I owe you an apology for all that garbage I said in front of Charlie's house." He looked at her with his familiar warm, teasing smile, and she melted.

"Thank you."

He reached out and pulled her into his arms. "Now I think I can still show you a move or two."

Lexy's brain flashed a triumphant message. She lifted her chin to meet his cocky challenge. "You think?"

"Oh, yeah. But I don't think we can get the full benefit of the program yet." He started tugging her along toward the library's circulation desk.

"We can't?"

"According to the author, partners need to be in a committed relationship."

"Oh."

"Of course . . . Would you like to be my home fitness partner? I have a house here. It's a good place for a family."

Lexy dug in her heels, and Sam stopped at a panel on the wall behind the main desk.

"Wait a minute. What are you suggesting?"

"Marriage." He hit some buttons on the panel, and the lights in the library began to fade, leaving them wrapped in rose-scented darkness. He pulled her against him, the man who made *tactile* one of Lexy's favorite sensations. "I love you."

"I heard a rumor about that." She tried to still her wildly beating heart.

"Believe it. Now it's time for something new." He was extracting her from her sweater.

"What are you doing?"

"Are you going to marry me?"

Her sweater slid to the floor, and Lexy flattened her palm against his chest to stop him. She had to be sure about this, sure that he knew who she really was. He gave her a look that was unmistakable, even in the gray half-light. "It's funny. Six months ago I didn't want to be Sexy Lexy anymore. At first I liked the head-turning attention. It was new and exciting, but all along I knew that she wasn't me, that I couldn't live up to the hype, that I'd be discovered and revealed as a fraud. Then I came here and met Flo and, in a way, your mother, and they helped me figure out that being Sexy Lexy was a way to learn about myself, to stretch my boundaries a bit, to become stronger, more daring."

"How daring?"

"Daring enough to marry you."

He grinned. "Good . . . You've had enough bunker sex, my wife-to-be. What about library sex?" He kissed her thoroughly. "Interested?"

"I love you," was all that she said.

Lexy could not quite explain how they went from vertical to horizontal, but she did have to share a nagging idea before she lost all coherent thought: "I've learned so much in Drake's Point. I might have to write a second edition, revised. You wouldn't mind?"

"No problem." He paused, holding himself above

her on those strong arms she admired. "As long as I'm your one and only Workout Sex hunk."

"Oh, you are," Lexy whispered, and he closed the gap between them.

He smiled down at her. "Let's get to work on that next book, my love."

Turn the page
for a special sneak
preview of

CONFESSIONS
of a
LINGERIE
ADDICT

by

JENNIFER ASHLEY

On sale now!

New Year's

On New Year's morning, I woke up with a man I didn't know.

I sat up. He sat up. We stared at each other.

He had blond hair sticking out every which way, bloodshot blue eyes, and a chin stubbled with red-gold bristles. He also had a very nice chest and muscular shoulders, which were all bronzed and tanned.

We were in my bed in my apartment and the New Year's party that had raged all night in the living room was finally quiet. We were both stark naked.

I had no clue who he was.

He said, "Unh."

I said, "Oh, God."

He scrambled out of bed, holding part of the sheet over him. I got a wonderful view of his chest and arms and lower abdomen, that slice between the belly button and what a nice girl shouldn't want to see.

He grabbed his clothes. He held them over himself and dropped the sheet. Then he ran.

He had the nicest butt I'd ever seen in my life.

I sat there, bewildered and in pain. I, Brenda Scott, mousy, quiet, never-rocks-the-boat Brenda had just slept with a beautiful-bodied blond man whose name she didn't know.

And I didn't remember anything about it.

The day before, December 31, my boss Tony Beale, the program manager of KCLP FM, had decided that the best way for him to get a ratings bounce was to see how high he could make the DJs bounce.

He drove all of us to Coronado Bridge to set up a remote broadcast in the freezing wind from San Diego Bay.

"This will work, Brenda," he said, rubbing his hands. His eyes lit with that fanatic glow they got when he was excited about one of his crazy ideas. "This is going to be great."

"Sure, Tony," I said, my teeth chattering.

Tony was always trying to get KCLP into the top five ranked stations in the city, and he had idea after stupid idea to help us claw our way up. None of them ever worked, of course.

Today, he'd decided to hook up the DJs with wireless mikes, strap them to bungee cords, and throw them over the side of the Coronado Bridge. He didn't throw me over because I wasn't one of the stars. All I had to do was stand at the top, shivering, and describe the scene.

So, I told San Diego which DJ was going over, then I turned off the mike and cried, because that morning, my boyfriend, Mr. Perfect, had called me and said, "This isn't going to work, Brenda."

He meant that he wanted to break up with me but couldn't think of a good excuse why. The truth was that he, Larry Bryant, one of the richest men in southern California, had gotten tired of mousy, nobody little Brenda Scott.

I'd seen the breakup coming. Larry Bryant, perfect man with a perfect career, a perfect life, a perfect house, and perfect looks had expected his girlfriend to be perfect, too.

I'm not perfect. I'm five-foot-four and have red hair that mostly sticks out. My eyes are blue, kind of a washed-out blue, not deep, dark, and soulful. I have a good nose, but it's freckled. I wear a size eight, and that's all I'm going to say about that.

I suppose Larry wanted me to get tucked and sucked and lifted until I was five-nine with a great figure and glowing blonde hair. I wouldn't, I couldn't, and so he didn't want me around any more.

Tony, when he'd found out about the breakup, had been livid. "For God's sake, Brenda, get him back! He's our best advertiser."

Larry was one of the few businessmen that bothered to advertise with KCLP. Probably because our rates were so cheap, and Tony gave him extra spots for free. That's how I'd met Larry; he had come to the station to talk to Tony about landing the choicest times for his spots. Larry's family owned a successful local chain of sporting goods stores, and he was ready to open branches in Los Angeles. Yes, *that* Larry Bryant.

"I know you're upset," Mr. Perfect had said that morning in his I-know-what's-best-for-you voice.

"You tell Tony you need a little time to pull yourself together, then you'll be all right."

I'd hung up on him.

Tony had decided that the breakup had been my fault and refused to give me any sympathy.

Out on the bridge, the morning show host, Tim, refused to jump. Tony got him finally shoved into place, turned on Tim's microphone, and told him to jump. Tim wouldn't do it, so Tony pushed him over.

The people of San Diego got to hear scream after terrified scream as Tim went down, down, down—and then—nothing. They got to hear me stand up top bleating, "There goes Tim. Sounds like he's having fun." And then "Oh, God."

And then silence. Dead air is one of the scariest things for radio stations. According to the engineers back in the studio and the FCC, I treated greater San Diego to one minute and twelve seconds of dead air before I finally said, shakily, "He's still breathing, isn't he?"

Tim *was* still breathing when they pulled him back up to the bridge. His cord hadn't been too long, he hadn't hit his head or banged into the side of the bridge, or any of those things I'd feared. He'd passed out from terror.

He woke up as they pulled him back over the side, snarling every foul word he knew at Tony Beale. His mike was still on. The engineers were laughing so hard that no one thought to cut him off the air.

More FCC fines for KCLP.

The day dragged on, the sun went down, the weather grew colder, and still I stood on the bridge while the DJs joked and laughed and pushed each other over the side.

I missed lunch, then I missed dinner. Someone brought sub sandwiches, but the jumpers ate them all while I kept up the on-air chatter.

My stomach growled, the hours went by and I thought of the New Year's party my roommate would be throwing. I had planned to spend New Year's Eve at an expensive restaurant with Mr. Perfect. Instead, I'd be spending it at home with my weird roommate and her even weirder friends.

Finally the day was over. Marty the producer wrapped up the mike cords, and I hurried to my car, hoping the heater would work.

Tony caught up to me as I unlocked my car. Tony, at fifty, had round eyes, a good paunch, and barely any hair on the top of his head. "Talk to Larry, Brenda," he said. "That's a good girl. You tell him you're sorry for whatever you did and that you won't do it again."

"Mind your own business, Tony," I growled.

"It is my business. I want his money."

I got into my car. "Happy New Year," I said.

He leaned down and called through the window. "I'll expect good news on Monday, Brenda."

I started the car and gunned it. Tony jumped out of the way, and I peeled out and slid into traffic heading back toward San Diego.

By the time I got home, it was dark and Clarissa's crowded, ear-splitting party was in full swing. My living room was crammed with people I didn't know, many looking like they could try out for parts in a bondage flick. As I dragged myself in, a dominatrix-looking woman I didn't know handed me a martini.

I downed it. It burned all the way to my stomach, almost straight vodka. I headed for the food, which was mostly gone except for a few tortilla chips and the remnants of salsa that smelled like stale onions.

Before I could eat even that, someone put another martini into my hand. I drank it while I yelled over the music to Clarissa, making up some excuse why I'd decided to come instead of going out with Larry. She looked at me with her eyeliner-black eyes and smiled. I have no idea if she even heard me.

I could have lived with the dominatrixes and the music and the lack of food. I could have just shut myself in my bedroom with my martini to have a private cry. But the next time I looked up, I saw Larry walk in.

I jumped. What was he doing here? Sure, Clarissa had invited him, but why would he come when we'd broken up? Had he not had enough of humiliating me that he had to come and give me some more in person?

He scanned the crowd, looking for me, probably. I grabbed martini number three and hid myself behind two guys with very white faces wearing black leather and chains.

As Larry made his way through the teaming crowd, the third martini went down the hatch, and then all pain went away.

And so did I. At least the conscious part of me. As far as I know I went over like a tree in a high wind.

The next thing I remember is waking up next to my

tight-butted blond man, who took one look at me and fled into the dawn.

I grabbed my clothes and jerked them on, leaving off half my underwear. I stumbled out of the room—and straight into Mr. Perfect.

To this day, I have no clue what he was doing there, why he'd come back. Clarissa shouldn't have let him in. He was shaved and dressed and looked like he was ready to go to work—on New Year's Day when the rest of the world was still climbing out of its fuzzy cocoon and mumbling, "hunh?"

I knew by his expression that he'd seen my mystery man run out of the room. He gazed down at me, baffled, his perfect brows arched.

"Brenda?"

I stood there, my mouth open, my panties in my hand while Larry stared at me in a mixture of horror and fascination. "*Brenda?* What do you think you're doing?"

I don't know where it came from. Brenda Scott had always been quiet, shy, and mousy. I did what I was told, showed up to work on time, laughed at everyone's jokes. I had been the obedient and obliging girlfriend, going to parties I didn't want to go to and talking to people I didn't want to talk to, to make my boyfriend look good.

But standing there with my stockings falling down and my shirt half-buttoned, while Mr. Perfect gave me the what-has-my-stupid-girlfriend-gotten-herself-into-now look, a new Brenda Scott woke up.

This Brenda Scott threw back martinis and slept

317

with men she didn't know. This Brenda Scott was wild, sexy, and daring—this Brenda was a woman who could do anything.

I looked Mr. Perfect right in the eye.

"Hey, Larry," I said. "Hand me my bra, will you?"

The next day, I waltzed into the San Diego branch of Lili Duoma, an exclusive lingerie clothier from Beverly Hills. I don't know why I decided to go in there, but while I was driving by, a parking space opened up right in front of the store.

I took that as a sign. Parking spaces in downtown San Diego don't just appear for no reason. I would have been thumbing my nose at Fate if I hadn't taken it.

Ten minutes later, I stood in front of a mannequin modeling a camisole and thong that were mostly sheer, mostly black, and covered mostly nothing.

Under my dress today, I wore white (boring), high-waisted briefs and a large bra that could have doubled as a slingshot. I bought my underwear at discount stores, one pair for every day of the week, with one left over for laundry day. I'd never in a million years wear panties that were skimpy and sexy and not machine-washable.

But this was the new Brenda. The wild Brenda who gulped martinis and seduced men under her ex-boyfriend's nose.

Before I knew what happened, my hand reached out of its own accord and picked up a sheer silk thong.

I looked at the slinky thing in my hands, felt the

silk caress my skin, and heard the black-haired sales-woman, whose name was either Zoe or Chloe, say, "Ah, yes, zo excellent a choice for you."

I bought it. I took home said thong and a catalog that Zoe (or Chloe) pushed on me, and entered a New World.

No one but me knew I wore that skimpy, silky thong the next day at work under my skirt and sweater. I felt just a little wicked, walking around looking frumpy on top and sexy underneath.

Right then and there I knew—no more pale high-waisted boring briefs for Brenda Scott.

I thumbed through that Italian catalog until it was dog-eared, called stores in New York and L.A., ordered whisper-soft camisoles, silken tanks, sheer slips, body stockings, lace hosiery, and sweet little teddies. I made pilgrimages to Beverly Hills and La Jolla and shopped and shopped.

I shopped, I bought, I brought it home. Then I bought a lingerie chest to keep it all in.

Me. The girl who got through college in the wimp-iest cotton briefs and thought even colored panty hose were way too sexy.

Some people smoke, some people get drunk, I buy lingerie.

It doesn't matter. It's only me who ever sees it.

Now, about my family.

About two months after my New Year's adventure, my brother David moved back to San Diego.

David had gone off to Chicago seven years before to get rich and he had. He'd found a yuppie job, made lots of yuppie money, and married a yuppie wife. Alicia had sleek blonde hair and a stick-thin figure, came from the right family and knew all the right people. Mr. Perfect would have loved her.

In March, David returned to San Diego without her. He carried a red duffel bag with all his worldly goods and nothing else. It turned out that he'd lost his yuppie job and all his pretty stocks and all his money, and in the end, his yuppie wife had thrown his yuppie butt out.

He moved back in with my mom in the house we'd grown up in, a rambling suburban place that sat up on a hill overlooking Mission Bay.

My mother had lived in that house for more than thirty years. After my dad passed away, she'd stayed up there alone. She liked it there, she said. She didn't change anything in the house, but I noticed that after my dad died, she started buying fresh flowers, drinking wine coolers, and eating organic vegetables.

My father had kept a sailboat down in Mission Bay, and my mom still had it, although she never used it. Whenever my dad had sailed out, my mother had sat up on the patio with her binoculars and watched him.

Mom rarely went out in the boat because she said she got too seasick. I just think she didn't want to listen to my father yell. He liked to do that when he got on the boat. Captain Bligh had nothing on my dad.

After my father died, my mom still sat on her patio every afternoon and watched the boats going in and out of Mission Bay.

David had been my father's pride and joy. David had gone through college with honors; then he landed a job as an engineer at a company that made incredibly sophisticated computer terminals for airlines.

What happened to him wasn't his fault. David explained that the airlines had started getting crunched and many then decided to go with an alternate company that offered the same service as David's, but for less. David's company got fewer and fewer orders and finally folded altogether.

Poor David. Mom welcomed him with open arms. David ran straight into them and gave her all his laundry.

David didn't come home alone. He brought a friend with him, called Jerry Murphy. Mom invited Jerry to stay up at the house with David for a while. I finally met Jerry when we all sat down to have a welcome home dinner at the house for David.

David introduced Jerry to the new, improved Brenda. Jerry was in his thirties. Jerry was good looking. Jerry had dark hair and gorgeous brown eyes. Jerry wasn't married, and he was thinking about moving to San Diego permanently. I liked Jerry.

I sat across from him wearing a leather skirt, not too short, and a satin blouse. Underneath I wore black lace thigh-highs, a lace camisole and black silk bikinis. I stared at Jerry and daydreamed about him taking them off me.

I need to give up on daydreams.

I had to admit that Mom looked better since David's return. She'd got her hair cut short, and it looked good. Tonight she had on jeans and a turtleneck and had put on makeup. I was glad. She had been hanging out on the patio in her robe for too long.

"Jerry had a boat repair business in Chicago," Mom announced as she handed around the chicken.

Jerry smiled and thanked her as he took the platter. *Polite to parents,* I noted. Another plus for Jerry.

"He thinks he'll do better starting one out here," David added. "It's warmer here anyway."

"Brenda works for a radio station," Mom said. "Maybe she can get you advertising on the radio."

"Does Jerry talk?" I asked, sending Jerry a coy smile. He gave me a dark-eyed wink.

A good beginning, I thought.

I was so wrong.

Jerry came down to KCLP the next day. He had a smooth way about him and made friends easily with everyone. Even Tony Beale liked him. Tony shook his hand. Told him it was a pleasure doing business with him. Told me to take him out to lunch.

"Keep him happy, Brenda," Tony said warningly. He was still annoyed with me for breaking up with Mr. Perfect. I kept reminding him that Mr. Perfect had broken up with *me,* but he insisted that if I'd been more of an obliging female, Larry would have stayed around.

I obliged now and took Jerry to lunch. I would do my best to keep him happy. No problem, Tony.

I took Jerry to Saba's, a gourmet sandwich place. I was wearing black satin panties, a matching lace bustier and pinstripe tights under a denim skirt and black cashmere sweater. Jerry wore a sweatshirt that stretched across his muscles. I enjoyed myself looking at his muscles.

"My dad had a boat," I said as we ate.

"I know. Sarah was telling me."

It took me two heartbeats to figure out that Sarah was my mother.

"We still have it," I said around my arugula and raspberry salad. "It probably needs your expert repairing."

I daydreamed about me showing Jerry the boat, the cabin, the bunks. Just me and him and the water and the sunshine.

"I know," he said. "I've seen it. We're going to take it out Saturday."

"Oh." My dream died. "Who's we?"

"Your mom said she'd let me sail it. Why don't you come along?"

I sat silently. I didn't want a family trip. But I supposed it was better than nothing. Mom could be nostalgic, David could show off everything he knew about sailing, and I could smile at Jerry and his muscles.

"Sure," I said. I tried to sound bright. "Saturday. Can't wait."

On Saturday afternoon, David called me. "Hey Brenda." He sounded tired and annoyed. "Can you pick me up?"

"Where are you?" I asked. "I thought we were going out to Dad's boat."

David said, *huh?*

"Aren't you calling from Dad's boat?" I asked.

"No, I had a job interview. I don't have enough

323

money to take the bus back to Mom's house. Can you give me a ride?"

I held onto the phone, trying to stem my disappointment. "Sure. Where are you?"

"Garnet Street," he said, and gave me the directions.

I growled something and hung up the phone. I had resigned myself to going out on the water as a family party, but maybe Mom and David had changed their minds about going at all.

Then I perked up. I'd take David home and convince Jerry to go out to the boat with me. I could show it to him alone, as I'd originally planned. We could take it out, have wine on the deck while we watched the sun set . . .

Happy in my fantasy, I drove to Garnet Street, picked up David, and drove him up the hill to Mom's house.

We got there. We parked the car. We got out. David unlocked the door with his key. Everything was quiet.

Maybe Jerry was sunbathing on the patio, I thought. In a skimpy bathing suit. I started to go look.

Just then, Jerry Murphy walked out of my mom's bedroom. In his underwear. Bright red bikini briefs that looked great on him.

Mom walked out behind him. In her robe.

David and I froze to the living room carpet.

After a long, tense moment, Mom said, "You two really should have called first."

David turned as red as Jerry's underwear. He shouted, "What the *hell?*"

KATE ANGELL
DRIVE ME CRAZY

Cade Nyland doesn't think that anything good can come of the new dent in his classic black Sting Ray, even if it does happen at the hands of a sexy young woman. He is determined to win his twelfth road rally race of the year.

TZ Blake only enters Chugger Charlie's tight butt competition to win enough money to keep her auto repair shop open. What she ends up with is a position as navigator in a rally race. All she has to do is pretend she knows where she is going. All factors indicate that the unlikely duo is in for a bumpy ride . . . and each eagerly anticipates the jostling that will bring them closer together.

Darlene Gardner
snoops in the city

Tori Whitley is possibly the world's worst snoop. Who else would fall for the man she was investigating? As a favor to her private-detective cousin, she agrees to tail Seahaven businessman Grady Palmer. How hard can it be—especially following a man with such a cute rear end? But checking out Grady proves easy on the eyes and hard on her heart. He's packing charm, intelligence, and too many secrets. Tori has no choice but to discover the truth—by going undercover instead of going under the covers. And all the clues lead to one conclusion: To be a successful private eye, sometimes you have to follow your instincts . . . and hope you bag the man of your dreams.
